ESTHER

A BOOK FOR GIRLS.

ROSA NOUCHETTE CAREY

1st WORLD
LIBRARY
Literary Society

Esther : A Book for Girls

Rosa Nouchette Carey

© 1st World Library – Literary Society, 2004
PO Box 2211
Fairfield, IA 52556
www.1stworldlibrary.org
First Edition

LCCN: 2004091271

Softcover ISBN: 1-59540-689-1
eBook ISBN: 1-59540-789-8

Purchase *"Esther: A Book for Girls"*
as a traditional bound book at:
www.1stWorldLibrary.org/purchase.asp?ISBN=1-59540-689-1

1st World Library Literary Society is a nonprofit
organization dedicated to promoting literacy by:

- Creating a free internet library accessible from any
  computer worldwide.
- Hosting writing competitions and offering book
  publishing scholarships.

Readers interested in supporting literacy
through sponsorship, donations or
membership please contact:
literacy@1stworldlibrary.org
Check us out at: www.1stworldlibrary.org

Esther: A Book for Girls
contributed by the Mahaney Family
in support of
1st World Library Literary Society

CONTENTS.

CHAPTER I. 9
The Last Day at Redmayne House.

CHAPTER II. 21
The Arrival at Combe Manor.

CHAPTER III. 32
Dot.

CHAPTER IV. 43
Uncle Geoffrey.

CHAPTER V. 55
The Old House at Milnthorpe.

CHAPTER VI. 66
The Flitting.

CHAPTER VII. 78
Over the Way.

CHAPTER VIII. 89
Flurry and Flossy.

CHAPTER IX. 100
The Cedars.

CHAPTER X. 112
"I Wish I Had a Dot of My Own."

CHAPTER XI. 124
Miss Ruth's Nurse.

CHAPTER XII. 135
I Was Not Like Other Girls.

CHAPTER XIII. 147
"We Have Missed Dame Bustle."

CHAPTER XIV. 159
Playing in Tom Tidler's Ground.

CHAPTER XV. 171
Life at the Brambles.

CHAPTER XVI. 183
The Smugglers' Cave.

CHAPTER XVII. 196
A Long Night.

CHAPTER XVIII. 208
"You Brave Girl!"

CHAPTER XIX. 221
A Letter from Home.

CHAPTER XX. 233
"You Were Right, Esther."

CHAPTER XXI. 246
Santa Claus.

CHAPTER XXII. 259
Allan and I Walk to Eltham Green.

CHAPTER XXIII. 273
Told in the Sunset.

CHAPTER XXIV. 285
Ringing the Changes.

CHAPTER I.

THE LAST DAY AT REDMAYNE HOUSE.

What trifles vex one!

I was always sorry that my name was Esther; not that I found fault with the name itself, but it was too grave, too full of meaning for such an insignificant person. Some one who was learned in such matters - I think it was Allan - told me once that it meant a star, or good fortune.

It may be so, but the real meaning lay for me in the marginal note of my Bible: Esther, fair of form and good in countenance, that Hadassah, who was brought to the palace of Shushan, the beautiful Jewish queen who loved and succored her suffering people; truly a bright particular star among them.

Girls, even the best of them, have their whims and fancies, and I never looked at myself in the glass on high days and holidays, when a festive garb was desirable, without a scornful protest, dumbly uttered, against so shining a name. There was such a choice, and I would rather have been Deborah or Leah, or even plain Susan, or Molly; anything homely, that would have suited my dark, low-browed face. Tall and angular, and hard-featured - what business had I with such a name?

"My dear, beauty is only skin-deep, and common sense is worth its weight in gold; and you are my good sensible Esther," my mother said once, when I had hinted rather too strongly at my plainness. Dear soul, she was anxious to appease the pangs of injured vanity, and was full of such sweet, balmy speeches; but girls in the ugly duckling stage are not alive to moral compliments; and, well - perhaps I hoped my mother might find contradiction possible.

Well, I am older and wiser now, less troublesomely introspective, and by no means so addicted to taking my internal structure to pieces, to find out how the motives and feelings work; but all the same, I hold strongly to diversity of gifts. I believe beauty is a gift, one of the good things of God; a very special talent, for which the owner must give account. But enough of this moralizing, for I want to speak of a certain fine afternoon in the year of our Lord, 18 - well, never mind the date.

It was one of our red-letter days at Redmayne House - in other words, a whole holiday; we always had a whole holiday on Miss Majoribanks' birthday. The French governess had made a grand toilette, and had gone out for the day. Fraulein had retired to her own room, and was writing a long sentimental effusion to a certain "liebe Anna," who lived at Heidelberg. As Fraulein had taken several of us into confidence, we had heard a great deal of this Anna von Hummel, a little round-faced German, with flaxen plaits and china-blue eyes, like a doll; and Jessie and I had often wondered at this strong Teutonic attachment. Most of the girls were playing croquet - they played croquet then - on the square lawn before the drawing-room windows; the younger ones were swinging in the lime-walk. Jessie and I had betaken ourselves with our books to a corner we much affected, where there was a bench under a may-tree.

Jessie was my school friend - chum, I think we called it; she was a fair, pretty girl, with a thoroughly English face, a neat compact figure, and manners which every one pronounced charming and lady-like; her mind was lady-like too, which was the best of all.

Jessie read industriously - her book seemed to rivet her attention; but I was restless and distrait. The sun was shining on the limes, and the fresh green leaves seemed to thrill and shiver with life: a lazy breeze kept up a faint soughing, a white butterfly was hovering over the pink may, the girls' shrill voices sounded everywhere; a thousand undeveloped thoughts, vague and unsubstantial as the sunshine above us, seemed to blend with the sunshine and voices.

"Jessie, do put down your book - I want to talk." Jessie raised her eyebrows a little quizzically but she was always amiable; she had that rare unselfishness of giving up her own will ungrudgingly; I think this was why I loved her so. Her story was interesting, but she put down her book without a sigh.

"You are always talking, Esther," she said, with a provoking little smile; "but then," she added, quickly, as though she were afraid that I should think her unkind, "I never heard other girls talk so well."

"Nonsense," was my hasty response: "don't put me out of temper with myself. I was indulging in a little bit of philosophy while you were deep in the 'Daisy Chain.' I was thinking what constituted a great mind."

Jessie opened her eyes widely, but she did not at once reply; she was not, strictly speaking, a clever girl, and did not at once grasp any new idea; our conversations were generally rather one-sided. Emma Hardy, who was our school wag, once observed that I used Jessie's brains as an airing-place for my ideas. Certainly Jessie listened more than she talked, but then, she listened so sweetly.

"Of course, Alfred the Great, and Sir Philip Sidney, and Princess Elizabeth of France, and all the heroes and heroines of old time - all the people who did such great things and lived such wonderful lives - may be said to have had great minds; but I am not thinking about them. I want to know what makes a great mind, and how one is to get it. There is Carrie, now, you know how good she is; I think she may be said to have one."

"Carrie - your sister?"

"Why, yes," I returned, a little impatiently; for certainly Jessie could not think I meant that stupid, peevish little Carrie Steadman, the dullest girl in the school; and whom else should I mean, but Carrie, my own dear sister, who was two years older than I, and who was as good as she was pretty, and who set us all such an example of unworldliness and self-denial; and Jessie had spent the Christmas holidays at our house, and had grown to know and love her too; and yet she could doubt of whom I was speaking; it could not be denied that Jessie was a little slow.

Rosa Nouchette Carey

"Carrie is so good," I went on, when I had cooled a little, "I am sure she has a great mind. When I read of Mrs. Judson and Elizabeth Fry, or of any of those grand creatures, I always think of Carrie. How few girls of nineteen would deprive themselves of half their dress allowance, that they might devote it to the poor; she has given up parties because she thinks them frivolous and a waste of time; and though she plays so beautifully, mother can hardly get her to practice, because she says it is a pity to devote so much time to a mere accomplishment, when she might be at school, or reading to poor old Betty Martin."

"She might do both," put in Jessie, rather timidly; for she never liked contradicting any of my notions, however far-fetched and ill-assorted they might be. "Do you know, Esther, I fancy your mother is a little sorry that Carrie is so unlike other girls; she told me once that she thought it such a pity that she had let her talents rust after all the money that had been spent on her education."

"You must have misunderstood my mother," I returned, somewhat loftily; "I heard her once say to Uncle Geoffrey that she thought Carrie was almost perfection. You have no idea how much Mr. Arnold thinks of her; he is always holding her up as his pattern young lady in the parish, and declares that he should not know what to do without her. She plays the organ at all the week-day services, and teaches at the Sunday school, and she has a district now, and a Bible-class for the younger girls. No wonder she cannot find time to practice, or to keep up her drawing." And I looked triumphantly at Jessie; but her manner did not quite please me. She might not be clever, but she had a good solid set of opinions to which she could hold stoutly enough.

"Don't think me disagreeable, Esther," she pleaded. "I think a great deal of Carrie; she is very sweet, and pretty, and good, and we should all be better if we were more like her; but no one is quite faultless, and I think even Carrie makes mistakes at times."

"Oh, of course!" I answered a little crossly, for I could not bear her finding fault with Carrie, who was such a paragon in my eyes. But Jessie took no notice of my manner, she was such a wise little creature; and I cannot help thinking that the less importance we attach to people's manner the better. Under a little roughness there is often good stuff, and some good people are singularly unfortunate in manner.

So Jessie went on in her gentle way, "Do you remember Miss Majoribanks' favorite copy: 'Moderation in all things'? I think this ought to apply to everything we do. We had an old nurse once, who used to say such droll things to us children. I remember I had been very good, and done something very wonderful, as I thought, and nursie said to me in her dry way, 'Well, Miss Jessie, my dear, duty is not a hedgehog, that you should be bristling all over in that way. There is no getting at you to-day, you are too fully armed at all points for praise.' And she would not say another word; and another time, when I thought I ought to have been commended; she said, 'Least done is soonest mended; and well done is not ill done, and that is all about it.' Poor old nurse! she would never praise any one."

"But, Jessie - how does this apply to Carrie?"

"Well, not very much, I dare say; only I think Carrie overdoes her duty sometimes. I remember one evening your mother look so disappointed when Carrie said she was too tired to sing."

"You mean the evening when the Scobells were there, and Carrie had been doing parish work all the day, and she came in looking so pale and fagged? I thought mother was hard on her that night. Carrie cried about it afterward in my room."

"Oh, Esther, I thought she spoke so gently! She only said, 'Would it not have been better to have done a little less to-day, and reserved yourself for our friends? We ought never to disappoint people if we can help it.'"

"Yes; only mother looked as if she were really displeased; and Carrie could not bear that; she said in her last letter that mother did not sympathize entirely in her work, and that she missed me dreadfully, for the whole atmosphere was rather chilling sometimes."

Jessie looked a little sorry at this. "No one could think that of your home, Esther." And she sighed, for her home was very different from ours. Her parents were dead, and as she was an only child, she had never known the love of brother or sister; and the aunt who brought her up was a strict narrow-minded sort of person, with manners that must have been singularly uncongenial to my affectionate, simple-minded Jessie. Poor Jessie! I could not help giving her one of my bear-like hugs at this, so well did I know the meaning of that sigh; and there is no telling into what channel our talk would have drifted, only just at that moment Belle Martin, the pupil-teacher, appeared in sight, walking very straight and fast, and carrying her chin in an elevated fashion, a sort of practical exposition of Madame's "Heads up, young ladies!" But this was only her way, and Belle was a good creature.

"You are to go in at once, Miss Cameron," she called out, almost before she reached us. "Miss Majoribanks has sent me to look for you; your uncle is with her in the drawing-room."

"Uncle Geoffrey? Oh, my dear Uncle Geoff!" I exclaimed, joyfully. "Do you really mean it, Belle?"

"Yes, Dr. Cameron is in the drawing-room," repeated Belle. But I never noticed how grave her voice was. She commenced whispering to Jessie almost before I was a yard away, and I thought I heard an exclamation in Jessie's voice; but I only said to myself, "Oh, my dear Uncle Geoff!" in a tone of suppressed ecstasy, and I looked round on the croquet players as I threaded the lawn with a sense of pity that not one of them possessed an uncle like mine.

Miss Majoribanks was seated in state, in her well-preserved black satin gown, with her black gloves reposing in her lap, looking rather like a feminine mute; but on this occasion I took no notice of her. I actually forgot my courtesy, and I am afraid I made one of my awkward rushes, for Miss Majoribanks groaned slightly, though afterward she turned it into a cough.

"Why, Esther, you are almost a woman now," said my uncle, putting me in front of him, and laying his heavy hand on my shoulder. "Bless me, how the child has grown, and how unlike she is to Carrie!"

"I was seventeen yesterday," I answered, pouting a little, for I understood the reference to Carrie; and was I not the ugly duckling? - but I would not keep up the sore feeling a minute, I was so pleased to see him.

No one would call Uncle Geoffrey handsome - oh, dear, no! his features were too rugged for that; but he had a droll, clever face, and a pair of honest eyes, and his gray hair was so closely cropped that it looked like a silver cap. He was a little restless and fidgety in his movements, too, and had ways that appeared singular to strangers, but I always regarded his habits respectfully. Clever men, I thought, were often eccentric; and I was quite angry with my mother when she used to say, "Geoff was an old bachelor, and he wanted a wife to polish him; I should like to see any woman dare to marry Uncle Geoff."

"Seventeen, sweet seventeen! Eh, Esther?" but he still held my hand and looked at me thoughtfully. It was then I first noticed how grave he looked.

"Have you come from Combe Manor, Uncle Geoff, and are they all quite well at home?" I asked, rather anxiously, for he seemed decidedly nervous.

"Well, no," he returned, rather slowly; "I am sorry to spoil your holiday, child, but I have come by your mother's express desire to fetch you home. Frank - your father, I mean - is not well, and they will be glad of your help and - bless me" - Uncle Geoff's favorite exclamation - "how pale the girl looks!"

"You are keeping something from me - he is very ill - I know he is very ill!" I exclaimed, passionately. "Oh, uncle, do speak out! he is - " but I could not finish my sentence, only Uncle Geoffrey understood.

"No, no, it is not so bad as that," putting his arm round me, for I was trembling and shaking all over; "he is very ill - I dare not deny that there is much ground for fear; but Esther, we ought to lose no time in getting away from here. Will you swallow this glass of wine, like a good, brave child, and then pack up your things as soon as possible?"

There was no resisting Uncle Geoffrey's coaxing voice; all his patients did what he told them, so I drank the wine, and tried to hurry from the room, only my knees felt so weak.

"Miss Martin will assist you," whispered Miss Majoribanks, as I passed her; and, sure enough, as I entered the dormitory, there was Belle emptying my drawers, with Jessie helping her. Even in my bewildered state of wretchedness I wondered why Miss Majoribanks thought it necessary for me to take all my things. Was I bidding good-by to Redmayne House?

Belle looked very kindly at me as she folded my dresses, but Jessie came up to me with tears in her eyes. "Oh, Esther!" she whispered, "how strange to think we were talking as we were, and now the opportunity has come?" and though her speech was a little vague, I understood it; she meant the time for me to display my greatness of mind - ah, me! my greatness of mind - where was it? I was of no use at all; the girls did it all between them, while I sat on the edge of my little bed and watched them. They were as quick as possible, and yet it seemed hours before the box was locked, and Belle had handed me the key; by-and-by, Miss Majoribanks came and fetched me down, for she said the fly was at the door, and Dr. Cameron was waiting.

We girls had never cared much for Miss Majoribanks, but nothing could exceed her kindness then. I think the reason why schoolmistresses are not often beloved by their pupils - though there certainly are exceptions to that rule - is that they do not often show their good hearts.

When Miss Majoribanks buttoned my gloves for me, and smoothed my hair, and gave me that motherly kiss, I felt I loved her. "God bless you my dear child! we shall all miss you; you have worked well and been a credit to the establishment. I am sorry indeed to part with you." Actually these were Miss Majoribanks' words, and spoken, too, in a husky voice!

And when I got downstairs, there were all the girls, many of them with their croquet mallets in their hands, gathered in the front garden, and little Susie Pierrepoint, the baby of the school, carrying a large bunch of lavender and sweet-william from her own little garden, which she thrust into my hands.

"They are for you," cried Susie; and then they all crowded round and kissed me.

"Good-by, Esther; we are so sorry to lose you; write to us and let us know how you are."

Jessie's pale little face came last. "Oh, my darling! how I shall be thinking of you!" cried the affectionate creature; and then I broke down, and Uncle Geoffrey led me away.

"I am glad to see your school-fellows love you," he said, as we drove off, and Redmayne House became lost to sight. "Human affection is a great boon, Esther."

Dear Uncle Geoffrey! he wanted to comfort me; but for some time I would not speak or listen.

CHAPTER II.

THE ARRIVAL AT COMBE MANOR.

The great secret of Uncle Geoffrey's influence with people was a certain quiet undemonstrative sympathy. He did not talk much; he was rather given to letting people alone, but his kindliness of look made his few spoken words more precious than the voluble condolences of others.

He made no effort to check the torrent of tears that followed my first stunned feelings; indeed, his "Poor child!" so tenderly uttered, only made them flow more quickly. It was not until we were seated in the railway compartment, and I had dried them of my own accord, that he attempted to rouse me by entering into conversation, and yet there was much that he knew must be said, only "great haste, small speed," was always Uncle Geoffrey's favorite motto. "There is time for all things, and much more," as he used to tell us.

"Are you better now?" he asked, kindly. "That is right; put your handkerchief away, and we can have a little talk together. You are a sensible girl, Esther, and have a wise little head on your shoulders. Tell me, my child, had you any idea of any special anxiety or trouble that was preying on your father's mind?"

"No, indeed," I returned, astonished. "I knew the farm was doing badly, and father used to complain now and then of Fred's extravagance, and mother looked once or twice very worried, but we did not think much about it."

"Then I am afraid what I am going to tell you will be a great shock," he returned, gravely. "Your father and mother must have had heavy anxieties lately, though they have kept it from you children. The cause of your father's illness is mental trouble. I must not hide from you, Esther, that he is ruined."

"Ruined!" I tried to repeat the word aloud, but it died on my lips.

"A man with a family ought not to speculate," went on my uncle, speaking more to himself than me. "What did Frank know about the business? About as much as Fred does about art. He has spent thousands on the farm, and it has been a dead loss from the beginning. He knew as much about farming as Carrie does. Stuff and nonsense! And then he must needs dabble in shares for Spanish mines; and that new-fangled Wheal Catherine affair that has gone to smash lately. Every penny gone; and a wife, and - how many of you are there, Esther?"

But I was too much overwhelmed to help him in his calculation, so he commenced striking off on his fingers, one by one.

"Let me see; there's Fred, brought up, young coxcomb! to think himself a fine gentleman and an artist, with almost as much notion of work as I have of piano playing; and Allan, who has more brains than the rest of you put together; and Carrie, who is half a saint and slightly hysterical; and your poor little self; and then comes that nondescript article Jack. Why in the world do you call a feminine creature Jack? And poor little Dot, who will never earn a penny for himself - humph, six of you to clothe and feed - "

"Oh, Uncle Geoff!" I burst out, taking no notice of this long tirade; and what did it matter if Dot never earned anything when I would work my fingers to the bone for him, the darling! "oh, Uncle Geoff, are things really so bad as that? Will Fred be obliged to give up his painting, when he has been to Rome, too; and shall we have to leave Combe Manor, and the farm? Oh, what will they all do? and Carrie, too?"

"Work," was the somewhat grim reply, and then he went on in a milder tone. "Things are very bad, Esther; about as bad as they can be - for we must look matters in the face - and your father is very ill, and there is no knowing where the mischief may end; but you must all put your shoulders to the domestic wheel, and push it up the Hill Difficulty. It is a crisis, and a very painful one, but it will prove which of you has the right mettle.

"I am not afraid of Allan," he went on; "the lad has plenty of good stuff in him; and I am not much afraid of you, Esther, at least I think not; but - " He hesitated, and then stopped, and I knew he was thinking of Fred and Carrie; but he need not. Of course Carrie would work as heartily as any of us; idling was never her forte; and Fred - well, perhaps Fred was not always industrious.

I seemed to have lost myself in a perfect tangle of doubt and dread. Uncle Geoffrey went on with his talk, half sad and half moralizing, but I could not follow all he said. Two thoughts were buzzing about me like hornets. Father was ill, very ill, and we should have to leave Combe Manor. The sting of these thoughts was dreadful.

I seemed to rouse out of a nightmare when Uncle Geoffrey suddenly announced that we were at Crowbridge. No one was waiting for us at the station, which somewhat surprised me; but Combe Manor was not a quarter of a mile off, so the luggage was wheeled away on a truck, and Uncle Geoffrey and I walked after it, up the sandy lane, and round by the hazel copse. And there were the fields, where Dapple, the gray mare, was feeding; and there were Cherry and Spot, and Brindle, and all the rest of the dear creatures, rubbing their horned heads against the hedge as usual; and two or three of them standing knee-deep in the great shallow pool, where Fred and Allan used to sail their boats, and make believe it was the Atlantic. We always called the little bit of sedgy ground under the willow America, and used to send freights of paper and cardboard across the mimic ocean, which did not always arrive safely.

How lovely and peaceful it all looked on this June evening! The sun shone on the red brick house and old-fashioned casements; roses were climbing everywhere, on the walls, round the porch, over the very gateway. Fred was leaning against the gate, in his brown velveteen coat and slouched hat, looking so handsome and picturesque, poor fellow! He had a Gloire de Dijon in his button-hole. I remember I wondered vaguely how he had had the heart to pick it.

"How is he?" called out Uncle Geoffrey. And Fred

started, for though he was watching for us he had not seen us turn the corner of the lane.

"No better," was the disconsolate answer, as he unlatched the gate, and stooped over it to kiss me. "We are expecting Allan down by the next train, and Carrie asked me to look out for you; how do you do, Esther? What have you done to yourself?" eyeing me with a mixture of chagrin and astonishment. I suppose crying had not improved my appearance; still, Fred need not have noticed my red eyes; but he was one who always "looked on the outward appearance."

"She is tired and unhappy, poor little thing," repeated Uncle Geoffrey, answering for me, as he drew my arm through his. "I hope Carrie has got some tea for her;" and as he spoke Carrie came out in the porch to meet us. How sweet she looked, the "little nun," as Fred always called her, in her gray dress; with her smooth fair hair and pale pretty face.

"Poor Esther, how tired you look!" she said, kissing me affectionately, but quietly - Carrie was always a little undemonstrative - "but I have got tea for you in the brown room" (we always called it the brown room, because it was wainscoted in oak); "will you have it now, or would you like to see mother?"

"You had better have tea first and see your mother afterward," observed Uncle Geoffrey; but I would not take this prudent counsel. On the stairs I came upon Jack, curled up on a window-sill, with Smudge, our old black cat, in her arms, and was welcomed by both of them with much effusion. Jack was a tall, thin girl, all legs and arms, with a droll, freckled face and round blue eyes, with all the awkwardness of fourteen, and none of its precocity. Her real name was Jacqueline, but we had always called her Jack, for brevity, and because, with her cropped head and rough ways, she resembled a boy more than a girl; her hair was growing now, and hung about her neck in short ungainly lengths, but I doubt whether in its present stage it was any improvement. I am not at all sure strangers considered Jack a prepossessing child, she was so awkward and overgrown, but I liked her droll face immensely. Fred was always finding fault with her and snubbing her, which brought him nothing but pert replies; then he would entreat mother to send her to school, but somehow she never went. Dot could not spare her, and mother thought there was plenty of time, so Jack still roamed about at her own sweet will; riding Dapple barebacked round the paddock, milking Cherry, and feeding the chickens; carrying on some pretense at lessons with Carrie, who was not a very strict mistress, and plaguing Fred, who had nice ways and hated any form of untidiness.

"Oh, you dear thing!" cried Jack, leaping from the window-seat and nearly strangling me, while Smudge rubbed himself lovingly against my dress; "oh, you dear, darling, delightful old Esther, how pleased I am to see you!" (Certainly Jack was not undemonstrative.) "Oh, it has been so horrid the last few days - father ill, and mother always with him, and Fred as cross as two sticks, and Carrie always too busy or too tired for any one to speak to her; and Dot complaining of pain in his back and not caring to play, oh!" finished Jack, with a long-drawn sigh, "it has been almost too horrid."

"Hush, Jack," was my sole reply; for there was dear mother coming down the passage toward us. I had only been away from her two months, and yet it struck me

Rosa Nouchette Carey

that her hair was grayer and her face was thinner than it used to be, and there were lines on her forehead that I never remember to have seen before; but she greeted me in her old affectionate way, putting back my hair from my face to look at me, and calling me her dear child. "But I must not stop a moment, Esther," she said hurriedly, "or father will miss me; take off your hat, and rest and refresh yourself, and then you shall come up and see him."

"But, mother, where is Dot?"

"In there," motioning toward the sick room; "he is always there, we cannot keep him out," and her lip trembled. When Jack and I returned to the brown room, we found the others gathered round the table. Carrie, who was pouring out the tea, pointed to the seat beside her.

It was the first dreary meal I had ever remembered in the brown room; my first evening at home had always been so happy. The shallow blue teacups and tiny plates always seemed prettier than other people's china, and nothing ever tasted so delicious as our home-made brown bread and butter.

But this evening the flavor seemed spoiled. Carrie sat in mother's place looking sad and abstracted, and fingering her little silver cross nervously. Fred was downcast and out of spirits, returning only brief replies to Uncle Geoffrey's questions, and only waking up to snub Jack if she spoke a word. Oh, how I wished Allan would make his appearance and put us all right! It was quite a relief when I heard mother's voice calling me, and she took me into the great cool room where father lay.

Dot was curled up in mother's great arm-chair, with his favorite book of natural history; he slipped a hot little hand in mine as I passed him.

Dot was our name for him because he was so little, but he had been called Frank, after our father; he was eight years old, but he hardly looked bigger than a child of six. His poor back was crooked, and he was lame from hip-disease; sometimes for weeks together the cruel abscesses wasted his strength, at other times he was tolerably free from pain; even at his worst times Dot was a cheery invalid, for he was a bright, patient little fellow. He had a beautiful little face, too, though perhaps the eyes were a trifle too large for the thin features; but Dot was my pet, and I could see no fault in him; nothing angered me more than when people pitied him or lamented over his infirmity. When I first came home the sound of his crutch on the floor was the sweetest music in my ear. But I had no eyes even for Dot after my first look at father. Oh, how changed, how terribly changed he was! The great wave of brown hair over his forehead was gray, his features were pinched and haggard, and when he spoke to me his voice was different, and he seemed hardly able to articulate.

"Poor children - poor children!" he groaned; and as I kissed his cheek he said, "Be a good girl, Esther, and try to be a comfort to your mother."

"When I am a man I shall try and be a comfort too," cried Dot, in his sharp chirpy voice; it quite startled father.

"That's my brave boy," said father, faintly, and I think there were tears in his eyes. "Dora" - my mother's name was Dora - "I am too tired to talk; let the children go now, and come and sit by me while I go to sleep;" and mother gently dismissed us.

I had rather a difficulty with Dot when I got outside, for he suddenly lowered his crutch and sat down on the floor.

"I don't want to go to bed," he announced, decidedly. "I shall sit here all night, in case mother wants me; when it gets dark she may feel lonely."

"But, Dot, mother will be grieved if she comes out and finds you here; she has anxiety enough as it is; and if you make yourself ill, too, you will only add to her trouble. Come, be a good boy, and let me help you to undress." But I might as well have talked to Smudge. Dot had these obstinate fits at times; he was tired, and his nerves were shaken by being so many hours in the sick room, and nothing would have induced him to move. I was so tired at last that I sat down on the floor, too, and rested my head against the door, and Dot sat bolt upright like a watchful little dog, and in this ridiculous position we were discovered by Allan. I had not heard of his arrival; and when he came toward us, springing lightly up two stairs at a time, I could not help uttering a suppressed exclamation of delight.

He stopped at once and looked at us in astonishment. "Dot and Esther! in the name of all that is mysterious; huddled up like two Chinese gods on the matting. Why, I took Esther for a heap of clothes in the twilight." Of course I told him how it happened. Dot was naughty and would not move, and I was keeping him company. Allan hardly heard me out before he had shouldered Dot, crutch and all, and was walking off with him down the passage. "Wait for me a few minutes, Esther," he whispered; and I betook myself to the window-seat and looked over the dusky garden, where the tall white lilies looked like ghostly flowers in the gloom.

It was a long time before Allan rejoined me. "That is a curious little body," he said, half laughing, as he sat down beside me. "I had quite a piece of work with him for carrying him off in that fashion; he said 'I was a savage, a great uncivilized man, to take such a mean advantage of him; If I were big I would fight you,' he said, doubling his fists; he looked such a miserable little atom of a chap as he said it."

"Was he really angry?" I asked, for Dot was so seldom out of temper.

"Angry, I believe you. He was in a towering rage; but he is all right now, so you need not go to him. I stroked him down, and praised him for his good intentions, and then I told him I was a doctor now, and no one contradicted my orders, and that he must be a good boy and let me help him to bed. Poor little fellow; he sobbed all the time he was undressing, he is so fond of father. I am afraid it will go badly with him if things turn out as I fear they will," and Allan's voice was very grave.

We had a long talk after that, until Uncle Geoffrey came upstairs and dislodged us, by carrying Allan off. It was such a comfort to have him all to myself; we had been so much separated of late years.

Allan was five years older than I; he was only a year younger than Fred, but the difference between them was very great. Allan looked the elder of the two; he was not so tall as Fred, but he was strongly built and sturdy; he was dark-complexioned, and his features were almost as irregular as mine; but in a man that did not so much matter, and very few people called Allan plain.

Allan had always been my special brother - most sisters know what I mean by that term. Allan was undemonstrative; he seldom petted or made much of me, but a word from him was worth a hundred from Fred; and there was a quiet unspoken sympathy between us that was sufficiently palpable. If Allan wanted his gloves mended he always came to me, and not to Carrie. I was his chief correspondent, and he made me the confidante of his professional hopes and fears. In return, he good-humoredly interested himself in my studies, directed my reading, and considered himself at liberty to find fault with everything that did not please him. He was a little peremptory sometimes, but I did not mind that half so much as Fred's sarcasms; and he never distressed me as Fred did, by laughing at my large hands, or wondering why I was not so natty in my dress as Carrie.

CHAPTER III.

DOT.

I went to my room to unpack my things, and by-and-by Carrie joined me.

I half hoped that she meant to help me, but she sat down by the window and said, with a sigh, how tired she was; and certainly her eyes had a weary look.

She watched me for some time in silence, but once or twice she sighed very heavily.

"I wish you could leave those things, Esther," she said, at last, not pettishly - Carrie was never pettish - but a little too plaintively. "I have not had a creature to whom I could talk since you left home in April."

The implied compliment was very nice, but I did not half like leaving my things - I was rather old-maidish in my ways, and never liked half measures; but I remembered reading once about "the lust of finishing," and what a test of unselfishness it was to put by a half-completed task cheerfully at the call of another duty. Perhaps it was my duty to leave my unpacking and listen to Carrie, but there was one little point in her speech that did not please me.

"You could talk to mother," I objected; for mother always listened to one so nicely.

"I tried it once, but mother did not understand," sighed Carrie. I used to wish she did not sigh so much. "We had quite an argument, but I saw it was no use - that I should never bring her to my way of thinking. She was brought up so differently; girls were allowed so little liberty then. My notions seemed to distress her. She said that I was peculiar, and that I carried things too far, and that she wished I were more like other girls; and then she kissed me, and said I was very good, and she did not mean to hurt me; but she thought home had the first claim; and so on. You know mother's way."

"I think mother was right there - you think so yourself, do you not Carrie?" I asked anxiously, for this seemed to me the A B C of common sense.

"Oh, of course," rather hastily. "Charity begins at home, but it ought not to stop there. If I chose to waste my time practicing for Fred's violin, and attending to all his thousand and one fads and fancies, what would become of all my parish work? You should have heard Mr. Arnold's sermon last Sunday, Esther; he spoke of the misery and poverty and ignorance that lay around us outside our homes, and of the loiterers and idlers within those homes." And Carrie's eyes looked sad and serious.

"That is true," I returned, and then I stopped, and Jessie's words came to my mind, "Even Carrie makes mistakes at times." For the first time in my life the thought crossed me; in my absence would it not have been better for Carrie to have been a little more at home? It was Jessie's words and mother's careworn face that put the thought into my head; but the next moment I had dismissed it as heresy. My good, unselfish Carrie, it was impossible that she could make mistakes! Carrie's next speech chimed in well with my unspoken thoughts.

"Home duties come first, of course, Esther - no one in their senses could deny such a thing; but we must be on our guard against make-believe duties. It is my duty to help mother by teaching Jack, and I give her two hours every morning; but when Fred comes into the schoolroom with some nonsensical request that would rob me of an hour or so, I am quite right not to give way to him. Do you think," warming into enthusiasm over her subject, "that Fred's violin playing ought to stand in the way of any real work that will benefit souls as well as bodies - that will help to reclaim ignorance and teach virtue?" And Carrie's beautiful eyes grew dark and dewy with feeling. I wish mother could have seen her; something in her expression reminded me of a picture of Faith I had once seen.

"Oh, Esther," she continued, for I was too moved to answer her, "every day I live I long to give myself more entirely to benefiting my fellow creatures. Girl as I am, I mean to join the grand army of workers - that is what Mr. Arnold called them. Oh, how I wish I could remember all he said! He told us not to be disheartened by petty difficulties, or to feel lonely because, perhaps, those who were our nearest and dearest discouraged our efforts or put obstacles in our way. 'You think you are alone,' he said, 'when you are one of the rank and file in that glorious battalion. There are thousands working with you and around you, although you cannot see them.' And then he exhorted us who were young to enter this crusade."

"But, Carrie," I interrupted, somewhat mournfully, for I was tired and a little depressed, "I am afraid our work is already cut out for us, and we shall have to do it however little pleased we may be with the pattern. From what Uncle Geoffrey tells me, we shall be very poor."

"I am not afraid of poverty, Esther."

"But still you will be grieved to leave Combe Manor," I persisted. "Perhaps we shall have to live in a little pokey house somewhere, and to go out as governesses."

"Perhaps so," she answered, serenely; "but I shall still find time for higher duties. I shall be a miser, and treasure all my minutes. But I have wasted nearly half-an-hour now; but it is such a luxury to talk to somebody who can understand." And then she kissed me affectionately and bade me hasten to bed, for it was getting late, and I looked sadly tired; but it never entered into her head to help me put away the clothes that strewed my room, though I was aching in every limb from grief and fatigue. If one looks up too much at the clouds one stumbles against rough stones sometimes. Star gazing is very sweet and elevating, but it is as well sometimes to pick up the homely flowers that grow round our feet. "What does Carrie mean by higher duties?" I grumbled, as I sought wearily to evoke order out of chaos. "To work for one's family is as much a duty as visiting the poor." I could not solve the problem; Carrie was too vague for me there; but I went to bed at last, and dreamed that we two were building houses on the seashore. Carrie's was the prettier, for it was all of sea-weed and bright-colored shells that looked as though the sun were shining on them, while mine was made of clay, tempered by mortar.

"Oh, Carrie, I like yours best" I cried, disconsolately; yet as I spoke a long tidal wave came up and washed the frail building away. But though mine filled with foamy water, the rough walls remained entire, and then I looked at it again the receding wave had strewn its floors with small shining pearls.

I must pass over the record of the next few days, for they were so sad - so sad, even now, I cannot think of them without tears. On the second day after my return, dear father had another attack, and before many hours were over we knew we were orphans.

Two things stood out most prominently during that terrible week; dear mother's exceeding patience and Dot's despair. Mother gave us little trouble. She lay on her couch weeping silently, but no word of complaint or rebellion crossed her lips; she liked us to sit beside her and read her soothing passages of Scripture, and she was very thoughtful and full of pity for us all. Her health was never very good, and just now her strength had given way utterly. Uncle Geoffrey would not hear of her exerting herself, and, indeed, she looked so frail and broken that even Fred got alarmed about her.

Carrie was her principal companion, for Dot took all my attention; and, indeed, it nearly broke our hearts to see him.

Uncle Geoffrey had carried him from the room when father's last attack had come on. Jack was left in charge of him, and the rest of us were gathered in the sick room. I was the first to leave when all was over, for I thought of Dot and trembled; but as I opened the door there he was, crouched down in a little heap at the entrance, with Jack sobbing beside him.

"I took away his crutch, but he crawled all the way on his hands and knees," whispered Jack; and then Allan came out and stood beside me.

"Poor little fellow!" he muttered; and Dot lifted his miserable little white face, and held out his arms.

"Take me in," he implored. "Father's dead, for I heard you all crying; but I must kiss him once more."

"I don't think it will hurt him," observed Allan, in a low voice. "He will only imagine all sorts of horrors - and he looks so peaceful," motioning toward the closed door.

"I will be so good," implored the poor child, "if you only take me in." And Allan, unable to resist any longer, lifted him in his arms.

I did not go in, for I could not have borne it. Carrie told me afterward that Allan cried like a child when Dot nestled up to the dead face and began kissing and stroking it.

"You are my own father, though you look so different," he whispered. "I wish you were not so cold. I wish you could look and speak to me - I am your little boy Dot - you were always so fond of Dot, father. Let me go with you; I don't want to live any longer without you," and so on, until Uncle Geoffrey made Allan take him away.

Oh, how good Allan was to him! He lay down by his side all night, soothing him and talking to him, for Dot never slept. The next day we took turns to be with him, and so on day after day; but I think Dot liked Allan best.

"He is most like father," he said once, which, perhaps, explained the preference; but then Allan had so much tact and gentleness. Fred did not understand him at all; he called him odd and uncanny, which displeased us both.

One evening I had been reading to mother, and afterward I went up to Dot. He had been very feverish and had suffered much all day, and Allan had scarcely left him; but toward evening he had grown quieter. I found Jack beside him; they were making up garlands for the grave; it was Dot's only occupation just now.

"Look here, Essie," he cried, eagerly. "Is not this a splendid wreath? We are making it all of pansies - they were father's favorite flowers. He always called them floral butterflies. Fancy a wreath of butterflies!" and Dot gave a weak little laugh. It was a very ghost of a laugh, but it was his first, and I hailed it joyfully. I praised the quaint stiff wreath. In its way it was picturesque. The rich hues of the pansies blended well - violet and gold; it was a pretty idea, laying heartsease on the breast that would never know anxiety again.

"When I get better," continued Dot, "I am going to make such a beautiful little garden by dear father. Jack and I have been planning it. We are going to have rose-trees and lilies of the valley and sweet peas - father was so fond of sweet peas; and in the spring snow-drops and crocuses and violets. Allan says I may do it."

"Yes, surely, Dot."

"I wonder what father is doing now?" he exclaimed, suddenly, putting by the unfinished wreath a little wearily. "I think the worst of people dying is that we cannot find out what they are doing," and his eyes grew large and wistful. Alas! Dot, herein lies the sting of death - silence so insupportable and unbroken!

"Shall I read you your favorite chapter?" I asked, softly; for every day Dot made us read to him the description of that City with its golden streets and gem-built walls; but he shook his head,

"It glitters too much for my head to-night," he said, quaintly; "it is too bright and shining. I would rather think of dear father walking in those green pastures, with all the good people who have died. It must be very beautiful there, Esther. But I think father would be happier if I were with him."

"Oh, Dot, no!" for the bare idea pained me; and I felt I must argue this notion away. "Allan and I could not spare you, or mother either; and there's Jack - what would poor Jack do without her playfellow?"

"I don't feel I shall ever play again," said Dot, leaning his chin on his mites of hands and peering at us in his shrewd way. "Jack is a girl, and she cannot understand; but when one is only a Dot, and has an ugly crutch and a back that never leaves off aching, and a father that has gone to heaven, one does not care to be left behind."

"But you are not thinking of us, Dot, and how unhappy it would make us to lose you too," I returned. And now the tears would come one by one; Dot saw them, and wiped them off with his sleeve.

"Don't be silly, Esther," he said, in a coaxing little voice. "I am not going yet. Allan says I may live to be a man. He said so last night; and then he told me he was afraid we should be very poor; and that made me sorry, for I knew I should never be able to work, with my poor back."

"But Allan and I will work for you, my darling," I exclaimed, throwing my arms round him; "only you must not leave us, Dot, even for father;" and as I said this I began to sob bitterly. I was terribly ashamed of myself when Allan came in and discovered me in the act; and there was Jack keeping me company, and frowning away her tears dreadfully.

I thought Allan would have scolded us all round; but no, he did nothing of the kind. He patted Jack's wet cheeks and laughed at the hole in her handkerchief; and he then seated himself on the bed, and asked me very gently what was the matter with us all. Dot was spokesman: he stated the facts of the case rather lugubriously and in a slightly injured voice.

"Esther is crying because she is selfish, and I am afraid I am selfish too."

"Most likely," returned Allan, dryly; "it is a human failing. What is the case in point, Frankie?"

Allan was the only one of us who ever called Dot by his proper name.

"I should not mind growing up to be a man," replied

Rosa Nouchette Carey

Dot, fencing a little, "if I were big and strong like you," taking hold of the huge sinewy hand. "I could work then for mother and the girls; but now you will be always obliged to take care of me, and so - and so - " and here Dot's lips quivered a little, "I would rather go with dear father, if Esther would not cry about it so."

"No, no, you must stay with us, Sonny," returned Allan, cheerily. "Esther and I are not going to give you up so easily. Why, look here, Frankie; I will tell you a secret. One of these days I mean to have a nice little house of my own, and Esther and you shall come and live with me, and I will go among my patients all the morning, and in the evening I shall come home very lazy and tired, and Esther shall fetch me my slippers and light the lamp, and I shall get my books, and you will have your drawing, and Esther will mend our clothes, and we shall be as cozy as possible."

"Yes, yes," exclaimed Dot, clapping his hands. The snug picture had fascinated his childish fancy; Allan's fireside had obscured the lights of paradise. From this time this imaginary home of Allan's became his favorite castle in the air. When we were together he would often talk of it as though it were reality. We had planted the garden and furnished the parlor a dozen times over before the year was out; and so strong is a settled imagination that I am almost sure Dot believed that somewhere there existed the little white cottage with the porch covered with honeysuckle, and the low bay-window with the great pots of flowering plants, beside which Dot's couch was to stand.

I don't think Jack enjoyed these talks so much as Dot and I did, as we made no room for her in our castle-building.

"You must not live with us, Jack," Dot would say, very gravely; "you are only a girl, and we don't want girls" - what was I, I wonder? - "but you shall come and see us once a week, and Esther will give you brown bread and honey out of our beehives; for we had arranged there must be a row of beehives under a southern wall where peaches were to grow; and as for white lilies, we were to have dozens of them. Dear, dear, how harmless all these fancies were, and yet they kept us cheerful and warded off many an hour of depression from pain when Dot's back was bad. I remember one more thing that Allan said that night, when we were all better and more cheerful, for it was rather a grave speech for a young man; but then Allan had these fits of gravity.

"Never mind thinking if you will grow up to be a man, Dot. Wishing won't help us to die an hour sooner, and the longest life must have an end some day. What we have to do is to take up our life, and do the best we can with it while it lasts, and to be kind and patient, and help one another. Most likely Esther and I will have to work hard enough all our lives - we shall work, and you may have to suffer; but we cannot do without you any more than you can do without us. There, Frankie!"

CHAPTER IV.

UNCLE GEOFFREY.

The day after the funeral Uncle Geoffrey held a family council, at which we were all present, except mother and Dot; he preferred talking to her alone afterward.

Oh, what changes! what incredible changes! We must leave Combe Manor at once. With the exception of a few hundred pounds that had been mother's portion, the only dowry that her good old father, a naval captain, had been able to give her, we were literally penniless. The boys were not able to help us much. Allan was only a house-surgeon in one of the London hospitals; and Fred, who called himself an artist, had never earned a penny. He was a fair copyist, and talked the ordinary art jargon, and went about all day in his brown velveteen coat, and wore his hair rather long; but we never saw much result from his Roman studies; latterly he had somewhat neglected his painting, and had taken to violin playing and musical composition. Uncle Geoffrey used to shake his head and say he was "Jack of all trades and master of none," which was not far from the mark. There was a great deal of talk between the three, before anything was settled.

Fred was terribly aggravating to Uncle Geoffrey, I could see; but then he was so miserable, poor fellow;

he would not look at things in their proper light, and he had a way with him as though he thought Uncle Geoffrey was putting upon him. The discussion grew very warm at last, for Allan sided with Uncle Geoffrey, and then Fred said every one was against him. It struck me Uncle Geoffrey pooh-poohed Fred's whim of being an artist; he wanted him to go into an office; there was a vacant berth he could secure by speaking to an old friend of his, who was in a China tea-house, a most respectable money-making firm, and Fred would have a salary at once, with good prospects of rising; but Fred passionately scouted the notion. He would rather enlist; he would drown, or hang himself sooner. There were no end of naughty things he said; only Carrie cried and begged him not to be so wicked, and that checked him.

Uncle Geoffrey lost his patience at last, and very nearly told him he was an idiot, to his face; but Fred looked so handsome and miserable, that he relented; and at last it was arranged that Fred was to take a hundred pounds of mother's money - she would have given him the whole if she could, poor dear - and take cheap rooms in London, and try how he could get on by teaching drawing and taking copying orders.

"Remember, Fred," continued Uncle Geoffrey, rather sternly, "you are taking a sixth part of your mother's entire income; all that she has for herself and these girls; if you squander it rashly, you will be robbing the widow and the fatherless. You have scouted my well-meant advice, and Allan's" - he went on - "and are marking out your own path in life very foolishly, as we think; remember, you have only yourself to blame, if you make that life a failure. Artists are of the same stuff as other men, and ought to be sober, steady, and

Rosa Nouchette Carey

persevering; without patience and effort you cannot succeed."

"When my picture is accepted by the hanging committee, you and Allan will repent your sneers," answered Fred, bitterly.

"We do not sneer, my boy," returned Uncle Geoffrey, more mildly - for he remembered Fred's father had only been dead a week - "we are only doubtful of the wisdom of your choice; but there, work hard at your daubs, and keep out of debt and bad company, and you may yet triumph over your cranky old uncle." And so the matter was amicably settled.

Allan's arrangements were far more simple. He was to leave the hospital in another year, and become Uncle Geoffrey's assistant, with a view to partnership. It was not quite Allan's taste, a practice in a sleepy country town; but, as he remarked rather curtly, "beggars must not be choosers," and he would as soon work under Uncle Geoffrey as any other man. I think Allan was rather ambitious in his secret views. He wanted to remain longer at the hospital and get into a London practice; he would have liked to have been higher up the tree than Uncle Geoffrey, who was quite content with his quiet position at Milnthorpe. But the most astonishing part of the domestic programme was, that we were all going to live with Uncle Geoffrey. I could scarcely believe my ears when I heard it, and Carrie was just as surprised. Could any of us credit such unselfish generosity? He had not prepared us for it in the least.

"Now, girls, you must just pack up your things, you, and the mother, and Dot; of course we must take Dot, and you must manage to shake yourselves down in the old house at Milnthorpe" - that is how he put it; "it is not so big as Combe Manor, and I daresay we shall be rather a tight fit when Allan comes; but the more the merrier, eh, Jack?"

"Oh, Uncle Geoff, do you mean it?" gasped Jack, growing scarlet; but Carrie and I could not speak for surprise.

"Mean it! Of course. What is the good of being a bachelor uncle, if one is not to be tyrannized over by an army of nephews and nieces? Do you think the plan will answer, Esther?" he said, rather more seriously.

"If you and Deborah do not mind it, Uncle Geoffrey, I am sure it ought to answer; but we shall crowd you, and put you and Deborah to sad inconvenience, I am afraid;" for I was half afraid of Deborah, who had lived with Uncle Geoffrey for five-and-twenty years, and was used to her own ways, and not over fond of young people.

"I shall not ask Deb's opinion," he answered, rather roguishly; "we must smooth her down afterward, eh, girls? Seriously, Allan, I think it is the best plan under the circumstances. I am not fond of being alone," and here Uncle Geoffrey gave a quick sigh. Poor Uncle Geoff! he had never meant to be an old bachelor, only She died while he was furnishing the old house at Milnthorpe, and he never could fix his mind on any one else.

"I like young folks about me," he continued, cheerfully. "When I get old and rheumatic, I can keep Dot company, and Jack can wait on us both. Of course

I am not a rich man, children, and we must all help to keep the kettle boiling; but the house is my own, and you can all shelter in it if you like; it will save house-rent and taxes, at any rate for the present."

"Carrie and I will work," I replied, eagerly; for, though Uncle Geoffrey was not a poor man, he was very far from being rich, and he could not possibly afford to keep us all. A third of his income went to poor Aunt Prue, who had married foolishly, and was now a widow with a large family.

Aunt Prue would have been penniless, only father and Uncle Geoff agreed to allow her a fixed maintenance. As Uncle Geoff explained to us afterward, she would now lose half her income.

"There are eight children, and two or three of them are very delicate, and take after their father. I have been thinking about it all, Esther," he said, when Allan and I were alone with him, "and I have made up my mind that I must allow her another hundred a year. Poor soul, she works hard at that school-keeping of hers, and none of the children are old enough to help her except Lawrence, and he is going into a decline, the doctors say. I am afraid we shall have to pinch a bit, unless you and Carrie get some teaching."

"Oh, Uncle Geoff, of course we shall work; and Jack, too, when she is old enough." Could he think we should be a burden on him, when we were all young and strong?

I had forgotten poor Aunt Prue, who lived a long way off, and whom we saw but seldom. She was a pretty, subdued little woman, who always wore shabby black gowns; I never saw her in a good dress in my life. Well, we were as poor as Aunt Prue now, and I wondered if we should make such a gallant fight against misfortune as she did.

We arranged matters after that - Allan and Uncle Geoff and I; for Carrie had gone to sit with mother, and Fred had strolled off somewhere. They wanted me to try my hand at housekeeping; at least, until mother was stronger and more able to bear things.

"Carrie hates it, and you have a good head for accounts," Allan observed, quietly. It seemed rather strange that they should make me take the head, when Carrie was two years older, and a week ago I was only a schoolgirl; but I felt they were right, for I liked planning and contriving, and Carrie detested anything she called domestic drudgery.

We considered ways and means after that. Uncle Geoffrey told us the exact amount of his income, He had always lived very comfortably, but when he had deducted the extra allowance for poor Aunt Prue, we saw clearly that there was not enough for so large a party; but at the first hint of this from Allan Uncle Geoffrey got quite warm and eager. Dear, generous Uncle Geoff! he was determined to share his last crust with his dead brother's widow and children.

"Nonsense, fiddlesticks!" he kept on saying; "what do I want with luxuries? Ask Deborah if I care what I eat and drink; we shall do very well, if you and Esther are not so faint-hearted." And when we found out how our protests seemed to hurt him, we let him have his own way; only Allan and I exchanged looks, which said as plainly as looks could, "Is he not the best uncle that ever lived, and will we not work our hardest to help him?"

I had a long talk with Carrie that night; she was very submissive and very sad, and seemed rather downhearted over things. She was quite as grateful for Uncle Geoff's generosity as we were, but I could see the notion of being a governess distressed her greatly. "I am very glad you will undertake the housekeeping, Esther," she said, rather plaintively; "it will leave me free for other things," and then she sighed very bitterly, and got up and left me. I was a little sorry that she did not tell me all that was in her mind, for, if we are "to bear each other's burdens," it is necessary to break down the reserve that keeps us out of even a sister's heart sometimes.

But though Carrie left me to my own thoughts, I was not able to quiet myself for hours. If I had only Jessie to whom I could talk! and then it seemed to me as though it were months since we sat together in the garden of Redmayne House talking out our girlish philosophy.

Only a fortnight ago, and yet how much had happened since then! What a revolution in our home-world! Dear father lying in his quiet grave; ourselves penniless orphans, obliged to leave Combe Manor, and indebted to our generous benefactor for the very roof that was to cover us and the food that we were to eat.

Ah, well! I was only a schoolgirl, barely seventeen. No wonder I shrank back a little appalled from the responsibilities that awaited me. I was to be Uncle Geoff's housekeeper, his trusted right-hand and referee. I was to manage that formidable Deborah, and the stolid, broad-faced Martha; and there was mother so broken in health and spirits, and Dot, and Jack, with her hoidenish ways and torn frocks, and Allan miles away from me, and Carrie - well, I felt half afraid of Carrie to-night; she seemed meditating great things when I wanted her to compass daily duties. I hoped she would volunteer to go on with Jack's lessons and help with the mending, and I wondered with more forebodings what things she was planning for which I was to leave her free.

All these things tired me, and I sat rather dismally in the moonlight looking out at the closed white lilies and the swaying branches of the limes, until a text suddenly flashed into my mind, "As thy day, so shall thy strength be." I lit my candle and opened my Bible, that I might read over the words for myself. Yes, there they were shining before my eyes, like "apples of gold in pictures of silver," refreshing and comforting my worn-out spirits. Strength promised for the day, but not beforehand, supplies of heavenly manna, not to be hoarded or put by; the daily measure, daily gathered.

An old verse of Bishop Ken's came to my mind. Very quaint and rich in wisdom it was:

"Does each day upon its wing
Its appointed burden bring?
Load it not besides with sorrow
That belongeth to the morrow.
When by God the heart is riven,
Strength is promised, strength is given:
But fore-date the day of woe,
And alone thou bear'st the blow."

When I had said this over to myself, I laid my head on

Rosa Nouchette Carey

the pillow and slept soundly.

Mother and I had a nice little talk the next day. It was arranged that I was to go over to Milnthorpe with Uncle Geoffrey, who was obliged to return home somewhat hastily, in order to talk to Deborah and see what furniture would be required for the rooms that were placed at our disposal. As I was somewhat aghast at the amount of business entrusted to my inexperienced hands, Allan volunteered to help me, as Carrie could not be spared.

We were to stay two or three days, make all the arrangements that were necessary, and then come back and prepare for the flitting. If Allan were beside me, I felt that I could accomplish wonders; nevertheless, I carried rather a harassed face into dear mother's dressing-room that morning.

"Oh, Esther, how pale and tired you look!" were her first words as I came toward her couch. "Poor child, we are making you a woman before your time!" and her eyes filled with tears.

"I am seventeen," I returned, with an odd little choke in my voice, for I could have cried with her readily at that moment. "That is quite a great age, mother; I feel terribly old, I assure you."

"You are our dear, unselfish Esther," she returned, lovingly. Dear soul, she always thought the best of us all, and my heart swelled how proudly, and oh! how gratefully, when she told me in her sweet gentle way what a comfort I was to her.

"You are so reliable, Esther," she went on, "that we all

look to you as though you were older. You must be Uncle Geoffrey's favorite, I think, from the way he talks about you. Carrie is very sweet and good too, but she is not so practical."

"Oh, mother, she is ever so much better than I!" I cried, for I could not bear the least disparagement of my darling Carrie. "Think how pretty she is, and how little she cares for dress and admiration. If I were like that," I added, flushing a little over my words, "I'm afraid I should be terribly vain."

Mother smiled a little at that.

"Be thankful then that you are saved that temptation." And then she stroked my hot cheek and went on softly: "Don't think so much about your looks, child; plain women are just as vain as pretty ones. Not that you are plain, Esther, in my eyes, or in the eyes of any one who loves you." But even that did not quite comfort me, for in my secret heart my want of beauty troubled me sadly. There, I have owned the worst of myself - it is out now.

We talked for a long time after that about the new life that lay before us, and again I marveled at mother's patience and submission; but when I told her so she only hid her face and wept.

"What does it matter?" she said, at last, when she had recovered herself a little. "No home can be quite a home to me now without him. If I could live within sight of his grave, I should be thankful; but Combe Manor and Milnthrope are the same to me now." And though these words struck me as strange at first, I understood afterward; for in the void and waste of her widowed life no outer change of circumstances seemed to disturb her, except for our sakes and for us.

She seemed to feel Uncle Geoffrey's kindness as a sort of stay and source of endless comfort. "Such goodness - such unselfishness!" she kept murmuring to herself; and then she wanted to hear all that Allan and I proposed.

"How I wish I could get strong and help you," she said, wistfully, when I had finished. "With all that teaching and housekeeping, I am afraid you will overtax your strength."

"Oh, no, Carrie will help me," I returned, confidently. "Uncle Geoffrey is going to speak to some of his patients about us. He rather thinks those Thornes who live opposite to him want a governess."

"That will be nice and handy, and save you a walk," she returned, brightening up at the notion that one of us would be so near her; but though I would not have hinted at such a thing, I should rather have enjoyed the daily walk. I was fond of fresh air, and exercise, and rushing about, after the manner of girls, and it seemed rather tame and monotonous just to cross the street to one's work; but I remembered Allan's favorite speech, "Beggars must not be choosers," and held my peace.

On the whole, I felt somewhat comforted by my talk with mother. If she and Uncle Geoffrey thought so well of me, I must try and live up to their good opinion. There is nothing so good as to fix a high standard for one's self. True, we may never reach it, never satisfy ourselves, but the continued effort strengthens and elevates us.

I went into Carrie's room to tell her about the Thornes, and lay our plans together, but she was reading Thomas a Kempis, and did not seem inclined to be disturbed, so I retreated somewhat discomforted.

But I forgot my disappointment a moment afterward, when I went into the schoolroom and found Dot fractious and weary, and Jack vainly trying to amuse him. Allan was busy, and the two children had passed a solitary morning.

"Dot wanted Carrie to read to him, but she said she was too tired, and I could do it," grumbled Jack, disconsolately.

"I don't like Jack's reading; it is too jerky, and her voice is too loud," returned Dot; but his countenance smoothed when I got the book and read to him, and soon he fell into a sound sleep.

CHAPTER V.

THE OLD HOUSE AT MILNTHORPE.

The following afternoon Uncle Geoffrey, Allan, and I, started for Milnthorpe. Youthful grief is addicted to restlessness - it is only the old who can sit so silently and weep; it was perfectly natural, then, that I should hail a few days' change with feelings of relief.

It was rather late in the evening when we arrived. As we drove through the market place there was the usual group of idlers loitering on the steps of the Red Lion, who stared at us lazily as we passed. Milnthorpe was an odd, primitive little place - the sunniest and sleepiest of country towns. It had a steep, straggling Highstreet, which ended in a wide, deserted-looking square, which rather reminded one of the Place in some Continental town. The weekly markets were held here, on which occasion the large white portico of the Red Lion was never empty. Milnthorpe woke with brief spasms of life on Monday morning; broad-shouldered men jostled each other on the grass-grown pavements; large country wagons, sweet-smelling in haymaking seasons, blocked up the central spaces; country women, with gay-colored handkerchiefs, sold eggs, and butter, and poultry In the square; and two or three farmers, with their dogs at their heels, lingered under the windows of the Red Lion, fingering the samples in their pockets, and exchanging dismal prognostications concerning the crops and the weather. One side of the square was occupied by St. Barnabas, with its pretty shaded churchyard and old gray vicarage. On the opposite side was the handsome red brick house occupied by Mr. Lucas, the banker, and two or three other houses, more or less pretentious, inhabited by the gentry of Milnthorpe.

Uncle Geoffrey lived at the lower end of the High street. It was a tall, narrow house, with old-fashioned windows and wire blinds. These blinds, which were my detestation, were absolutely necessary, as the street door opened directly on the street. There was one smooth, long step, and that was all. It had rather a dull outside look, but the moment one entered the narrow wainscoted hall, there was a cheery vista of green lawn and neatly graveled paths through the glass door.

The garden was the delight of Uncle Geoffrey's heart. It was somewhat narrow, to match the house; but in the center of the lawn, there was a glorious mulberry tree, the joy of us children. Behind was a wonderful intricacy of slim, oddly-shaped flower-beds, inter-sected by miniature walks, where two people could with difficulty walk abreast; and beyond this lay a tolerable kitchen garden, where Deborah grew cabbages and all sorts of homely herbs, and where tiny pink roses and sturdy sweet-williams blossomed among the gooseberry bushes.

On one side of the house were two roomy parlors, divided by folding doors. We never called them anything but parlors, for the shabby wainscoted walls and old-fashioned furniture forbade any similitude to the modern drawing-room.

On the other side of the hall was Uncle Geoffrey's study - a somewhat grim, dingy apartment, with brown shelves full of ponderous tomes, a pipe-rack filled with fantastic pipes, deep old cupboards full of hetereo-geneous rubbish, and wide easy-chairs that one could hardly lift, one of which was always occupied by Jumbles, Uncle Geoffrey's dog.

Jumbles was a great favorite with us all. He was a solemn, wise-looking dog of the terrier breed, indeed, I believe Uncle Geoff called him a Dandy Dinmont - blue-gray in color, with a great head, and deep-set intelligent eyes. It was Uncle Geoffrey's opinion that Jumbles understood all one said to him. He would sit with his head slightly on one side, thumping his tail against the floor, with a sort of glimmer of fun in his eyes, as though he comprehended our conversation, and interposed a "Hear, hear!" and when he had had enough of it, and we were growing prosy, he would turn over on his back with an expression of abject weariness, as though canine reticence objected to human garrulity.

Jumbles was a rare old philosopher - a sort of four-footed Diogenes. He was discerning in his friendships, somewhat aggressive and splenetic to his equals; intolerant of cats, whom he hunted like vermin, and rather disdainfully condescending to the small dogs of Milnthorpe. Jumbles always accompanied Uncle Geoffrey in his rounds. He used to take his place in the gig with undeviating punctuality; nothing induced him to desert his post when the night-bell rang. He would rouse up from his sleep, and go out in the coldest weather. We used to hear his deep bark under the window as they sallied out in the midnight gloom.

The morning after we arrived, Allan and I made a tour of inspection through the house. There were only three rooms on the first floor - Uncle Geoffrey's, with its huge four-post bed; a large front room, that we both decided would just do for mother; and a smaller one at the back, that, after a few minutes' deliberation, I allotted to Carrie.

It caused me an envious pang or two before I yielded it, for I knew I must share a large upper room with Jack; the little room behind it must be for Dot, and the larger one would by-and-by be Allan's. I confess my heart sank a little when I thought of Jack's noisiness and thriftless ways; but when I remembered how fond she was of good books, and the great red-leaved diary that lay on her little table, I thought it better that Carrie should have a quiet corner to herself, and then she would be near mother.

If only Jack could be taught to hold her tongue sometimes, and keep her drawers in order, instead of strewing her room with muddy boots and odd items of attire! Well, perhaps it might be my mission to train Jack to more orderly habits. I would set her a good example, and coax her to follow it. She was good-tempered and affectionate, and perhaps I should find her sufficiently pliable. I was so lost in these anxious thoughts that Allan had left me unperceived. I found him in the back parlor, seated on the table, and looking about him rather gloomily.

"I say, Esther!" he called out, as soon as he caught sight of me, "I am afraid mother and Carrie will find this rather shabby after the dear old rooms at Combe Manor. Could we not furbish it up a little?" And Allan looked discontentedly at the ugly curtains and little,

Rosa Nouchette Carey

straight horse-hair sofa. Everything had grown rather shabby, only Uncle Geoffrey had not found it out.

"Oh, of course!" I exclaimed, joyfully, for all sorts of brilliant thoughts had come to me while I tossed rather wakefully in the early morning hours. "Don't you know, Allan, that Uncle Geoffrey has decided to send mother and Carrie and Dot down to the sea for a week, while you and I and Jack make things comfortable for them? Now, why should we not help ourselves to the best of the furniture at Combe Manor, and make Uncle Geoff turn out all these ugly things? We might have our pretty carpet from the drawing-room, and the curtains, and mother's couch, and some of the easy-chairs, and the dear little carved cabinet with our purple china; it need not all be sold when we want it so badly for mother."

Allan was so delighted at the idea that we propounded our views to Uncle Geoffrey at dinner-time; but he did not see the thing quite in our light.

"Of course you will need furniture for the bedrooms," he returned, rather dubiously; "but I wanted to sell the rest of the things that were not absolutely needed, and invest the money."

But this sensible view of the matter did not please me or Allan. We had a long argument, which ended in a compromise - the question of carpets might rest. Uncle Geoffrey's was a good Brussels, although it was dingy; but I might retain, if I liked, the pretty striped curtains from our drawing-room at Combe Manor, and mother's couch, and a few of the easy-chairs, and the little cabinet with the purple china; and then there was mother's inlaid work-table, and Carrie's davenport, and books belonging to both of us, and a little gilt clock that father had given mother on her last wedding-day - all these things would make an entire renovation in the shabby parlors.

I was quite excited by all these arrangements; but an interview with Deborah soon cooled my ardor.

Allan and Jumbles had gone out with Uncle Geoffrey, and I was sitting at the window looking over the lawn and the mulberry tree, when a sudden tap at the door startled me from my reverie. Of course it was Deborah; no one else's knuckles sounded as though they were iron. Deborah was a tall, angular woman, very spare and erect of figure, with a severe cast of countenance, and heavy black curls pinned up under her net cap; her print dresses were always starched until they crackled, and on Sunday her black silk dress rustled as I never heard any silk dress rustle before.

"Yes, Deborah, what is it?" I asked, half-frightened; for surely my hour had come. Deborah was standing so very erect, with the basket of keys in her hands, and her mouth drawn down at the corners.

"Master said this morning," began Deborah, grimly, "as how there was a new family coming to live here, and that I was to go to Miss Esther for orders. Five-and-twenty years have I cooked master's dinners for him, and received his orders, and never had a word of complaint from his lips, and now he is putting a mistress over me and Martha."

"Oh, Deborah," I faltered, and then I came to a full stop; for was it not trying to a woman of her age and disposition, used to Uncle Geoffrey's bachelor ways, to

Rosa Nouchette Carey

have a houseful of young people turned on her hands? She and Martha would have to work harder, and they were both getting old. I felt so much for her that the tears came into my eyes, and my voice trembled.

"It is hard!" I burst out; "it is very hard for you and Martha to have your quiet life disturbed. But how could we help coming here, when we had no home and no money, and Uncle Geoffrey was so generous? And then there was Dot and mother so ailing." And at the thought of all our helplessness, and Uncle Geoffrey's gcodness a great tear rolled down my cheek. It was very babyish and undignified; but, after all, no assumption of womanliness would have helped me so much. Deborah's grim mouth relaxed; under her severe exterior, and with her sharp tongue, there beat a very kind heart, and Dot was her weak point.

"Well, well, crying won't help the pot to boil, Miss Esther!" she said, brusquely enough; but I could see she was coming round. "Master was always that kind-hearted that he would have sheltered the whole parish if he could. I am not blaming him, though it goes hard with Martha and me, who have led peaceable, orderly lives, and never had a mistress or thought of one since Miss Blake died, and the master took up thoughts of single blessedness in earnest."

"What sort of woman was Miss Blake?" I asked, eagerly, forgetting my few troubled tears at the thought of Uncle Geoffrey's one romance. The romance of middle-aged people always came with a faint, far-away odor to us young ones, like some old garment laid up in rose-leaves or lavender, which must needs be of quaint fashion and material, but doubtless precious in the eyes of the wearer.

"Woman!" returned Deborah, with an angry snort; "she was a lady, if there ever was one. We don't see her sort every day, I can tell you that, Miss Esther; a pretty-spoken, dainty creature, with long fair curls, that one longed to twine round one's fingers."

"She was pretty, then?" I hazarded more timidly.

"Pretty! she was downright beautiful. Miss Carrie reminds me of her sometimes, but she is not near so handsome as poor Miss Rose. She used to come here sometimes with her mother, and she and master would sit under that mulberry tree. I can see her now walking over the grass in her white gown, with some apple blossoms in her hand, talking and laughing with him. It was a sad day when she lay in the fever, and did not know him, for all his calling to her 'Rose! Rose!' I was with her when she died, and I thought he would never hold up his head again."

"Poor Uncle Geoffrey! But he is cheerful and contented now."

"But there, I must not stand gossiping," continued Deborah, interrupting herself. "I have only brought you the keys, and wish to know what preserve you and Mr. Allan might favor for tea."

But here I caught hold, not of the key-basket, but of the hard, work-worn hand that held it.

"Oh, Deborah! do be good to us!" I broke out: "we will trouble you and Martha as little as possible, and we are all going to put our shoulders to the wheel and help ourselves; and we have no home but this, and no one to take care of us but Uncle Geoffrey."

"I don't know but I will make some girdle cakes for tea," returned Deborah, in the most imperturbable voice; and she turned herself round abruptly, and walked out of the room without another word. But I was quite well satisfied and triumphant. When Deborah baked girdle cakes, she meant the warmest of welcomes, and no end of honor to Uncle Geoffrey's guests.

"Humph! girdle cakes!" observed Uncle Geoffrey, with a smile, as he regarded them. "Deb is in a first-rate humor, then. You have played your cards well, old lady," and his eyes twinkled merrily.

I went into the kitchen after tea, and had another long talk with Deborah. Dear old kitchen! How many happy hours we children had spent in it! It was very low and dark, and its two windows looked out on the stable-yard; but in the evening, when the fire burned clear and the blinds were drawn, it was a pleasant place. Deborah and Martha used to sit in the brown Windsor chairs knitting, with Puff, the great tabby cat, beside them, and the firelight would play on the red brick floor and snug crimson curtains.

Deborah and I had a grand talk that night. She was a trifle obstinate and dogmatical, but we got on fairly well. To do her justice, her chief care seemed to be that her master should not be interfered with in any of his ways. "He will work harder than ever," she groaned, "now there are all these mouths to feed. He and Jumbles will be fairly worn out."

But our talk contented me. I had enlisted Deborah's sympathies on our side. I felt the battle was over. I was only a "bit thing" as Deborah herself called me, and I was tolerably tired when I went up to my room that night.

Not that I felt inclined for sleep. Oh dear no! I just dragged the big easy-chair to the window, and sat there listening to the patter of summer rain on the leaves.

It was very dark, for the moon had hidden her face; but through the cool dampness there crept a delicious fragrance of wet jasmine and lilies. I wanted to have a good "think;" not to sit down and take myself to pieces. Oh no, that was Carrie's way. Such introspection bored me and did me little good, for it only made me think more of myself and less of the Master; but I wanted to review the past fortnight, and look the future in the face. Foolish Esther! As though we can look at a veiled face. Only the past and the present is ours; the future is hidden with God.

Yes, a fortnight ago I was a merry, heedless schoolgirl, with no responsibilities and few duties, except that laborious one of self-improvement, which must go on, under some form or other, until we die. And now, on my shrinking shoulders lay the weight of a woman's work. I was to teach others, when I knew so little myself; it was I who was to have the largest share of home administration - I, who was so faulty, so imperfect.

Then I remembered a sentence Carrie had once read to me out of one of her innumerable books, and which had struck me very greatly at the time.

"Happy should I think myself," said St. Francis de Sales, "if I could rid myself of my imperfections but one quarter of an hour previous to my death."

Well, if a saint could say that, why should I lose heart thinking about my faults? What was the good of stirring up muddy water to try and see one's own miserable reflection, when one could look up into the serene blue of Divine Providence? If I had faults - and, alas! how many they were - I must try to remedy them; if I slipped, I must pray for strength to rise again.

Courage, Esther! "Little by little," as Uncle Geoffrey says; "small beginnings make great endings." And when I had cheered myself with these words I went tranquilly to bed.

CHAPTER VI.

THE FLITTING.

So the old Combe Manor days were over, and with them the girlhood of Esther Cameron.

Ah me! it was sad to say good-by to the dear old home of our childhood; to go round to our haunts, one by one, and look our last at every cherished nook and corner; to bid farewell to our four-footed pets, Dapple and Cherry and Brindle, and the dear little spotted calves; to caress our favorite pigeons for the last time, and to feed the greedy old turkey-cock, who had been the terror of our younger days. It was well, perhaps, that we were too busy for a prolonged leave-taking. Fred had gone to London, and his handsome lugubrious face no longer overlooked us as we packed books and china. Carrie and mother and Dot were cozily established in the little sea-side lodging, and only Allan, Jack, and I sat down to our meals in the dismantled rooms.

It was hard work trying to keep cheerful, when Allan left off whistling, as he hammered at the heavy cases, and when Jack was discovered sobbing in odd corners, with Smudge in her arms - of course Smudge would accompany us to Milnthorpe; no one could imagine Jack without her favorite sable attendant, and then Dot

Rosa Nouchette Carey

was devoted to him. Jack used to come to us with piteous pleadings to take first one and then another of her pets; now it was the lame chicken she had nursed in a little basket by the kitchen fire, then a pair of guinea pigs that belonged to Dot, and some carrier pigeons that they specially fancied; after that, she was bent on the removal of a young family of hedgehogs, and some kittens that had been discovered in the hay-loft, belonging to the stable cat.

We made a compromise at last, and entrusted to her care Carrie's tame canaries, and a cage of dormice that belonged to Dot, in whose fate Smudge look a vast amount of interest, though he never ventured to look at the canaries. The care of these interesting captives was consolatory to Jack, though she rained tears over them in secret, and was overheard by Allan telling them between her sobs that "they were all going to live in a little pokey house, without chickens or cows, or anything that would make life pleasant, and that she and they must never expect to be happy again." Ah, well! the longest day must have an end, and by-and-by the evening came when we turned away from dear old Combe Manor forever.

It was far more cheerful work fitting up the new rooms at Milnthorpe, with Deborah's strong arms to help, and Uncle Geoffrey standing by to encourage our efforts; even Jack plucked up heart then, and hung up the canaries, and hid away the dormice out of Smudge's and Jumbles' reach, and consented to stretch her long legs in our behalf. Allan and I thought we had done wonders when all was finished, and even Deborah gave an approving word.

"I think mother and Carrie will be pleased," I said, as I

put some finishing touches to the tea-table on the evening we expected them. Allan had gone to the station to meet them, and only Uncle Geoffrey was my auditor. There was a great bowl of roses on the table, great crimson-hearted, delicious roses, and a basket of nectarines, that some patient had sent to Uncle Geoffrey. The parlors looked very pretty and snug; we had arranged our books on the shelves, and had hung up two or three choice engravings, and there was the gleam of purple and gold china from the dark oak cabinet, and by the garden window there were mother's little blue couch and her table and workbox, and Carrie's davenport, and an inviting easy-chair. The new curtains looked so well, too. No wonder Uncle Geoffrey declared that he did not recognize his old room.

"I am sure they will be pleased," I repeated, as I moved the old-fashioned glass dish full of our delicious Combe Manor honey; but Uncle Geoffrey did not answer; he was listening to some wheels in the distance.

"There they are," he said, snatching up his felt wide-awake. "Don't expect your mother to notice much to-night, Esther; poor thing, this is a sad coming home to her."

I need not have worked so hard; that was my first thought when I saw mother's face as she entered the room. She was trembling like a leaf, and her face was all puckered and drawn, as I kissed her; but Uncle Geoffrey would not let her sit down or look at anything.

"No, no, you shall not make efforts for us to-night," he

Rosa Nouchette Carey

said, patting her as though she were a child. "Take your mother upstairs, children, and let her have quiet! do you hear, nothing but quiet to-night." And then Allan drew her arm through his.

I cried shame on myself for a selfish, disappointed pang, as I followed them. Of course Uncle Geoffrey was right and wise, as he always was, and I was still more ashamed of myself when I entered the room and found mother crying as though her heart would break, and clinging to Allan.

"Oh, children, children! how can I live without your father?" she exclaimed, hysterically. Well, it was wise of Allan, for he let that pass and never said a word; he only helped me remove the heavy widow's bonnet and cloak, and moved the big chintz couch nearer to the window, and then he told me to be quick and bring her some tea; and when I returned he was sitting by her, fanning and talking to her in his pleasant boyish way; and though the tears were still flowing down her pale cheeks she sobbed less convulsively.

"You have both been so good, and worked so hard, and I cannot thank you," she whispered, taking my hand, as I stood near her.

"Esther does not want to be thanked," returned Allan, sturdily. "Now you will take your tea, won't you, mother? and by-and-by one of the girls shall come and sit with you."

"Are we to go down and leave her?" I observed, dubiously, as Allan rose from his seat.

"Yes, go, both of you, I shall be better alone; Allan

knows that," with a grateful glance as I reluctantly obeyed her. I was too young to understand the healing effects of quiet and silence in a great grief; to me the thought of such loneliness was dreadful, until, later on, she explained the whole matter.

"I am never less alone than when I am alone," she said once, very simply to me. "I have the remembrance of your dear father and his words and looks ever before me, and God is so near - one feels that most when one is solitary." And her words remained with me long afterward.

It was not such a very sad evening, after all. The sea air had done Dot good, and he was in better spirits; and then Carrie was so good and sweet, and so pleased with everything.

"How kind of you, Esther," she said, with tears in her eyes, as I led her into her little bedroom. "I hardly dared hope for this, and so near dear mother." Well, it was very tiny, but very pretty, too. Carrie had her own little bed, in which she had slept from a child, and the evening sun streamed full on it, and a pleasant smell of white jasmine pervaded it; part of the window was framed with the delicate tendrils and tiny buds; and there was her little prayer-desk, with its shelf of devotional books, and her little round table and easy-chair standing just as it used; only, if one looked out of the window, instead of the belt of green circling meadows, dotted over by grazing cattle there was the lawn and the mulberry tree - a little narrow and homely, but still pleasant.

Carrie's eyes looked very vague and misty when I left her and went down to Dot. Allan had put him to bed, but he would not hear of going to sleep; he had his dormice beside him, and Jumbles was curled up at the foot of the bed; he wanted to show me his seaweed and shells, and tell me about the sea.

"I can't get it out of my head, Essie," he said, sitting up among his pillows and looking very wide-awake and excited. "I used to fall asleep listening to the long wash and roll of the waves, and in the morning there it was again. Don't you love the sea?"

"Yes, dearly, Dot; and so does Allan."

"It reminded me of the "Pilgrim's Progress" - just the last part. Don't you remember the river that every one was obliged to cross? Carrie told me it meant death." I nodded; Dot did not always need an answer to his childish fancies, he used to like to tell them all out to Allan and me. "One night," he went on, "my back was bad, and I could not sleep, and Carrie made me up a nest of pillows in a big chair by the window, and we sat there ever so long after mother was fast asleep.

"It was so light - almost as light as day - and there were all sorts of sparkles over the water, as though it were shaking out tiny stars in play; and there was one broad golden path - oh! it was so beautiful - and then I thought of Christian and Christiana, and Mr. Ready-to-halt, and father, and they all crossed the river, you know."

"Yes, Dot," I whispered. And then I repeated softly the well-known verse we had so often sung:

"One army of the living God,
  To His command we bow;

Part of the host have crossed the flood,
And part are crossing now."

"Yes, yes," he repeated, eagerly; "it seemed as though I could see father walking down the long golden path; it shone so, he could not have missed his way or fallen into the dark waters. Carrie told me that by-and-by there would be "no more sea," somehow; I was sorry for that - aren't you, Essie?"

"Oh, no, don't be sorry," I burst out, for I had often talked about this with Carrie. "It is beautiful, but it is too shifting, too treacherous, too changeable, to belong to the higher life. Think of all the cruel wrecks, of all the drowned people it has swallowed up in its rage; it devours men and women, and little children, Dot, and hides its mischief with a smile. Oh, no, it is false in its beauty, and there shall be an end of it, with all that is not true and perfect."

And when Dot had fallen asleep, I went down to Uncle Geoffrey and repeated our conversation, to which he listened with a great deal of interest.

"You are perfectly right, Esther," he said, thoughtfully; "but I think there is another meaning involved in the words 'There shall be no more sea.'"

"The sea divides us often from those we love," he went on musingly; "it is our great earthly barrier. In that perfected life that lies before us there can be no barrier, no division, no separating boundaries. In the new earth there will be no fierce torrents or engulfing ocean, no restless moaning of waves. Do you not see this?"

"Yes, indeed, Uncle Geoffrey;" but all the same I

thought in my own mind that it was a pretty fancy of the child's, thinking that he saw father walking across the moonlight sea. No, he could not have fallen in the dark water, no fear of that, Dot, when the angel of His mercy would hold him by the hand; and then I remembered a certain lake and a solemn figure walking quietly on its watery floor, and the words, "It is I, be not afraid," that have comforted many a dying heart!

Allan had to leave us the next day, and go back to his work; it was a pity, as his mere presence, the very sound of his bright, young voice, seemed to rouse mother and do her good. As for me, I knew when Allan went some of the sunshine would go with him, and the world would have a dull, work-a-day look. I tried to tell him so as we took our last walk together. There was a little lane just by Uncle Geoffrey's house; you turned right into it from the High street, and it led into the country, within half a mile of the house. There were some haystacks and a farmyard, a place that went by the name of Grubbings' Farm; the soft litter of straw tempted us to sit down for a little, and listen to the quiet lowing of the cattle as they came up from their pasture to be milked.

"It reminds me of Combe Manor," I said, and there was something wet on my cheek as I spoke; "and oh, Allan! how I shall miss you to-morrow," and I touched his coat sleeve furtively, for Allan was not one to love demonstration. But, to my surprise, he gave me a kind little pat.

"Not more than I shall miss you," he returned, cheerily. "We always get along well, you and I, don't we, little woman?" And as I nodded my head, for something seemed to impede my utterance at that moment, he went on more seriously, "You have a tough piece of work before you, Esther, you and Carrie; you will have to put your Combe Manor pride in your pockets, and summon up all your Cameron strength of mind before you learn to submit to the will of strangers.

"Our poor, pretty Carrie," he continued, regretfully; "the little saint, as Uncle Geoffrey used to call her. I am afraid her work will not be quite to her mind, but you must smoothe her way as much as possible; but there, I won't preach on my last evening; let me have your plans instead, my dear."

But I had no plans to tell him, and so we drifted by degrees into Allan's own work; and as he told me about the hospital and his student friends, and the great bustling world in which we lived, I forgot my own cares. If I had not much of a life of my own to lead, I could still live in his.

The pleasure of this talk lingered long in my memory; it was so nice to feel that Allan and I understood each other so well and had no divided interests; it always seems to me that a sister ought to dwell in the heart of a brother and keep it warm for that other and sacred love that must come by-and-by; not that the wife need drive the sister into outer darkness, but that there must be a humbler abiding in the outer court, perchance a little guest-chamber on the wall; the nearer and more royal abode must be for the elected woman among women.

There is too little giving up and coming down in this world, too much jealous assertion of right, too little yielding of the scepter in love. It may be hard - God

Rosa Nouchette Carey

knows it is hard, to our poor human nature, for some cherished sister to stand a little aside while another takes possession of the goodly mansion, yet if she be wise and bend gently to the new influence, there will be a "come up higher," long before the dregs of the feast are reached. Old bonds are not easily broken, early days have a sweetness of their own; by-and-by the sister will find her place ready for her, and welcoming hands stretched out without grudging.

The next morning I rose early to see Allan off Just at the last moment Carrie came down in her pretty white wrapper to bid him good-by. Allan was strapping up his portmanteau in the hall, and shook his head at her in comic disapproval. "Fie, what pale cheeks, Miss Carrie! One would think you had been burning the midnight oil." I wonder if Allan's jesting words approached the truth, for Carrie's face flushed suddenly, and she did not answer.

Allan did not seem to notice her confusion. He bade us both good-by very affectionately, and told us to be good girls and take care of ourselves, and then in a moment he was gone.

Breakfast was rather a miserable business after that; I was glad Uncle Geoffrey read his paper so industriously and did not peep behind the urn. Dot did, and slipped a hot little hand in mine, in an old-fashioned sympathizing way. Carrie, who was sitting in her usual dreamy, abstracted way, suddenly startled us all by addressing Uncle Geoffrey rather abruptly.

"Uncle Geoffrey, don't you think either Esther or I ought to go over to the Thornes? They want a governess, you know."

"Eh, what?" returned Uncle Geoffrey, a little disturbed at the interruption in the middle of the leading article. "The Thornes? Oh, yes, somebody was saying something to me the other day about them; what was it?" And he rubbed his hair a little irritably.

"We need not trouble Uncle Geoffrey," I put in, softly; "you and I can go across before mother comes down. I must speak to Deborah, and then I meant to hear Jack's lessons, but they can wait."

"Very well," returned Carrie, nonchalantly; and then she added, in her composed, elder sisterly way, "I may as well tell you, Esther, that I mean to apply for the place myself; it will be so handy, the house being just opposite; far more convenient than if I had a longer walk."

"Very well," was my response, but I could not help feeling a little relief at her decision; the absence of any walk was an evil in my eyes. The Thornes' windows looked into ours; already I had had a sufficient glimpse of three rather untidy little heads over the wire blind, and the spectacle had not attracted me. I ventured to hint my fears to Carrie that they were not very interesting children; but, to my dismay, she answered that few children are interesting, and that one was as good as another.

"But I mean to be fond of my pupils," I hazarded, rather timidly, as I took my basket of keys. I thought Uncle Geoffrey was deep in his paper again. "I think a governess ought to have a good moral influence over them. Mother always said so."

"We can have a good moral influence without any

personal fondness," returned Carrie, rather dryly. Poor girl! her work outside was distasteful to her, and she could not help showing it sometimes.

"One cannot take interest in a child without loving it in time," I returned, with a little heat, for I did not enjoy this slavish notion of duty - pure labor, and nothing else. Carrie did not answer, she leaned rather wearily against the window, and looked absently out. Uncle Geoffrey gave her a shrewd glance as he folded up the newspaper and whistled to Jumbles.

"Settle it between yourselves girls," he observed, suddenly, as he opened the door; "but if I were little Annie Thorne, I know I should choose Esther;" and with this parting thrust he left the room, making us feel terribly abashed.

CHAPTER VII.

OVER THE WAY.

I cannot say that I was prepossessed with the Thorne family, neither was Carrie.

Mrs. Thorne was what I call a loud woman; her voice was loud, and she was full of words, and rather inquisitive on the subject of her neighbors.

She was somewhat good-looking, but decidedly over-dressed. Early as it was, she was in a heavily-flounced silk dress, a little the worse for wear. I guessed that first day, with a sort of feminine intuition, that Mrs. Thorne wore out all her second-best clothes in the morning. Perhaps it was my country bringing up, but I thought how pure and fresh Carrie's modest dress looked beside it; and as for the quiet face under the neatly-trimmed bonnet, I could see Mrs. Thorne fell in love with it at once. She scarcely looked at or spoke to me, except when civility demanded it; and perhaps she was right, for who would care to look at me when Carrie was by? Then Carrie played, and I knew her exquisite touch would demand instant admiration. I was a mere bungler, a beginner beside her; she even sang a charming little *chanson*. No wonder Mrs. Thorne was delighted to secure such an accomplished person for her children's governess. The three little girls came in by-and-by - shy, awkward children, with their mother's black eyes, but without her fine complexion; plain, uninteresting little girls, with a sort of solemn non-intelligence in their blank countenances, and a perceptible shrinking from their mother's sharp voice.

"Shake hands with Miss Cameron, Lucy; she is going to teach you all manner of nice things. Hold yourself straight, Annie. What will these young ladies think of you, Belle, if they look at your dirty pinafore? Mine are such troublesome children," she continued, in a complaining voice; "they are never nice and tidy and obedient, like other children. Mr. Thorne spoils them, and then finds fault with me."

"What is your name, dear?" I whispered to the youngest, when Mrs. Thorne had withdrawn with Carrie for a few minutes. They were certainly very unattractive children; nevertheless, my heart warmed to them, as it did to all children. I was child-lover all my life.

"Annie," returned the little one, shyly rolling her fat arms in her pinafore. She was less plain than the others, and had not outgrown her plumpness.

"Do you know I have a little brother at home, who is a sad invalid;" and then I told them about Dot, about his patience and his sweet ways, and how he amused himself when he could not get off his couch for weeks; and as I warmed and grew eloquent with my subject, their eyes became round and fixed, and a sort of dawning interest woke up on their solemn faces; they forgot I was a stranger, and came closer, and Belle laid a podgy and a very dirty hand on my lap.

"How old is your little boy?" asked Lucy, in a shrill whisper. And as I answered her Mrs. Thorne and Carrie re-entered the room. They both looked surprised when they saw the children grouped round me; Carrie's eyebrows elevated themselves a little quizzically, and Mrs. Thorne called them away rather sharply.

"Don't take liberties with strangers, children. What will Miss Cameron think of such manners?" And then she dismissed them rather summarily. I saw Annie steal a little wistful look at me as she followed her sisters.

We took our leave after that. Mrs. Thorne shook hands with us very graciously, but her parting words were addressed to Carrie. "On Monday, then. Please give my kind regards to Dr. Cameron, and tell him how thoroughly satisfied I am with the proposed arrangement." And Carrie answered very prettily, but as the door closed she sighed heavily.

"Oh, what children! and what a mother!" she gasped, as she took my arm, and turned my foot-steps away from the house. "Never mind Jack, I am going to the service at St. Barnabas; I want some refreshment after what I have been through." And she sighed again.

"But, Carrie," I remonstrated, "I have no time to spare. You know how Jack has been neglected, and how I have promised Allan to do my best for her until we can afford to send her to school."

"You can walk with me to the church door," she returned, decidedly. I was beginning to find out that Carrie could be self-willed sometimes. "I must talk to you, Esther; I must tell you how I hate it. Fancy trying to hammer French and music into those children's heads, when I might - I might - " But here she stopped, actually on the verge of crying.

"Oh, my darling, Carrie!" I burst out, for I never could bear to see her sweet face clouded for a moment, and she so seldom cried or gave way to any emotion. "Why would you not let me speak? I might have saved you this. I might have offered myself in your stead, and set you free for pleasanter work." But she shook her head, and struggled for composure.

"You would not have done for Mrs. Thorne, Esther. Don't think me vain if I say that I play and sing far better than you."

"A thousand times better," I interposed. "And then you can draw."

"Well, Mrs. Thorne is a woman who values accomplishments. You are clever at some things; you speak French fairly, and then you are a good Latin scholar" (for Allan and I studied that together); "you can lay a solid foundation, as Uncle Geoffrey says; but Mrs. Thorne does not care about that," continued Carrie a little bitterly; "she wants a flimsy super-structure of accomplishments - music, and French, and drawing, as much as I can teach a useful life-work, Esther."

"Well, why not?" I returned, with a little spirit, for here was one of Carrie's old arguments. "If it be the work given us to do, it must be a useful life-work. It might be our duty to make artificial flowers for our livelihood - hundreds of poor creatures do that - and you would not scold them for waste of time, I suppose?"

"Anyhow, it is not work enough for me," replied Carrie firmly, and passing over my clever argument with a dignified silence; "it is the drudgery of mere ornamentation that I hate. I will do my best for those dreadful children, Esther. Are they not pitiful little overdressed creatures? And I will try and please their mother though I have not a thought in common with her. And when I have finished my ornamental brick-making - told my tales of the bricks - " here she paused, and looked at me with a heightened color.

"And what then?" I asked, rather crossly, for there was a flaw in her speech somewhere, and I could not find it out.

"We shall see, my wise little sister," she said, letting go my arm with a kind pressure. "See, here is St. Barnabas; is it not a dear old building? Must you go back to Jack?"

"Yes, I must," I answered, shortly. "*Laborare est orare* - to labor is to pray, in my case, Carrie;" and with that I left her.

But Carrie's arguments had seriously discomposed me. I longed to talk it all out with Allan, and I do not think I ever missed him so much as I did that day. I am afraid I was rather impatient with Jack that morning; to be sure she was terribly awkward and inattentive; she would put her elbows on the table, and ink her fingers, and then she had a way of jerking her hair out of her eyes, which drove me nearly frantic. I began to think we really must send her to school. We had done away with the folding doors, they always creaked so, and had hung up some curtains in their stead; through the folds I could catch glimpses of dear mother leaning back in her chair, with Dot beside her. He was spelling over his lesson to her, in a queer, little sing-song voice, and they looked so cool and quiet that the contrast was quite provoking; and there was Carrie kneeling in some dim corner, and soothing her perturbed spirits with softly-uttered psalms and prayers.

"Jack," I returned, for the sixth time, "I cannot have you kick the table in that schoolboy fashion."

Jack looked at me with roguish malice in her eyes. "You are not quite well, Esther; you have got a pain in your temper, haven't you, now?"

I don't know what I might have answered, for Jack was right, and I was as cross as possible, only just at that moment Uncle Geoffrey put his head in at the door, and stood beaming on us like an angel of deliverance.

"Fee-fo-fum," for he sometimes called Jack by that charming *sobriquet*, indeed, he was always inventing names for her, "it is too hot for work, isn't it? I think I must give you a holiday, for I want Esther to go out with me." Uncle Geoffrey's wishes were law, and I rose at once; but not all my secret feelings of relief could prevent me from indulging in a parting thrust.

"I don't think Jack deserves the holiday," I remarked, with a severe look at the culprit; and Jack jerked her hair over her eyes this time in some confusion.

"Hullo, Fee-fo-fum, what have you been up to? Giving Esther trouble? Oh, fie! fie!"

"I only kicked the table," returned Jack, sullenly, "because I hate lessons - that I do, Uncle Geoffrey -

and I inked my fingers because I liked it; and I put my elbows on the copy-book because Esther said I wasn't to do it; and my hair got in my eyes; and William the Conqueror had six wives, I know he had; and I told Esther she had a pain in her temper, because she was as cross as two sticks; and I don't remember any more, and I don't care," finished Jack, who could be like a mule on occasions.

Uncle Geoffrey laughed - he could not help it - and then he patted Jack kindly on her rough locks. "Clever little Fee-fo-fum; so William the Conqueror had six wives, had he? Come, this is capital; we must send you to school, Jack, that is what we must do. Esther cannot be in two places at once." What did he mean by that, I wonder! And then he bid me run off and put on my hat, and not keep him waiting.

Jack's brief sullenness soon vanished, and she followed me out of the room to give me a penitent hug - that was so like Jack; the inky caress was a doubtful consolation, but I liked it, somehow.

"Where are you going, Uncle Geoff?" I asked, as we walked up the High street, followed by Jumbles, while Jack and Smudge watched us from the door.

"Miss Lucas wants to see you," he returned, briefly. "Bless me, there is Carrie, deep in conversation with Mr. Smedley. Where on earth has the girl picked him up?" And there, true enough, was Carrie, standing in the porch, talking eagerly to a fresh-colored, benevolent-looking man, whom I knew by sight as the vicar of St. Barnabas.

She must have waylaid him after service, for the other

worshipers had dropped off; we had met two or three of them in the High street. I do not know why the sight displeased me, for of course she had a right to speak to her clergyman. Uncle Geoffrey whistled under his breath, and then laughed and wondered "what the little saint had to say to her pastor;" but I did not let him go on, for I was too excited with our errand.

"Why does Miss Lucas want to see me?" I asked, with a little beating of the heart. The Lucas family were the richest people in Milnthorpe.

Mr. Lucas was the banker, and kept his carriage, and had a pretty cottage somewhere by the seaside; they were Uncle Geoffrey's patients, I knew, but what had that to do with poor little me?

"Miss Lucas wants to find some one to teach her little niece," returned Uncle Geoffrey; and then I remembered all at once that Mr. Lucas was a widower with one little girl. He had lost his wife about a year ago, and his sister had come to live with him and take care of his motherless child. What a chance this would have been for Carrie! but now it was too late. I was half afraid as we came up to the great red brick house, it was so grand and imposing, and so was the solemn-looking butler who opened the door and ushered us into the drawing-room.

As we crossed the hall some one came suddenly out on us from a dark lobby, and paused when he saw us. "Dr. Cameron! This is your niece, I suppose, whom my sister Ruth is expecting?" and as he shook hands with us he looked at me a little keenly, I thought. He was younger than I expected; it flashed across me suddenly that I had once seen his poor wife. I was standing looking out of the window one cold winter's day, when a carriage drove up to the door with a lady wrapped in furs. I remember Uncle Geoffrey went out to speak to her, and what a smile came over her face when she saw him. She was very pale, but very beautiful; every one said so in Milnthorpe, for she had been much beloved.

"My sister is in the drawing-room; you must excuse me if I say I am in a great hurry," and then he passed on with a bow. I thought him very formidable, the sort of man who would be feared as well as respected by his dependants. He had the character of being a very reserved man, with a great many acquaintances and few intimate friends. I had no idea at that time that no one understood him so well as Uncle Geoffrey.

I was decidedly nervous when I followed Uncle Geoffrey meekly into the drawing-room. Its size and splendor did not diminish my fears, and I little imagined then how I should get to love that room.

It was a little low, in spite of its spaciousness, and its three long windows opened in French fashion on to the garden. I had a glimpse of the lawn, with a grand old cedar in the middle, before my eyes were attracted to a lady in deep mourning, writing in a little alcove, half curtained off from the rest of the room, and looking decidedly cozy.

The moment she turned her face toward us at the mention of our names, my unpleasant feelings of nervousness vanished. She was such a little woman - slightly deformed, too - with a pale, sickly-looking face, and large, clear eyes, that seemed to attract sympathy at once, for they seemed to say to one, "I am only a timid, simple little creature. You need not be

Rosa Nouchette Carey

afraid of me."

I was not very tall, but I almost looked down on her as she gave me her hand.

"I was expecting you, Miss Cameron," she said, in such a sweet tone that it quite won my heart. "Your uncle kindly promised to introduce us to each other."

And then she looked at me, not keenly and scrutinizingly, as her brother had done, but with a kindly inquisitiveness, as though she wanted to know all about me, and to put me at my ease as soon as possible. I flushed a little at that, and my unfortunate sensitiveness took alarm. If it were only Carrie, I thought, with her pretty face and soft voice; but I was so sadly unattractive, no one would be taken with me at first sight. Fred had once said so in my hearing, and how I had cried over that speech!

"Esther looks older than she is; but she is only seventeen," interposed Uncle Geoffrey, as he saw that unlucky blush. "She is a good girl, and very industrious, and her mother's right hand," went on the simple man. If I only could have plucked up spirit and contradicted him, but I felt tongue-tied.

"She looks very reliable," returned Miss Lucas, in the kindest way. To this day I believe she could not find any compliment compatible with truth. I once told her so months afterward, when we were very good friends, and she laughed and could not deny it.

"You were frowning so, Esther," she replied, "from excess of nervousness, I believe, that your forehead was quite lost in your hair, and your great eyes were looking at me in such a funny, frightened way, and the corners of your mouth all coming down, I thought you were five-and-twenty at least, and wondered what I was to do with such a proud, repellant-looking young woman; but when you smiled I began to see then."

I had not reached the smiling stage just then, and was revolving her speech in rather a dispirited way. Reliable! I knew I was that; when all at once she left off looking at me, and began talking to Uncle Geoffrey.

"And so you have finished all your Good Samaritan arrangements, Dr. Cameron; and your poor sister-in-law and her family are really settled in your house? You must let me know when I may call, or if I can be of any use. Giles told me all about it, and I was so interested."

"Is it not good of Uncle Geoffrey?" I broke in. And then it must have been that I smiled; but I never could have passed that over in silence, to hear strangers praise him, and not join in.

"I think it is noble of Dr. Cameron - we both think so," she answered, warmly; and then she turned to me again. "I can understand how anxious you must all feel to help and lighten his burdens. When Dr. Cameron proposed your services for my little niece - for he knows what an invalid I am, and that systematic teaching would be impossible to me - I was quite charmed with the notion. But now, before we talk any more about it, supposing you and I go up to see Flurry."

CHAPTER VIII.

FLURRY AND FLOSSY.

What a funny little name! I could not help saying so to Miss Lucas as I followed her up the old oak staircase with its beautifully carved balustrades.

"It is her own baby abbreviation of Florence," she returned, pausing on the landing to take breath, for even that slight ascent seemed to weary her. She was quite pale and panting by the time we arrived at our destination. "It is nice to be young and strong," she observed, wistfully. "I am not very old, it is true" - she could not have been more than eight-and-twenty - "but I have never enjoyed good health, and Dr. Cameron says I never can hope to do so; but what can you expect of a crooked little creature like me?" with a smile that was quite natural and humorous, and seemed to ask no pity.

Miss Ruth was perfectly content with her life. I found out afterward she evoked rare beauty out of its quiet every-day monotony, storing up precious treasures in homely vessels.

Life was to her full of infinite possibilities, a gradual dawning and brightening of hopes that would meet their full fruition hereafter. "Some people have strength to work," she said once to me, "and then plenty of work is given to them; and some must just keep quiet and watch others work, and give them a bright word of encouragement now and then. I am one of those wayside loiterers," she finished, with a laugh; but all the same every one knew how much Miss Ruth did to help others, in spite of her failing strength.

The schoolroom, or nursery, as I believe it was called, was a large pleasant room just over the drawing-room, and commanding the same view of the garden and cedar-tree. It had three windows, only they were rather high up, and had cushioned window-seats. In one of them there was a little girl curled up in company with a large brown and white spaniel.

"Well, Flurry, what mischief are you and Flossy concocting?" asked Miss Lucas, in a playful voice, for the child was too busily engaged to notice our entrance.

"Why, it is my little auntie," exclaimed Flurry, joyously, and she scrambled down, while Flossy wagged his tail and barked. Evidently Miss Ruth was not a frequent visitor to the nursery.

Flurry was about six, not a pretty child by any means, though there might be a promise of future beauty in her face. She was a thin, serious-looking little creature, more like the father than the mother, and no one could call Mr. Lucas handsome. Her dark eyes - nearly black they were - matched oddly, in my opinion, with her long fair hair; such pretty fluffy hair it was, falling over her black frock. When her aunt bade her come and speak to the lady who was kind enough to promise to teach her, she stood for a moment regarding me

Rosa Nouchette Carey

gravely with childish inquisitiveness before she gave me her hand.

"What are you going to teach me?" she asked. "I don't think I want to be taught, auntie; I can read, I have been reading to Flossy, and I can write, and hem father's handkerchiefs. Ask nursie."

"But you would like to play to dear father, and to learn all sorts of pretty hymns to say to him, would you not, my darling! There are many things you will have to know before you are a woman."

"I don't mean to be a woman ever, I think," observed Flurry; "I like being a child better. Nursie is a woman, and nursie won't play; she says she is old and stupid."

A happy inspiration came to me. "If you are good and learn your lessons, I will play with you," I said, rather timidly; "that is, if you care for a grown-up playfellow."

I was only seventeen, in spite of my *pronounce* features, and I could still enter into the delights of a good drawn battle of battledore and shuttlecock. Perhaps it was the repressed enthusiasm of my tone, for I really meant what I said; but Flurry's brief coldness vanished, and she caught at my hand at once.

"Come and see them," she said; "I did not know you liked dolls, but you shall have one of your own if you like;" and she led me to a corner of the nursery where a quantity of dolls in odd costumes and wonderfully constrained attitudes were arranged round an inverted basket.

"Joseph and his brethren," whispered Flurry. "I am going to put him in the pit directly, only I wondered what I should do for the camels - this is Issachar, and this Gad. Look at Gad's turban."

It was almost impossible to retain my gravity. I could see Miss Lucas smiling in the window seat. Joseph and his brethren - what a droll idea for a child! But I did not know then that Flurry's dolls had to sustain a variety of bewildering parts. When I next saw them the smart turbans were all taken off the flaxen heads, a few dejected sawdust bodies hung limply round a miller's cart. "Ancient Britons," whispered Flurry. "Nurse would not let me paint them blue, but they did not wear clothes then, you know." In fact, our history lesson was generally followed by a series of touching *tableaux vivants*, the dolls sustaining their parts in several moving scenes of "Alfred and the Cakes," "Hubert and Arthur," and once "the Battle of Cressy."

Flurry and I parted the best of friends; and when we joined Uncle Geoffrey in the drawing-room I was quite ready to enter on my duties at once.

Miss Lucas stipulated for my services from ten till five; a few simple lessons in the morning were to be followed by a walk, I was to lunch with them, and in the afternoon I was to amuse Flurry or teach her a little - just as I liked.

"The fact is," observed Miss Lucas, as I looked a little surprised at this programme, "Nurse is a worthy woman, and we are all very much attached to her; but she is very ignorant, and my brother will not have Flurry thrown too much on her companionship. He wishes me to find some one who will take the sole

Rosa Nouchette Carey

charge of the child through the day; in the evening she always comes down to her father and sits with him until her bedtime." And then she named what seemed to me a surprisingly large sum for services. What! all that for playing with Flurry, and giving her a few baby lessons; poor Carrie could not have more for teaching the little Thornes. But when I hinted this to Uncle Geoffrey, he said quietly that they were rich people and could well afford it.

"Don't rate yourself so low, little woman," he added, good-humoredly; "you are giving plenty of time and interest, and surely that is worth something." And then he went on to say that Jack must go to school, he knew a very good one just by; some ladies who were patients of his would take her at easy terms, he knew. He would call that very afternoon and speak to Miss Martin.

Poor mother shed a few tears when I told her our plans. It was sad for her to see her girls reduced to work for themselves; but she cheered up after a little while, and begged me not to think her ungrateful and foolish. "For we have so many blessings, Esther," she went on, in her patient way. "We are all together, except poor Fred, and but for your uncle's goodness we might have been separated."

"And we shall have such nice cozy evenings," I returned, "when the day's work is over. I shall feel like a day laborer, mother, bringing home my wages in my pocket. I shall be thinking of you and Dot all day, and longing to get back to you."

But though I spoke and felt so cheerfully, I knew that the evenings would not be idle. There would be mending to do and linen to make, for we could not afford to buy our things ready-made; but, with mother's clever fingers and Carrie's help, I thought we should do very well. I must utilize every spare minute, I thought. I must get up early and help Deborah, so that things might go on smoothly for the rest of the day. There was Dot to dress, and mother was ailing, and had her breakfast in bed - there would be a hundred little things to set right before I started off for the Cedars, as Mr. Lucas' house was called.

"Never mind, it is better to wear out than to rust out," I said to myself. And then I picked up Jack's gloves from the floor, hung up her hat in its place, and tried to efface the marks of her muddy boots from the carpet (I cannot deny Jack was a thorn in my side just now), and then there came a tap at my door, and Carrie came in.

She looked so pretty and bright, that I could not help admiring her afresh. I am sure people must have called her beautiful.

"How happy you look, Carrie, in spite of your three little Thornes," I said rather mischievously. "Has mother told you about Miss Lucas?"

"Yes, I heard all about that," she returned, absently. "You are very fortunate, Esther, to find work in which you can take an interest. I am glad - very glad about that."

"I wish, for your sake, that we could exchange," I returned, feeling myself very generous in intention, but all the same delighted that my unselfishness should not be put to the proof.

"Oh, no, I have no wish of that sort," she replied,

hastily; "I could not quite bring myself to play with children in the nursery." I suppose mother had told her about the dolls. "Well, we both start on our separate treadmill on Monday - Black Monday, eh, Esther?"

"Not at all," I retorted, for I was far too pleased and excited with my prospects to be damped by Carrie's want of enthusiasm. I thought I would sit down and write to Jessie, and tell her all about it, but here was Carrie preparing herself for one of her chats.

"Did you see me talking to Mr. Smedley, Esther?" she began; and as I nodded she went on. "I had never spoken to him before since Uncle Geoffrey introduced us to him. He is such a nice, practical sort of man. He took me into the vicarage, and introduced me to his wife. She is very plain and homely, but so sensible."

I held my peace. I had rather a terror of Mrs. Smedley. She was one of those bustling workers whom one dreads by instinct. She had a habit of pouncing upon people, especially young ones, and driving them to work. Before many days were over she had made poor mother promise to do some cutting out for the clothing club, as though mother had not work enough for us all at home. I thought it very inconsiderate of Mrs. Smedley.

"I took to them at once," went on Carrie, "and indeed they were exceedingly kind. Mr. Smedley seemed to understand everything in a moment, how I wanted work, and - "

"But, Carrie," I demanded, aghast at this, "you have work: you have the little Thornes."

"Oh, don't drag them in at every word," she answered, pettishly - at least pettishly for her; "of course, I have my brick-making, and so have you. I am thinking of other things now, Esther; I have promised Mr. Smedley to be one of his district visitors."

I almost jumped off my chair at that, I was so startled and so indignant.

"Oh, Carrie! and when you know mother does not approve of girls of our age undertaking such work - she has said so over and over again - how can you go against her wishes?"

Carrie looked at me mildly, but she was not in the least discomposed at my words.

"Listen to me, you silly child," she said, good-humoredly; "this is one of mother's fancies; you cannot expect me with my settled views to agree with her in this."

I don't know what Carrie meant by her views, unless they consisted in a determination to make herself and every one else uncomfortable by an overstrained sense of duty.

"Middle-aged people are timid sometimes. Mother has never visited the poor herself, so she does not see the necessity for my doing it; but I am of a different opinion," continued Carrie, with a mild obstinacy that astonished me too much for any reply.

"When mother cried about it just now, and begged me to let her speak to Mr. Smedley, I told her that I was old enough to judge for myself, and that I thought one's conscience ought not to be slavishly bound even to one's parent. I was trying to do my duty to her and to every one, but I must not neglect the higher part of my vocation."

"Oh, Carrie, how could you? You will make her so unhappy."

"No; she only cried a good deal, and begged me to be prudent and not overtax my strength; and then she talked about you, and hoped I should help you as much as possible, as though I meant to shirk any part of my duty. I do not think she really disapproved, only she seemed nervous and timid about it; but I ask you, Esther, how I could help offering my services, when Mrs. Smedley told me about the neglected state of the parish, and how few ladies came forward to help?"

"But how will you find time?" I remonstrated; though what was the good of remonstrating when Carrie had once made up her mind?

"I have the whole of Saturday afternoon, and an hour on Wednesday, and now the evenings are light I might utilize them a little. I am to have Nightingale lane and the whole of Rowley street, so one afternoon in the week will scarcely be sufficient."

"Oh, Carrie," I groaned; but, actually, though the mending lay on my mind like a waking nightmare, I could not expostulate with her. I only looked at her in a dim, hopeless way and shook my head; if these were her views I must differ from them entirely. Not that I did not wish good - heavenly good - to the poor, but that I felt home duties would have to be left undone; and after all that uncle had done for us!

"And then I promised Mrs. Smedley that I would help in the Sunday-school," she continued, cheerfully. "She was so pleased, and kissed me quite gratefully. She says she and Mr. Smedley have had such up-hill work since they came to Milnthorpe - and there is so much lukewarmness and worldliness in the place. Even Miss Lucas, in spite of her goodness - and she owned she was very good, Esther - will not take their advice about things."

"I told her," she went on, hesitating, "that I would speak to you, and ask you to take a Sunday class in the infant school. You are so fond of children, I thought you would be sure to consent."

"So I would, and gladly too, if you would take my place at home," I returned, quickly; "but if you do so much yourself, you will prevent me from doing anything. Why not let me take the Sunday school class, while you stop with mother and Dot?"

"What nonsense!" she replied, flushing a little, for my proposition did not please her; "that is so like you, Esther, to raise obstacles for nothing. Why cannot we both teach; surely you can give one afternoon a week to God's work?"

"I hope I am giving not one afternoon, but every afternoon to it," I returned, and the tears rushed to my eyes, for her speech wounded me. "Oh, Carrie, why will you not understand that I think that all work that is given us to do is God's work? It is just as right for me to play with Flurry as it is to teach in the Sunday school."

"You can do both if you choose," she answered, coolly.

"Not unless you take my place," I returned, decidedly, for I had the Cameron spirit, and would not yield my point; "for in that case Dot would lose his Sunday lessons, and Jack would be listless and fret mother."

"Very well," was Carrie's response; but I could see she was displeased with my plain speaking; and I went downstairs very tired and dispirited, to find mother had cried herself into a bad headache.

"If I could only talk to your dear father about it," she whispered, when she had opened her heart to me on the subject of Carrie. "I am old-fashioned, as Carrie says, and it is still my creed that parents know best for their children; but she thinks differently, and she is so good that, perhaps, one ought to leave her to judge for herself. If I could only know what your father would say," she went on, plaintively.

I could give her no comfort, for I was only a girl myself, and my opinions were still immature and unfledged, and then I never had been as good as Carrie. But what I said seemed to console mother a little, for she drew down my face and kissed it.

"Always my good, sensible Esther," she said, and then Uncle Geoffrey came in and prescribed for the headache, and the subject dropped.

CHAPTER IX.

THE CEDARS.

I was almost ashamed of myself for being so happy, and yet it was a sober kind of happiness too. I did not forget my father, and I missed Allan with an intensity that surprised myself; but, in spite of hard work and the few daily vexations that hamper every one's lot, I continued to extract a great deal of enjoyment out of my life. To sum it up with a word, it was life - not mere existence - a life brimming over with duties and responsibilities and untried work, too busy for vacuum. Every corner and interstice of time filled up - heart, and head, and hands always fully employed; and youth and health, those two grand gifts of God, making all such work a delight.

Now I am older, and the sap of life does not run so freely in my veins, I almost marvel at the remembrance of those days, at my youthful exuberance and energy, and those words, "As thy day, so shall thy strength be," come to me with a strange force and illumination, for truly I needed it all then, and it was given to me. Time was a treasure trove, and I husbanded every minute with a miser's zeal. I had always been an early riser, and now I reaped the benefit of this habit. Jack used to murmur discontentedly in her sleep when I set the window open soon after six, and the fresh summer air

Rosa Nouchette Carey

fanned her hot face. But how cool and dewy the garden looked at that hour!

It was so bright and still, with the thrushes and blackbirds hopping over the wet lawn, and the leaves looking so fresh and green in the morning sun; such twitterings and chirpings came from the lilac trees, where the little brown sparrows twittered and plumed themselves. The bird music used to chime in in a sort of refrain to my morning prayers - a diminutive chorus of praise - the choral before the day's service commenced.

I always gave Jack a word of warning before I left the room (the reprimand used to find her in the middle of a dream), and then I went to Dot. I used to help him to dress and hear him repeat his prayers, and talk cheerfully to him when he was languid and fretful, and the small duties of life were too heavy for his feeble energies. Dot always took a large portion of my time; his movements were slow and full of tiny perversities; he liked to stand and philosophize in an infantile way when I wanted to be downstairs helping Deborah. Dot's fidgets, as I called them, were part of the day's work.

When he was ready to hobble downstairs with his crutch, I used to fly back to Jack, and put a few finishing touches to her toilet, for I knew by experience that she would make her appearance downstairs with a crooked parting and a collar awry, and be grievously plaintive when Carrie found fault with her. Talking never mended matters; Jack was at the hoiden age, and had to grow into tidiness and womanhood by-and-by.

After that I helped Deborah, and took up mother's breakfast. I always found her lying with her face to the window, and her open Bible beside her. Carrie had always been in before me and arranged the room. Mother slept badly, and at that early hour her face had a white, pining look, as though she had lost her way in the night, or waked to miss something. She used to turn with a sweet troubled smile to me as I entered.

"Here comes my busy little woman," she would say, with a pretense at cheerfulness, and then she would ask after Dot. She never spoke much of her sadness to us; with an unselfishness that was most rare she refused to dim our young cheerfulness by holding an unhealed grief too plainly before our eyes. Dear mother, I realize now what that silence must have cost her!

When breakfast was over, and Uncle Geoffrey busily engrossed with his paper, I used to steal into the kitchen and have a long confab with Deborah, and then Jack and I made our bed and dusted our room to save Martha, and by that time I was ready to start to the Cedars; but not until I had convoyed Jack to Miss Martin's, and left her and her books safely at the door.

Dot used to kiss me rather wistfully when I left him with his lesson-books and paint-box, waiting for mother to come down and keep him company. Poor little fellow, he had rather a dull life of it, for even Jumbles refused to stay with him, and Smudge was out in the garden, lazily watching the sparrows. Poor little lonely boy, deprived of the usual pleasures of boyhood, and looking out on our busy lives from a sort of sad twilight of pain and weakness, but keeping such a brave heart and silent tongue over it all.

Rosa Nouchette Carey

How I enjoyed my little walk up High street and across the wide, sunshiny square! When I reached the Cedars, and the butler admitted me, I used to run up the old oak staircase and tap at the nursery door.

Nurse used to courtesy and withdraw; Flurry and I had it all to ourselves. I never saw Miss Lucas until luncheon-time; she was more of an invalid than I knew at that time, and rarely left her room before noon. Flurry and I soon grew intimate; after a few days were over we were the best of friends. She was a clever child and fond of her lessons, but she was full of droll fancies. She always insisted on her dolls joining our studies. It used to be a little embarrassing to me at first to see myself surrounded by the vacant waxen faces staring at us, with every variety of smirk and bland fatuous expression: the flaxen heads nid-nodded over open lesson-books, propped up in limp, leathery arms. When Flossy grew impatient for a game of play, he would drag two or three of them down with a vicious snap and a stroke of his feathery paws. Flurry would shake her head at him disapprovingly, as she picked them up and shook out their smart frocks. The best behaved of the dolls always accompanied us in our walk before luncheon.

I used to think of Carrie's words, sometimes, as I played with Flurry in the afternoon; she would not hear of lessons then. Sometimes I would coax her to sew a little, or draw; and she always had her half hour at the piano, but during the rest of the afternoon I am afraid there was nothing but play.

How I wish Dot could have joined us sometimes as we built our famous brick castles, or worked in Flurry's little garden, where she grew all sorts of wonderful things. When I was tired or lazy I used to bring out my needle-work to the seat under the cedar, and tell Flurry stories, or talk to her as she dressed her dolls; she was very good and tractable, and never teased me to play when I was disinclined.

I told her about Dot very soon, and she gave me no peace after that until I took her to see him; there was quite a childish friendship between them soon. Flurry used to send him little gifts, which she purchased with her pocket-money - pictures, and knives, and pencils. I often begged Miss Lucas to put a stop to it, but she only laughed and praised Flurry, and put by choice little portions of fruit and other dainties for Flurry's boy friend.

Flurry prattled a great deal about her father, but I never saw him. He had his luncheon at the bank. Once when we were playing battledore and shuttle-cock in the hall - for Miss Lucas liked to hear us all over the house; she said it made her feel cheerful - I heard a door open overhead, and caught a glimpse of a dark face watching us; but I thought it was Morgan the butler, until Flurry called out joyfully, "Father! Father!" and then it disappeared. Now and then I met him in the square, and he always knew me and took off his hat; but I did not exchange a word with him for months.

Flurry loved him, and seemed deep in his confidence. She always put on her best frock and little pearl necklace to go down and sit with her father, while he ate his dinner. She generally followed him into his study, and chatted to him, until nurse fetched her at bed-time. When she had asked me some puzzling question that it was impossible to answer, she would refer it to her father with implicit faith. She would make me rather uncomfortable at times respecting little speeches of his.

"Father can't understand why you are so fond of play," she said once to me; "he says so few grown-up girls deign to amuse themselves with a game: but you do like it, don't you, Miss Cameron?" making up a very coaxing face. Of course I confessed to a great fondness for games, but all the same I wished Mr. Lucas had not said that. Perhaps he thought me too hoidenish for his child's governess, and for a whole week after that I refused to play with Flurry, until she began to mope, and my heart misgave me. We played at hide and seek that day all over the house - Flurry and Flossy and I.

Then another time, covering me with dire confusion, "Father thinks that such a pretty story, Miss Cameron, the one about Gretchen. He said I ought to try and remember it, and write it down; and then he asked if you had really made it up in your head."

"Oh, Flurry, that silly little story?"

"Not silly at all," retorted Flurry, with a little heat; "father had a headache, and he could not talk to me, so I told him stories to send him to sleep, and I thought he would like dear little Gretchen. He never went to sleep after all, but his eyes were wide open, staring at the fire; and then he told me he had been thinking of dear mamma, and he thought I should be very like her some day. And then he thanked me for my pretty stories, and then tiresome old nursie fetched me to bed."

That stupid little tale! To think of Mr. Lucas listening to that. I was not a very inventive storyteller, though I could warm into eloquence on occasions, but Flurry's demand was so excessive that I hit on a capital plan at last.

I created a wonderful child heroine, and called her Juliet and told a little fresh piece of her history every day. Never was there such a child for impossible adventures and hairbreadth escapes; what that unfortunate little creature went through was known only to Flurry and me.

She grew to love Juliet like a make-believe sister of her own, and talked of her at last as a living child. What long moral conversations took place between Juliet and her mother, what admirable remarks did that excellent mother make, referring to sundry small sins of omission and commission on Juliet's part! When I saw Flurry wince and turn red I knew the remarks had struck home.

It was astonishing how Juliet's behavior varied with Flurry's. If Flurry were inattentive, Juliet was listless; if her history lessons were ill-learned, Juliet's mamma had always a great deal to say about the battle of Agincourt or any other event that it was necessary to impress on her memory. I am afraid Flurry at last took a great dislike to that well-meaning lady, and begged to hear more about Juliet's little brother and sister. When I came to a very uninteresting part she would propose a game of ball or a scamper with Flossy; but all the same next day we would be back at it again.

The luncheon hour was very pleasant to me. I grew to like Miss Lucas excessively; she talked so pleasantly and seemed so interested in all I had to tell her about myself and Flurry; a quiet atmosphere of refinement surrounded her - a certain fitness and harmony of thought. Sometimes she would invite us into the drawing-room after luncheon, saying she felt lonely and would be glad of our society for a little. I used to enjoy those half-hours, though I am afraid Flurry found them a little wearisome. Our talk went over her head, and she would listen to it with a droll, half-bored expression, and take refuge at last with Flossy.

Sometimes, but not often, Miss Lucas would take us to drive with her. I think, until she knew me well, that she liked better to be alone with her own thoughts. As our knowledge of each other grew, I was struck with the flower-like unfolding of her ideas; they would bud and break forth into all manner of quaint fancies - their freshness and originality used to charm me.

I think there is no interest in life compared to knowing people - finding them out, their tastes, character, and so forth. I had an inquisitive delight, I called it thirst, for human knowledge, in drawing out a stranger; no traveler exploring unknown tracts of country ever pursued his researches with greater zeal and interest. Reserve only attracts me.

Impulsive people, who let out their feelings the first moment, do not interest me half so much as silent folk. I like to sit down before an enclosed citadel and besiege it; with such ramparts of defense there must be precious store in the heart of the city, some hidden jewels, perhaps; at least, so I argue with myself.

But, happy as I was with Miss Lucas and Flurry, five o'clock no sooner struck than I was flying down the oak staircase, with Flurry peeping at me between the balustrades, and waving a mite of a hand in token of adieu; for was I not going home to mother and Dot?

Oh, the dear, bright home scene that always awaited me! I wonder if Carrie loved it as I did! The homely, sunny little parlors; the cozy tea table, over which old Martha would be hovering with careful face and hands; mother in her low chair by the garden window; Uncle Geoffrey with his books and papers at the little round table; Dot and Jack hidden in some corner, out of which Dot would come stumping on his poor little crutches to kiss me, and ask after his little friend Flurry.

"Here comes our Dame Bustle," Uncle Geoffrey would say. It was his favorite name for me, and mother would look up and greet me with the same loving smile that was never wanting on her dear face.

On the stairs I generally came upon Carrie, coming down from her little room.

"How are the little Thornes?" I would ask her, cheerfully; but by-and-by I left off asking her about them. At first she used to shrug her shoulders and shake her head in a sort of disconsolate fashion, or answered indifferently: "Oh, much as usual, thank you." But once she returned, quite pettishly:

"Why do you ask after those odious children, Esther? Why cannot you let me forget them for a few hours? If we are brickmakers, we need not always be telling the tales of our bricks." She finished with a sort of weary tone in her tired voice, and after that I let the little Thornes alone.

What happy evenings those were! Not that we were idle, though - "the saints forbid," as old Biddy used to say. When tea was over, mother and I betook ourselves to the huge mending basket; sometimes Carrie joined us, when she was not engaged in district work, and then her clever fingers made the work light for us.

Then there were Jack's lessons to superintend, and sometimes I had to help Dot with his drawing, or copy out papers for Uncle Geoffrey: then by-and-by Dot had to be taken upstairs, and there were little things to do for mother when Carrie was too tired or busy to do them. Mother was Carrie's charge. As Dot and Jack were mine, it was a fair division of labor, only somehow Carrie had always so much to do.

Mother used to fret sometimes about it, and complain that Carrie sat up too late burning the midnight oil in her little room; but I never could find out what kept her up. I was much happier about Carrie now - she seemed brighter and in better spirits. If she loathed her daily drudgery, she said little about it, and complained less. All her interests were reserved for Nightingale lane and Rowley street. The hours spent in those unsavory neighborhoods were literally her times of refreshment. Her poor people were very close to her heart, and often she told us about them as we sat working together in the evening, until mother grew quite interested, and used to ask after them by name, which pleased Carrie, and made a bond of sympathy between them. At such times I somehow felt a little sad, though I would not have owned it for worlds, for it seemed to me as though my work were so trivial compared to Carrie's - as though I were a poor little Martha, "careful and troubled about many things" about, Deborah's crossness and Jack's reckless ways, occupied with small minor duties - dressing Dot, and tidying Jack's and Uncle Geoffrey's drawers; while Carrie was doing angel's work; reclaiming drunken women, and teaching miserable degraded children, and then coming home and playing sweet sacred fragments of Handel to soothe mother's worn spirits, or singing her the hymns she loved. Alas! I could not sing except in church, and my playing was a poor affair compared to Carrie's.

I felt it most on Sundays, when Carrie used to go off to the Sunday school morning and afternoon, and left me to the somewhat monotonous task of hearing Jack her catechism and giving Dot his Scripture lesson. Sunday was always a trial to Dot. He was not strong enough to go to church - the service would have wearied him too much - his few lessons were soon done, and then time used to hang heavily on his hands.

At last the grand idea came to me to set him to copy Scripture maps, and draw small illustrations of any Biblical scene that occurred in the lesson of the day. I have a book full of his childish fancies now, all elaborately colored on week-days - "Joseph and his Brethren" in gaudy turbans, and wonderfully inexpressive countenances, reminding me of Flurry's dolls; the queen of Sheba, coming before Solomon, in a marvelous green tiara and yellow garments; a headless Goliath, expressed with a painful degree of detail, more fit for the Wirtz Gallery than a child's scrap-book.

Dot used frequently to write letters to Allan, to which I often added copious postscripts. I never could coax Dot to write to Fred, though Fred sent him plenty of kind messages, and many a choice little parcel of scraps and odds and ends, such as Dot liked.

Fred was getting on tolerably, he always told us. He had rooms in St. John's Wood, which he shared with two other artists; he was working hard, and had some copying orders. Allan saw little of him; they had no friends in common, and no community of taste. Never were brothers less alike or with less sympathy.

CHAPTER X.

"I WISH I HAD A DOT OF MY OWN."

Months passed over, and found us the same busy, tranquil little household. I used to wonder how my letters could interest Allan so much as he said they did; I could find so little to narrate. And, talking of that, it strikes me that we are not sufficiently thankful for the monotony of life. I speak advisedly; I mean for the quiet uniformity and routine of our daily existence. In our youth we quarrel a little with its sameness and regularity; it is only when the storms of sudden crises and unlooked-for troubles break over our thankful heads that we look back with regret to those still days of old.

Nothing seemed to happen, nothing looked different. Mother grew a little stronger as the summer passed, and took a few more household duties on herself. Dot pined and pinched as the cold weather came on, as he always did, and looked a shivering, shabby Dot sometimes. Jack's legs grew longer, and her frocks shorter, and we had to tie her hair to keep it out of her eyes, and she stooped more, and grew round-shouldered, which added to her list of beauties; but no one expected grace from Jack.

At the Cedars things went on as usual, that Flurry left

off calling me Miss Cameron, and took to Esther instead, somewhat scandalizing Miss Lucas, until she began taking to it herself. "For you are so young, and you are more Flurry's playfellow than her governess," she said apologetically; "it is no good being stiff when we are such old friends." And after that I always called her Miss Ruth.

"Don't you want see to Roseberry, Esther?" asked Flurry, one day - that was the name of the little seaside place where Mr. Lucas had a cottage. "Aunt Ruth says you must come down with us next summer; she declares she has quite set her heart on it."

"Oh, Flurry, that would be delightful! - but how could I leave mother and Dot?" I added in a regretful parenthesis. That was always the burden of my song - Mother and Dot.

"Dot must come, too," pronounced Flurry, decidedly; and she actually proposed to Miss Ruth at luncheon that "Esther's little brother should be invited to Roseberry." Miss Ruth looked at me with kindly amused eyes, as I grew crimson and tried to hush Flurry.

"We shall see," she returned, in her gentle voice; "if Esther will not go without Dot, Dot must come too." But though the bare idea was too delightful, I begged Miss Ruth not to entertain such an idea for a moment.

I think Flurry's little speech put a kind thought into Miss Ruth's head, for when she next invited us to drive with her, the gray horses stopped for an instant at Uncle Geoffrey's door, and the footman lifted Dot in his little fur-lined coat, and placed him at Miss Ruth's side. And seeing the little lad's rapture, and Flurry's childish delight, she often called for him, sometimes when she was alone, for she said Dot never troubled her; he could be as quiet as a little mouse when her head ached and she was disinclined to talk.

I said nothing happened; but one day I had a pleasant surprise, just when I did not deserve it; for it was one of my fractious days - days of moods and tenses I used to called them - when nothing seemed quite right, when I was beset by that sort of grown-up fractiousness that wants to be petted and put to bed, and bidden to lie still like a tired child.

Winter had set in in downright earnest, and in those cold dark mornings early rising seemed an affront to the understanding, and a snare to be avoided by all right-minded persons; yet notwithstanding all that, a perverse, fidgety notion of duty drove me with a scourge of mental thorns from my warm bed. For I was young and healthy, and why should I lie there while Deborah and Martha broke the ice in their pitchers, and came downstairs with rasped red faces and acidulated tempers? I was thankful not to do likewise, to know I should hear in a few minutes a surly tap at the door, with the little hot-water can put down with protesting evidence. Even then it was hard work to flesh and blood, with no dewy lawn, no bird music now to swell my morning's devotion with tiny chorus of praise; only a hard frozen up world, with a trickle of meager sunshine running through it.

But my hardest work was with Dot; he used to argue drowsily with me while I stood shivering and awaiting his pleasure. Why did I not go down to the fire if I were cold? He was not going to get up in the middle of the night to please any one; never mind the robins - of which I reminded him gently - he wished he were a robin too, and could get up and go to bed with a neat little feather bed tacked to his skin - nice, cosy little fellows; and then he would draw the bedclothes round his thin little shoulders, and try to maintain his position.

He quite whimpered on the morning in question, when I lifted him out bodily - such a miserable Dot, looking like a starved dove in his white plumage; but he cheered up at the sight of the fire and hot coffee in the snug parlor, and whispered a little entreaty for forgiveness as I stooped over him to make him comfortable.

"You are tired, Esther," said my mother tenderly, when she saw my face that morning; "you must not get up so early this cold weather, my dear." But I held my peace, for who would dress Dot, and what would become of Jack? And then came a little lump in my throat, for I was tired and fractious.

When I got to the Cedars a solemn stillness reigned in the nursery, and instead of an orderly room a perfect chaos of doll revelry prevailed. All the chairs were turned into extempore beds, and the twelve dolls, with bandaged heads and arms, were tucked up with the greatest care.

Flurry met me with an air of great importance and her finger on her lip.

"Hush, Esther, you must not make a noise. I am Florence Nightingale, and these are all the poor sick and wounded soldiers; look at this one, this is Corporal

Trim, and he has had his two legs shot off."

I recognized Corporal Trim under his bandages; he was the very doll Flossy had so grievously maltreated and had robbed of an eye; the waxen tip of his nose was gone, and a great deal of his flaxen wig besides - quite a caricature of a mutilated veteran.

I called Flurry to account a little sternly, and insisted on her restoring order to the room. Flurry pouted and sulked; her heart was at Scutari, and her wits went wool-gathering, and refused dates and the multiplication table. To make matters worse, it commenced snowing, and there was no prospect of a walk before luncheon. Miss Ruth did not come down to that meal, and afterward I sat and knitted in grim silence. Discipline must be maintained, and as Flurry would not work, neither would I play with her; but I do not know which of us was punished the most.

"Oh, how cross you are, Esther, and it is Christmas eve!" cried Flurry at last, on the verge of crying. It was growing dusk, and already shadows lurked in the corner of the room, Flurry looked at me so wistfully that I am afraid I should have relented and gone on a little with Juliet, only at that moment she sprang up joyfully at the sound of her aunt's voice calling her, and ran out to the top of the dark staircase.

"We are to go down, you and I; Aunt Ruth wants us," she exclaimed, laying violent hands on my work. I felt rather surprised at the summons, for Miss Ruth never called us at this hour, and it would soon be time for me to go home.

The drawing-room looked the picture of warm comfort

Rosa Nouchette Carey

as we entered it; some glorious pine logs were crackling and spluttering in the grate, sending out showers of colored sparks.

Miss Ruth was half-buried in her easy-chair, with her feet on the white fleecy rug, and the little square tea-table stood near her, with its silver kettle and the tiny blue teacups.

"You have sent for us, Miss Ruth," I said, as I crossed the room to her; but at that instant another figure I had not seen started up from a dark corner, and caught hold of me in rough, boyish fashion.

"Allan! oh Allan! Allan!" my voice rising into a perfect crescendo of ecstasy at the sight of his dear dark face. Could anything be more deliciously unexpected? And there was Miss Ruth laughing very softly to herself at my pleasure.

"Oh, Allan, what does this mean," I demanded, "when you told us there was no chance of your spending Christmas with us? Have you been home? Have you seen mother and Dot? Have you come here to fetch me home?"

Allan held up his hands as he took a seat near me.

"One question at a time, Esther. I had unexpected leave of absence for a week, and that is why you see me; and as I wanted to surprise you all, I said nothing about it. I arrived about three hours ago, and as mother thought I might come and fetch you, why I thought I would, and that you would be pleased to see me; that is all my story," finished Allan, exchanging an amused glance with Miss Ruth. They had never met before, and yet they seemed already on excellent terms. All an made no sort of demur when Miss Ruth insisted that we should both have some tea to warm us before we went. I think he felt at home with her at once.

Flurry seemed astonished at our proceeding. She regarded Allan for a long time very solemnly, until he won her heart by admiring Flossy; then she condescended to converse with him.

"Are you Esther's brother, really?"

"Yes, Miss Florence - I believe that is your name."

"Florence Emmeline Lucas," she repeated glibly. "I'm Flurry for short; nobody calls me Florence except father sometimes. It was dear mamma's name, and he always sighs when he says it."

"Indeed," returned Allan in an embarrassed tone; and then he took Flossy on his knee and began to play with him.

"Esther is rich," went on Flurry, rather sadly. "She has three brothers; there's Fred, and you, and Dot. I think she likes Dot best, and so do I. What a pity I haven't a Dot of my own! No brothers; only father and Aunt Ruth."

"Poor little dear," observed Allan compassionately - he was always fond of children. His hearty tone made Flurry look up in his face. "He is a nice man," she said to me afterward; "he likes Flossy and me, and he was pleased when I kissed him."

I did not tell Flurry that Allan had been very much

　　　Rosa Nouchette Carey

astonished at her friendship.

"That is a droll little creature," he said, as we left the house together; "but there is something very attractive about her. You have a nice berth there, Esther. Miss Lucas seems a delightful person," an opinion in which I heartily agreed. Then he asked me about Mr. Lucas; but I had only Flurry's opinion to offer him on that subject, and he questioned me in his old way about my daily duties. "Mother thinks you are overworked, and you are certainly looking a little thin, Esther. Does not Carrie help you enough? And what is this I have just heard about the night school?"

Our last grievance, which I had hitherto kept from Allan; but of course mother had told him. It was so nice to be walking there by his side, with the crisp white snow beneath our feet, and the dark sky over our heads; no more fractiousness now, when I could pour out all my worries to Allan.

Such a long story I told him; but the gist of it was this; Carrie had been very imprudent; she would not let well alone, or be content with a sufficient round of duties. She worked hard with her pupils all day, and besides that she had a district and Sunday school; and now Mrs. Smedley had persuaded her to devote two evenings of her scanty leisure to the night school.

"I think it is very hard and unjust to us," I continued rather excitedly. "We have so little of Carrie - only just the odds and ends of time she can spare us. Mrs. Smedley has no right to dictate to us all, and to work Carrie in the way she does. She has got an influence over her, and she uses it for her own purposes, and Carrie is weak to yield so entirely to her judgment; she coaxes her and flatters her, and talks about her high standard and unselfish zeal for the work; but I can't understand it, and I don't think it right for Carrie to be Mrs. Smedley's parochial drudge."

"I will talk to Carrie," returned Allan, grimly; and he would not say another word on the subject. But I forgot all my grievances during the happy evening that followed.

Allan was in such spirits! As frolicsome as a boy, he would not let us be dull, and so his talk never flagged for a moment. Dot laughed till the tears ran down his cheeks when Allan kicked over the mending basket, and finally ordered Martha to take it away. When Carrie returned from the night school, she found us all gathered round the fire in peaceful idleness, listening to Allan's stories, with Dot on the rug, basking in the heat like a youthful salamander.

I think Allan must have followed her up to her room, for just as I was laying my head on the pillow there was a knock at the door, and Carrie entered with her candle, fully dressed, and with a dark circle round her eyes.

She put down the light, so as not to wake Jack, and sat down by my side with a weary sigh.

"Why did you all set Allan to talk to me?" she began reproachfully. "Why should I listen to him more than to you or mother? I begin to see that a man's foes are indeed of his own household."

I bit my lips to keep in a torrent of angry words. I was out of patience with Carrie, even a saint ought to have common sense, I thought, and I was so tired and sleepy, and to-morrow was Christmas Day.

"I could not sleep until I came and told you what I thought about it," she went on in her serious monotone. I don't think she even noticed my exasperated silence. "It is of no use for Allan to come and preach his wordly wisdom to me; we do not measure things by the same standard, he and I. You are better, Esther, but your hard matter-of-fact reasoning shocks me sometimes."

"Oh, Carrie! why don't you create a world of your own," I demanded, scornfully, "if we none of us please you - not even Allan?"

"Now you are angry without cause," she returned, gently, for Carrie rarely lost her temper in an argument; she was so meekly obstinate that we could do nothing with her. "We cannot create our own world, Esther; we can only do the best we can with this. When I am working so hard to do a little good in Milnthorpe, why do you all try to hinder and drag me back?"

"Because you are *over*doing it, and wearing yourself out," I returned, determined to have my say; but she stopped me with quiet peremptoriness.

"No more of that, Esther; I have heard it all from Allan. I am not afraid of wearing out; I hope to die in harness. Why, child, how can you be so faint-hearted? We cannot die until our time comes."

"But when we court death it is suicide," I answered, stubbornly; but Carrie only gave one of her sweet little laughs.

"You foolish Esther! who means to die, I should like to know? Why, the child is actually crying. Listen to me, you dear goosie. I was never so happy or well in my life." I shook my head sorrowfully, but she persisted in her statement. "Mrs. Smedley has given me new life. How I do love that woman! She is a perfect example to us - of unselfishness and energy. She says I am her right hand, and I do believe she means it, Esther." But I only groaned in answer. "She is doing a magnificent work in Milnthrope," she continued, "and I feel so proud that I am allowed to assist her. Do you know, I had twenty boys in my class this evening; they would come to me, though Miss Miles' class was nearly empty." And so she went on, until I felt all over prickles of suppressed nervousness. "Well, good-night," she said, at last, when I could not he roused into any semblance of interest; "we shall see which of us be right by-and-by."

"Yes, we shall see," I answered, drowsily; but long after she left I muttered the words over and over to myself, "We shall see."

Yes, by-and-by the light of Divine truth would flash over our actions, and in that pure radiance every unworthy work would wither up to naught - every unblessed deed retreat into outer darkness. Which would be right, she or I?

I know only too well that, taking the world as a whole, we ought to *encourage* Christian parochial work, because too many girls who possess the golden opportunity of leisure allow it to be wasted, and so commit the "sin of omission;" but there would have been quite as much good done had Carrie dutifully helped in our invalid home and cheered us all to health by her bright presence. And besides, I myself could then perhaps have taken a class at me night school if the stocking-mending and the other multitudinous domestic matters could have allowed it.

The chimes of St. Barnabas were pealing through the midnight air before I slept. Above was the soft light of countless stars, sown broadcast over the dark skies. Christmas was come, and the angel's song sounding over the sleeping earth.

"Peace and goodwill to men" - peace from weary arguments and fruitless regret, peace on mourning hearts, on divided homes, on mariners tossing afar on wintry seas, and peace surely on one troubled girlish heart that waited for the breaking of a more perfect day.

CHAPTER XI.

MISS RUTH'S NURSE.

Miss Ruth insisted on giving me a week's holiday, that I might avail myself of Allan's society; and as dear mother still persisted that I looked pale and in need of change, Allan gave me a course of bracing exercise in the shape of long country walks with him and Jack, when we plowed our way over half-frozen fields and down deep, muddy lanes, scrambling over gates and through hedges, and returning home laden with holly berries and bright red hips and haws.

On Allan's last evening we were invited to dine at the Cedars - just Uncle Geoffrey, Allan, and I. Miss Ruth wrote such a pretty letter. She said that her brother thought it was a long time since he had seen his old friend Dr. Cameron, and that he was anxious to make acquaintance with his nephew and Flurry's playfellow - this was Miss Ruth's name for me, for we had quite dropped the governess between us.

Allan looked quite pleased, and scouted my dubious looks; he had taken a fancy to Miss Ruth, and wanted to see her again. He laughed when I said regretfully that it was his last evening, and that I would rather have spent it quietly at home with him. I was shy at the notion of my first dinner-party; Mr. Lucas' presence would make it a formal affair.

And then mother fretted a little that I had no evening-dress ready. I could not wear white, so all my pretty gowns were useless; but I cheered her up by my assuring her that such things did not matter in our deep mourning. And when I had dressed myself in my black cashmere, with soft white ruffles and a little knot of Christmas roses and ferns which Carrie had arranged in my dress, mother gave a relieved sigh, and thought I should do nicely, and Allan twisted me round, and declared I was not half so bad after all, and that, though I was no beauty, I should pass, with which dubious compliment I was obliged to content myself.

"I wish you were going in my stead, Carrie," I whispered, as she wrapped me in mother's warm fleecy shawl, for the night was piercingly cold.

"I would rather stay with mother," she answered quietly. And then she kissed me, and told me to be a good child, and not to be frightened of any one, in her gentle, elder sisterly way. It never occurred to her to envy me my party or my pleasant position at the Cedars, or to compare her own uncongenial work with mine. These sorts of petty jealousies and small oppositions were impossible to her; her nature was large and slightly raised, and took in wider vistas of life than ours.

My heart sank a little when I heard the sharp vibrating sound of Mrs. Smedley's voice as we were announced. I had no idea that the vicar and his wife were to be invited, but they were the only guests beside ourselves. I never could like Mrs. Smedley and to the very last I never changed my girlish opinion of her. I have a curious instinctive repugnance to people who rustle through life; whose entrances and exits are environed with noise; who announce their intentions with the blast of the trumpet. Mrs. Smedley was a wordy woman. She talked much and well, but her voice was loud and jarring. She was not a bad-looking woman. I daresay in her younger days she had been handsome, for her features were very regular and her complexion good; but I always said that she had worn herself thin with talking. She was terribly straight and angular (I am afraid I called it bony); she had sharp high cheek bones, and her hands were long and lean. On this evening she wore a rich brown brocade, that creaked and rustled with every movement, and some Indian bangles that jingled every time she raised her arm. I could not help comparing her to Miss Ruth, who sat beside her, looking lovely in a black velvet gown, and as soft and noiseless as a little mouse. I am afraid Mrs. Smedley's clacking voice made her head ache terribly for she grew paler and paler before the long dinner was over. As Miss Ruth greeted me, I saw Mr. Lucas cross the room with Flurry holding his hand.

"Flurry must introduce me to her playfellow," he said, with a kind glance at us both, as the child ran up to me and clasped me close.

"Oh, Esther, how I have wanted you and Juliet," she whispered; but her father heard her.

"I am afraid Flurry has had a dull week of it," he said, taking a seat beside us, and lifting the little creature to his knee. How pretty Flurry looked in her dainty white frock, all embroidery and lace, with knots of black ribbons against her dimpled shoulders, and her hair flowing round her like a golden veil! Such a little fairy queen she looked!

"Father has been telling me stories," she observed, confidently; "they were very pretty ones, but I think I like Juliet best. And, oh! Esther, Flossy has broken Clementina's arm - that is your favorite doll, you know."

"Has Miss Cameron a doll, too?" asked Mr. Lucas, and I thought he looked a little quizzical.

"I always call it Esther's," returned Flurry, seriously. "She is quite fond of it, and nurses it sometimes at lessons."

But I could bear no more. Mrs. Smedley was listening, I was sure, and it did sound so silly and babyish, and yet I only did it to please Flurry.

"I am afraid you think me very childish," I stammered, for I remembered that game of battledore and shuttle-cock, and how excited I had been when I had achieved two hundred. But as I commenced my little speech, with burning cheeks and a lip that would quiver with nervousness, he quietly stopped me.

"I think nothing to your discredit, Miss Cameron. I am too grateful to you for making my little girl's life less lonely. I feel much happier about her now, and so does my sister." And then, as dinner was announced, he turned away and offered his arm to Mrs. Smedley.

Mr. Smedley took me in and sat by me, but after a few cursory observations he left me to my own devices and talked to Miss Ruth. I was a little disappointed at this, for I preferred him infinitely to his wife, and I had always found his sermons very helpful; but I heard afterward that he never liked talking to young ladies, and did not know what to say to them. Carrie was an exception. She was too great a favorite with them both ever to be neglected. Mr. Lucas' attention was fully occupied by his voluble neighbor. Now and then he addressed a word to me, that I might not feel myself slighted, but Mrs. Smedley never seconded his efforts.

Ever since I had refused to teach in the Sunday school she had regarded me with much head-shaking and severity. To her I was simply a frivolous, uninteresting young person, too headstrong to be guided. She always spoke pityingly of "your poor sister Esther" to Carrie, as though I were in a lamentable condition. I know she had heard of Flurry's doll, her look was so utterly contemptuous.

To my dismay she commenced talking to Mr. Lucas about Carrie. It was very bad taste, I thought, with her sister sitting opposite to her; but Carrie was Mrs. Smedley's present hobby, and she always rode her hobby to death. No one else heard her, for they were all engaged with Miss Ruth.

"Such an admirable creature," she was saying, when my attention was attracted to the conversation; "a most lovely person and mind, and yet so truly humble. I confess I love her as though she were a daughter of my own." Fancy being Mrs. Smedley's daughter! Happily, for their own sakes, she had no children. "Augustus feels just the same; he thinks so highly of her. Would you believe it, Mr. Lucas, that though she is a daily governess like her sister," with a sharp glance at poor little miserable me, "that that dear devoted girl takes house to house visitation in that dreadful Nightingale lane and Rowley street?" Was it my fancy, or did Mr. Lucas shrug his shoulders dubiously at this? As Mrs. Smedley paused here a moment, as though she expected an answer, he muttered, "Very praiseworthy, I am sure," in a slightly bored tone.

"She has a class in the Sunday-school besides, and now she gives two evenings a week to Mr. Smedley's night school. She is a pattern to all the young ladies of the place, as I do not fail to tell them."

Why Mr. Lucas looked at me at that moment I do not know, but something in my face seemed to strike him, for he said, in a curious sort of tone, that meant a great deal, if I had only understood it:

"You do not follow in your sister's footsteps, then, Miss Cameron?"

"No, I do not," I answered abruptly, far too abruptly, I am afraid; "human beings cannot be like sheep jumping through a hedge - if one jumps, they all jump, you know."

"And you do not like that," with a little laugh, as though he were amused.

"No, I must be sure it is a safe gap first, and not a short cut to nowhere," was my inexplicable response. I do not know if Mr. Lucas understood me, for just then Miss Ruth gave the signal for the ladies to rise. The rest of the evening was rather a tedious affair. I played a little, but no one seemed specially impressed, and I could hear Mrs. Smedley's voice talking loudly all the time.

Mr. Lucas did not address me again; he and Uncle Geoffrey talked politics on the rug. The Smedleys went early, and just as we were about to follow their example a strange thing happened; poor Miss Ruth was taken with one of her bad attacks.

I was very frightened, for she looked to me as though she were dying; but Uncle Geoffrey was her doctor, and understood all about it, and Allan quietly stood by and helped him.

Mr. Lucas rang for nurse, who always waited on Miss Ruth as well as Flurry, but she had gone to bed with a sick headache. The housemaid was young and awkward, and lost her head entirely, so Uncle Geoffrey sent her away to get her mistress' room ready, and he and Allan carried Miss Ruth up between them; and a few minutes afterward I heard Allan's whistle, and ran out into the hall.

"Good-night, Esther," he said, hurriedly; I am just going to the surgery for some medicine. Uncle Geoffrey thinks you ought to offer your services for the night, as that girl is no manner of use; you had better go up now."

"But, Allan, I do not understand nursing in the least," for this suggestion terrified me, and I wanted the walk home with Allan, and a cozy chat when every one had gone to bed; but, to my confusion, he merely looked at me and turned on his heel. Allan never wasted words on these occasions; if people would not do their duty he washed his hands of them. I could not bear him to be disappointed in me, or think me cowardly and selfish, so I went sorrowfully up to Miss Ruth's room, and found Uncle Geoffrey coming in search of me.

Rosa Nouchette Carey

"Oh, there you are, Esther," he said, in his most business-like tone, taking it for granted, as a matter of course, that I was going to stay. "I want you to help Miss Lucas to get comfortably to bed; she is in great pain, and cannot speak to you just yet; but you must try to assist her as well as you can. When the medicine comes, I will take a final look at her, and give you your orders." And then he nodded to me and went downstairs. There was no help for it; I must do my little best, and say nothing about it.

Strange to say, I had never been in Miss Ruth's room before. I knew where it was situated, and that its windows looked out on the garden, but I had no idea what sort of a place it was.

It was not large, but so prettily fitted up, and bore the stamp of refined taste, in every minute detail. I always think a room shows the character of its owner; one can judge in an instant, by looking round and noticing the little ornaments and small treasured possessions.

I once questioned Carrie rather curiously about Mrs. Smedley's room, and she answered, reluctantly, that it was a large, bare-looking apartment, with an ugly paper, and full of medicine chests and work-baskets; nothing very comfortable or tasteful in its arrangements. I knew it; I could have told her so without seeing it.

Miss Ruth's was very different; it was perfectly crowded with pretty things, and yet not too many of them. And such beautiful pictures hung on the walls, most of them sacred: but evidently chosen with a view to cheerfulness. Just opposite the bed was "The Flight into Egypt;" a portrait of Flurry; and some sunny little landscapes, most of them English scenes, finished the collection. There were some velvet lined shelves, filled with old china, and some dear little Dresden shepherdesses on the mantelpiece. A stand of Miss Ruth's favorite books stood beside her lounge chair, and her inlaid Indian desk was beside it.

I was glad Miss Ruth liked pretty things; it showed such charming harmony in her character. Poor Miss Ruth, she was evidently suffering severely, as she lay on her couch in front of the fire; her hair was unbound, and fell in thick short lengths over her pillow, reminding me of Flurry's soft fluff, but not quite so bright a gold.

I was sadly frightened when I found she did not open her eyes or speak to me. I am afraid I bungled sadly over my task, though she was quite patient and let me do what I liked with her. It seemed terribly long before I had her safely in her bed. When her head touched the pillows, she raised her eyelids with difficulty.

"Thank you," she whispered; "you have done it so nicely, dear, and have not hurt me more than you could help," and then she motioned me to kiss her. Dear patient Miss Ruth!

I had got the room all straight before Uncle Geoffrey came back, and then Mr. Lucas was with him. Miss Ruth spoke to them both, and took hold of her brother's hand as he leaned over her.

"Good-night, Giles; don't worry about me; Esther is going to take care of me." She took it for granted, too. "Dr. Cameron's medicine will soon take away the pain."

Uncle Geoffrey's orders were very simple; I must watch her and keep up the fire, and give her another dose if she were to awake in two hours' time; and if the attack came on again, I must wake nurse, in spite of her headache, as she knew what to do; and then he left me.

"You are very good to do this," Mr. Lucas said, as he shook hands with me. "Have you been used to nursing?"

I told him, briefly, no; but I was wise enough not to add that I feared I should never keep awake, in Spite of some very strong coffee Uncle Geoffrey had ordered me; but I was so young, and with such an appetite for sleep.

I took out my faded flowers when they left me, said my prayers, and drank my coffee, and then tried to read one of Miss Ruth's books, but the letters seemed to dance before my eyes. I am afraid I had a short doze over Hiawatha, for I had a confused idea that I was Minnehaha laughing-water; and I thought the forest leaves were rustling round me, when a coal dropped out of the fire and startled me.

It woke Miss Ruth from her refreshing sleep; but the pain had left her, and she looked quite bright and like herself.

"I am a bad sleeper, and often lie awake until morning," she said, as I shook up her pillows and begged her to lie down again. "No, it is no good trying again just now, I am so dreadfully wide awake. Poor Esther! how tired you look, being kept out of your bed in this way." And she wanted me to curl myself up on the couch and go to sleep, but I stoutly refused; Uncle Geoffrey had said I was to watch her until morning. When she found I was inexorable in my resolution to keep awake, she began to talk.

"I wonder if you know what pain is, Esther - real positive agony?" and when I assured her that a slight headache was the only form of suffering I had ever known, she gave a heavy sigh.

"How strange, how fortunate, singular too, it seems to me. No pain! that must be a foretaste of heaven;" and she repeated, dreamily, "no more pain there. Oh, Esther, if you knew how I long sometimes for heaven."

The words frightened me, somehow; they spoke such volumes of repressed longing. "Dear Miss Ruth, why?" I asked, almost timidly.

"Can you ask why, and see me as I am to-night?" she asked, with scarcely restrained surprise. "If I could only bear it more patiently and learn the lesson it is meant to teach me, 'perfect through suffering,' the works of His chisel!" And then she softly repeated the words,

"Shedding soft drops of pity
Where the sharp edges of the tool have been."

"I always loved that stanza so; it gave me the first idea I ever quite grasped how sorry He is when He is obliged to hurt us." And as I did not know how to answer her, she begged me to fetch the book, and she would show me the passage for myself.

CHAPTER XII.

I WAS NOT LIKE OTHER GIRLS.

I had no idea Miss Ruth could talk as she did that night. She seemed to open her heart to me with the simplicity of a child, giving me a deeper insight into a very lovely nature. Carrie had hitherto been my ideal, but on this night I caught myself wondering once or twice whether Carrie would ever exercise such patience and uncomplaining endurance under so many crossed purposes, such broken work.

"I was never quite like other people," she said to me when I had closed the book; "you know I was a mere infant in my nurse's arms, when that accident happened." I nodded, for I had heard the sad details from Uncle Geoffrey; how an unbroken pair of young horses had shied across the road just as the nurse who was carrying Miss Ruth was attempting to cross it; the nurse had been knocked down and dreadfully injured, and her little charge had been violently thrown against the curb, and it had been thought by the doctor that one of the horses must have kicked her. For a long time she lay in a state of great suffering, and it was soon known that her health had sustained permanent injury.

"I was always a crooked, stunted little thing," she went on, with a lovely smile. "My childhood was a sad ordeal; it was just battling with pain, and making believe that I did not mind. I used to try and bear it as cheerfully as I could, because mother fretted so over me; but in secret I was terribly rebellious, often I cried myself to sleep with angry passionate tears, because I was not like other girls.

"Do you care to hear all this?" interrupting herself to look at my attentive face. It must have been a sufficient answer, for she went on talking without waiting for me to speak.

"Giles was very good to me, but it was hard on him for his only sister to be such a useless invalid. He was active and strong, and I could not expect to keep him chained to my couch - I was always on a couch then - he had his friends and his cricket and football, and I could not expect to see much of him, I had to let him go with the rest.

"Things went on like this - outward submission and inward revolt - much affection, but little of the grace of patience, until the eve of my confirmation, when a stranger came to preach at the parish church. I never heard his name before, and I never have heard it since. People said he came from a distance; but I shall never forget that sermon to my dying day, or the silvery penetrating voice that delivered it.

"It was as though a message from heaven was brought straight to me, to the poor discontented child who sat so heart weary and desponding in the corner of the pew. I cannot oven remember the text; it was something about the suffering of Christ, but I knew that it was addressed to the suffering members of His church, and that he touched upon all physical and mental pain. And what struck me most was that he spoke of pain as a privilege, a high privilege and special training; something that called us into a fuller and inner fellowship with our suffering head.

"He told us the heathen might dread pain, but not the Christian; that one really worthy of the name must be content to be the cross bearer, to tread really and literally in the steps of the Master.

"What if He unfolded to us the mystery of pain? Would He not unfold the mystery of love too? What generous souls need fear that dread ordeal, that was to remove them from the outer to the inner court? Ought they not to rejoice that they were found worthy to share His reproach? He said much more than this, Esther, but memory is so weak and betrays one. But he had flung a torch into the darkest recesses of my soul, and the sudden light seemed to scorch and shrivel up all the discontent and bitterness; and, oh, the peace that succeeded; it was as though a drowning mariner left off struggling and buffeting with the waves that were carrying him to the shore, but just lay still and let himself be floated in."

"And you were happier," I faltered, as she suddenly broke off, as though exhausted.

"Yes, indeed," she returned softly. "Pain was not any more my enemy, but the stern life companion He had sent to accompany me - the cross that I must carry out of love to Him; oh, how different, how far more endurable! I took myself in hand by-and-by when I grew older and had a better judgment of things. I knew mine was a life apart, a separated life; by that I mean that I should never know the joy of wifehood or motherhood, that I must create my own little world, my own joys and interests."

"And you have done so."

"Yes, I have done so; I am a believer in happiness; I am quite sure in my mind that our beneficent Creator meant all His creatures to be happy, that whatever He gives them to bear, that He intends them to abide in the sunshine of His peace, and I determined to be happy. I surrounded my-self with pretty things, with pictures that were pleasant to the eye and recalled bright thoughts. I made my books my friends, and held sweet satisfying communion with minds of all ages. I cultivated music, and found intense enjoyment in the study of Handel and Beethoven.

"When I got a little stronger I determined to be a worker too, and glean a little sheaf or two after the reapers, if it were only a dropped ear now and then.

"I took up the Senana Mission. You have no idea how important I have grown, or what a vast correspondence I have kept up - the society begin to find me quite useful to them - and I have dear unknown correspondents whom I love as old friends, and whose faces I shall only see, perhaps, when we meet in heaven.

"When dear Florence died - that was my sister-in-law, you know - I came to live with Giles, and to look after Flurry. I am quite a responsible woman, having charge of the household, and trying to be a companion to Giles; confess now, Esther, it is not such a useless life after all?"

I do not know what I answered her. I have a dim

Rosa Nouchette Carey

recollection that I burst into some extravagant eulogium or other, for she colored to her temples and called me a foolish child, and begged me seriously never to say such things to her again.

"I do not deserve all that, Esther, but you are too young to judge dispassionately; you must recollect that I have fewer temptations than other people. If I were strong and well I might be worldly too."

"No, never," I answered indignantly; "you would always be better than other people, Miss Ruth - you and Carrie - oh, why are you both so good?" with a despairing inflection in my voice. "How you must both look down on me."

"I know some one who is good, too," returned Miss Ruth, stroking my hair. "I know a brave girl who works hard and wears herself out in loving service, who is often tired and never complains, who thinks little of herself, and yet who does much to brighten other lives, and I think you know her too, Esther?" But I would not let her go on; it was scant goodness to love her, and Allan, and Dot. How could any one do otherwise? And what merit could there be in that?

But though I disclaimed her praise, I was inwardly rejoiced that she should think such things of me, and should judge me worthy of her confidence. She was treating me as though I were her equal and friend, and, to do her justice the idea of my being a governess never seemed to enter into hers or Mr. Lucas' head.

They always treated me from this time as a young friend, who conferred a favor on them by coming. My salary seemed to pass into my hand with the freedom of a gift. Perhaps it was that Uncle Geoffrey was such an old and valued friend, and that Miss Ruth knew that in point of birth the Camerons were far above the Lucases, for we were an old family whom misfortune had robbed of our honors.

However this may be, my privileges were many, and the yoke of service lay lightly on my shoulders. Poor Carrie, indeed, had to eat the bitter bread of dependence, and to take many a severe rebuke from her employer. Mrs. Thorne was essentially a vulgar-minded woman. She was affected by the adventitious adjuncts of life; dress, mere station and wealth weighed largely in her view of things. Because we were poor, she denied our claim to equality; because Carrie taught her children, she snubbed and repressed her, to keep her in her place, as though Carrie were a sort of Jack-in-the-box to be jerked back with every movement.

When Miss Ruth called on mother, Mrs. Thorne shrugged her shoulders, and wondered at the liberality of some people's views. When we were asked to dinner at the Cedars (I suppose Mrs. Smedley told her, for Carrie never gossiped), Mrs. Thorne's eye brows were uplifted in a surprised way. Her scorn knew no bounds when she called one afternoon, and saw Carrie seated at Miss Ruth's little tea-table; she completely ignored her through the visit, except to ask once after her children's lessons. Carrie took her snubbing meekly, and seemed perfectly indifferent. Her quiet lady-like bearing seemed to impress Miss Ruth most favorably, for when Carrie took her leave she kissed her, a thing she had never done before. I looked across at Mrs. Thorne, and saw her tea-cup poised half-way to her lips. She was transfixed with astonishment.

"I envy you your sister, Esther," said Miss Ruth, busying herself with the silver kettle. "She is a dear girl - a very dear girl."

"Humph!" ejaculated Mrs. Thorne. She was past words, and soon after she took her departure in a high state of indignation and dudgeon.

I did not go home the next day. Allan came to say good-by to me, Uncle Geoffrey followed him, and he and Mr. Lucas both decided that I could not be spared. Nurse was somewhat ailing, and Uncle Geoffrey had to prescribe for her too; and as Miss Ruth recovered slowly from these attacks, she would be very lonely, shut up in her room.

Miss Ruth was overjoyed when I promised to stay with her as long as they wanted me. Allan had satisfied my scruples about Jack and Dot.

"They all think you ought to stay," he said. "Mother was the first to decide that. Martha has promised to attend to Dot in your absence. She grumbled a little, and so did he; but that will not matter. Jack must look after herself," finished this very decided young man, who was apt to settle feminine details in rather a summary fashion.

If mother said it was my duty to remain, I need not trouble my head about minor worries; the duty in hand, they all thought, was with Miss Ruth, and with Miss Ruth I would stay.

"It will be such a luxury to have you, Esther," she said, in her old bright way. "My head is generally bad after these attacks, and I cannot read much to myself, and with all my boasted resolution the hours do seem very long. Flurry must spare you to me after the morning, and we will have nice quiet times together."

So I took possession of the little room next hers, and put away the few necessaries that mother had sent me, with a little picture of Dot, that he had drawn for me; but I little thought that afternoon that it would be a whole month before I left it.

I am afraid that long visit spoiled me a little; it was so pleasant resuming some of the old luxuries. Instead of the cold bare room where Jack and I slept, for, in spite of all our efforts, it did look bare in the winter, I found a bright fire burning in my cozy little chamber, and casting warm ruddy gleams over the white china tiles; the wax candles stood ready for lighting on the toilet table; my dressing gown was aging in company with my slippers; everything so snug and essential to comfort, to the very eider-down quilt that looked so tempting.

Then in the morning, just to dress myself and go down to the pleasant dining-room, with the great logs spluttering out a bright welcome, and the breakfast table loaded with many a dainty. No shivering Dot to coerce into good humor; no feckless Jack to frown into order; no grim Deborah to coax and help. Was it very wicked that I felt all this a relief? Then how deliciously the days passed; the few lessons with Flurry, more play than work; the inspiriting ramble ending generally with a peep at mother and Dot!

The cozy luncheons, at which Flurry and I made our dinners, where Flurry sat in state at the bottom of the table and carved the pudding, and gave herself small airs of consequence, and then the long quiet afternoons with Miss Ruth.

I used to write letters at her dictation, and read to her, not altogether dry reading, for she dearly loved an amusing book. It was the "Chronicles of Carlingford" we read, I remember; and how she praised the whole series, calling them pleasant wholesome pictures of life. We used to be quite sorry when Rhoda, the rosy-cheeked housemaid, brought up the little brass kettle, and I had to leave off to make Miss Ruth's tea. Mr. Lucas always came up when that was over, to sit with his sister a little and tell her all the news of the day, while I went down to Flurry, whom I always found seated on the library sofa, with her white frock spreading out like wings, waiting to sit with father while he ate his dinner.

I always had supper in Miss Ruth's room, and never left her again till nurse came in to put her comfortable for the night. Flurry used to run in on her way to bed to hug us both and tell us what father had said.

"You are father's treasure, his one ewe lamb, are you not?" said Miss Ruth once, as she drew the child fondly toward her; and when she had gone, running off with her merry laugh, she spoke almost with a sigh of her brother's love for the child.

"Giles's love for her almost resembles idolatry. The child is like him, but she has poor Florence's eyes and her bright happy nature. I tremble sometimes to think what would become of him if he lost her. I have lived long enough to know that God sometimes takes away 'the desire of a man's eyes, all that he holds most dear.'"

"But not often," I whispered, kissing her troubled brow, for a look of great sadness came over her face at the idea; but her words recurred to me by-and-by when I heard a short conversation between Flurry and her father.

After the first fortnight Miss Ruth regained strength a little, and though still an invalid was enabled to spend some hours downstairs. Before I left the Cedars she had resumed all her old habits, and was able to preside at her brother's dinner-table.

I joined them on these occasions, both by hers and Mr. Lucas' request, and so became better acquainted with Flurry's father.

One Sunday afternoon I was reading in the drawing-room window, and trying to finish my book by the failing wintry light, when Flurry's voice caught my attention; she was sitting on a stool at her father's feet turning over the pages of her large picture Bible. Mr. Lucas had been dozing, I think, for there had been no conversation. Miss Ruth had gone upstairs.

"Father," said the little one, suddenly, in her eager voice, "I do love that story of Isaac. Abraham was such a good man to offer up his only son, only God stopped him, you know. I wonder what his mother would have done if he had come home, and told her he had killed her boy. Would she have believed him, do you think? Would she have ever liked him again?"

"My little Florence, what a strange idea to come into your small head." I could tell from Mr. Lucas' tone that such an idea had never occurred to him. What would Sarah have said as she looked upon her son's destroyer? Would she have acquiesced in that dread obedience, that sacrificial rite?

"But, father dear," still persisted Flurry, "I can't help thinking about it; it would have been so dreadful for poor Sarah. Do you think you would have been like Abraham, father; would you have taken the knife to slay your only child?"

"Hush, Florence," cried her father, hoarsely, and he suddenly caught her to him and kissed her, and bade her run away to her Aunt Ruth with some trifling message or other. I could see her childish question tortured him, by the strained look of his face, as he approached the window. He had not known I was there, but when he saw me he said almost irritably, only it was the irritability of suppressed pain:

"What can put such thoughts in the child's head? I hope you do not let her think too much, Miss Cameron?"

"Most children have strange fancies," I returned, quietly. "Flurry has a vivid imagination; she thinks more deeply than you could credit at her age; she often surprises me by the questions she asks. They show an amount of reasoning power that is very remarkable."

"Let her play more," he replied, in a still more annoyed voice. "I hate prodigies; I would not have Flurry an infant phenomenon for the world. She has too much brain-power; she is too excitable; you must keep her back Miss Cameron."

"I will do what I can," I returned humbly; and then, as he still looked anxious and ill at ease, I went on, "I do not think you need trouble about Flurry's precocity;

children often say these things. Dot, my little brother - Frankie, I mean - would astonish you with some of his remarks. And then there was Jack," warming up with my subject; "Jack used to talk about harps and angels in the most heavenly way, till mother cried and thought she would die young; and look at Jack now - a strong healthy girl, without an ounce of imagination." I could see Mr. Lucas smile quietly to himself in the dusk, for he knew Jack, and had made more than one quizzical remark on her; but I think my observation comforted him a little, for he said no more, only when Flurry returned he took her on his knees and told her about a wonderful performing poodle he had seen, as a sort of pleasant interlude after her severe Biblical studies.

Rosa Nouchette Carey

CHAPTER XIII.

"WE HAVE MISSED DAME BUSTLE."

One other conversation lingered long in my memory, and it took place on my last evening at the Cedars. On the next day I was going home to mother and Dot, and yet I sighed! Oh, Esther, for shame!

It was just before dinner. Miss Ruth had been summoned away to see an old servant of the family, and Flurry had run after her. Mr. Lucas was standing before the fire, warming himself after the manner of Englishmen, and I sat at Miss Ruth's little table working at a fleecy white shawl, that I was finishing to surprise mother.

There was a short silence between us, for though I was less afraid of Mr. Lucas than formerly, I never spoke to him unless he addressed me; but, looking up from my work a moment, I saw him contemplating me in a quiet, thoughtful way, but he smiled pleasantly when our eyes met.

"This is your last evening, I think, Miss Cameron?"

"Indeed it is," I returned, with a short sigh.

"You are sorry to leave us?" he questioned, very

kindly; for I think he had heard the sigh.

"I ought not to be sorry," I returned, stoutly; "for I am going home."

"Oh! and home means everything with you!"

"It means a great deal," knitting furiously, for I was angry at myself for being so sorry to leave; "but Miss Ruth has been so good to me that she has quite spoiled me. I shall not be half so fit for all the hard work I have at home.

"That is a pity," he returned, slowly, as though he were revolving not my words, but some thoughts in his own mind. "Do you know I was thinking of something when you looked up just now. I was wondering why you should not remain with us altogether." I put down my knitting at that, and looked him full in the face; I was so intensely surprised at his words. "You and my sister are such friends; it would be pleasant for her to have you for a constant companion, for I am often busy and tired, and - - " He paused as though he would have added something, but thought better of it. "And she is much alone. A young lively girl would rouse her and do her good, and Flurry would be glad of you."

"I should like it very much," I returned, hesitatingly, "if it were not for mother and Dot." Just for the moment the offer dazzled me and blinded my common sense. Always to occupy my snug little pink chamber; to sit with Miss Ruth in this warm, luxurious drawing-room; to be waited on, petted, spoiled, as Miss Ruth always spoiled people. No wonder such a prospect allured a girl of seventeen.

"Oh, they will do without you," he returned, with a man's indifference to female argument. He and Allan were alike in the facility with which they would knock over one's pet theories. "You are like other young people, Miss Cameron; you think the world cannot get on without you. When you are older you will get rid of this idea," he continued, turning amused eyes on my youthful perplexity. "It is only the young who think one cannot do without them," finished this worldly-wise observer of human nature.

Somehow that stung me and put me on my mettle, and in a moment I had arrayed the whole of my feeble forces against so arbitrary an arrangement of my destiny.

"I cannot help what other young people think," I said, in rather a perverse manner; "they may be wise or foolish as they like, but I am sure of one thing, that mother and Dot cannot do without me."

I am afraid my speech was rather rude and abrupt, but Mr. Lucas did not seem to mind it. His eyes still retained their amused twinkle, but he condescended to argue the point more seriously with me, and sat down in Miss Ruth's low chair, as though to bring himself more on a level with me.

"Let me give you a piece of advice, Miss Cameron; never be too sure of anything. Granted that your mother will miss you very badly at first (I can grant you that, if you like), but there is your sister to console her; and that irresistible Jack - how can your mother, a sensible woman in her way, let a girl go through life with such a name?"

"She will not answer to any other,'" I returned, half offended at this piece of plain speaking; but it was true we had tried Jacqueline, and Lina, and Jack had always remained obstinately deaf.

"Well, well, she will get wiser some day, when she grows into a woman; she will take more kindly to a sensible name then; but as I was saying, your mother may miss you, but all the same she may be thankful to have you so well established and in so comfortable a position. You will be a member of the family, and be treated as well as my sister herself; and the additional salary may be welcome just now, when there are school-bills to pay."

It seemed clear common sense, put in that way, but not for one instant would I entertain such a proposition seriously. The more tempting it looked, the more I distrusted it. Mr. Lucas might be worldly-wise, but here I knew better than he. Would a few pounds more reconcile mother to my vacant place, or cheer Dot's blank face when he knew Esther had deserted him?

"You are very good," I said, trying to keep myself well in hand, and to speak quietly - but now my cheeks burned with the effort; "and I thank you very much for your kind thought, but - "

"Give me no buts," he interrupted, smiling; "and don't thank me for a piece of selfishness, for I was thinking most of my sister and Flurry."

"But all the same I must thank you," I returned, firmly; "and I would like you to believe how happy I should have been if I could have done this conscientiously."

"It is really so impossible?" still incredulously.

"Really and truly, Mr. Lucas. I am worth little to other people, I know, but in their estimation I am worth much. Dot would fret badly; and though mother would make the best of it - she always does - she would never get over the missing, for Carrie is always busy, and Jack is so young, and - "

"There is the dinner bell, and Ruth still chattering with old nurse. That is the climax of our argument. I dare say no more, you are so terribly in earnest, Miss Cameron, and so evidently believe all you say; but all the same, mothers part with their daughters sometimes, very gladly, too, under other circumstances; but there, we will let the subject drop for the present." And then he looked again at me with kindly amused eyes, refusing to take umbrage at my obstinacy; and then, to my relief, Miss Ruth interrupted us.

I felt rather extinguished for the rest of the evening. I did not dare tell Miss Ruth, for fear she would upbraid me for my refusal. I knew she would side with her brother, and would think I could easily be spared from home. And if Carrie would only give up her parish work, and fit into the niche of the daughter of the house, she could easily fulfill all my duties. If - a great big "if" it was - an "if" that would spoil Carrie's life, and destroy all those sweet solemn hopes of hers. No, no; I must not entertain such a thought for a moment.

Mr. Lucas had spoiled my last evening for me, and I think he knew it, for he came to my side as I was putting away my work, and spoke a few contrite words.

"Don't let our talk worry you," he said, in so low a voice that Miss Ruth could not hear his words. "I am sure you were quite right to decide as you did - judging from your point of view, I mean, for of course I hold a different opinion. If you ever see fit to change your decision, you must promise to come and tell me." And of course I promised unhesitatingly.

Miss Ruth followed me to my room, and stood by the fire a few minutes.

"You look grave to-night, Esther, and I flatter myself that it is because you are sorry that your visit has come to an end."

"And you are right," I returned, throwing my arms round her light little figure. Oh, how dearly I had grown to love her! "I would like to be always with you, Miss Ruth; to wait upon you and be your servant. Nothing would be beneath me - nothing. You are fond of me a little, are you not?" for somehow I craved for some expression of affection on this last night. Miss Ruth was very affectionate, but a little undemonstrative sometimes in manner.

"I am very fond of you, Esther," she replied, turning her sweet eyes to me, "and I shall miss my kind, attentive nurse more than I can say. Poor Nurse Gill is getting quite jealous of you. She says Flurry is always wild to get to her playfellow, and will not stay with her if she can help it, and that now I can easily dispense with her services for myself. I had to smooth her down, Esther; the poor old creature quite cried about it, but I managed to console her at last."

"I was always afraid that Mrs. Gill did not like me," I

returned, in a pained voice, for somehow I always disliked hurting people's feelings.

"Oh, she likes you very much; you must not think that. She says Miss Cameron is a very superior young lady, high in manner, and quite the gentlewoman. I think nurse's expression was 'quite the lady, Miss Ruth.'"

"I have never been high in manner to her," I laughed. "We have a fine gossip sometimes over the nursery fire. I like Mrs. Gill, and would not injure her feelings for the world. She is so kind to Dot, too, when he comes to play with Flurry."

"Poor little man, he will be glad to get his dear Esther back," she returned, in a sympathizing voice; and then she bade me good-night, and begged me to hasten to bed, as St. Barnabas had just chimed eleven.

I woke the next morning with a weight upon me, as though I were expecting some ordeal; and though I scolded myself vigorously for my moral cowardice, and called myself a selfish, lazy girl, I could not shake off the feeling.

Never had Miss Ruth seemed so dear to me as she had that day. As the hour approached for my departure I felt quite unhappy at the thought of even leaving her for those few hours.

"We shall see you in the morning," she said, quite cheerfully, as I knelt on the rug, drawing on my warm gloves. I fancied she noticed my foolish, unaccountable depression, and would not add to it by any expression of regret.

"Oh, yes," I returned, with a sort of sigh, as I glanced round the room where I had passed the evenings so pleasantly of late, and thought of the mending basket at home. I was naughty, I confess it; there were absolutely tears in my eyes, as I ran out into the cold dusk of a February evening.

The streets were wet and gleaming, the shop lights glimmered on pools of rain-water; icy drops pattered down on my face; the brewers' horses steamed as they passed with the empty dray; the few foot passengers in High street shuffled along as hastily as they could; even Polly Pattison's rosy face looked puckered up with cold as she put up the shutters of the Dairy.

Uncle Geoffrey's voice hailed me on the doorstep.

"Here you are, little woman. Welcome home! We have missed Dame Bustle dreadfully;" and as he kissed me heartily I could not help stroking his rough, wet coat sleeve in a sort of penitent way.

"Have you really missed me? It is good of you to say so, Uncle Geoff."

"The house has not felt the same," he returned, pushing me in before him, and bidding me shake my cloak as I took it off in the passage.

And then the door opened, and dear mother came out to help me. As I felt her gentle touch, and heard Dot's feeble "Hurrah! here is Esther!" the uncomfortable, discontented feelings vanished, and my better self regained the mastery. Yes, it was homely and shabby; but oh! so sunny and warm! I forgot Miss Ruth when Dot's beautiful little face raised itself from the cushions of the sofa, on which I had placed him, and he put his arms round me as I knelt down beside him, and whispered that his back was bad, and his legs felt funny, and he was so glad I was home again, for Martha was cross, and had hard scrubby hands, and hurt him often, though she did not mean it. This and much more did Dot whisper in his childish confidence.

Then Jack came flying in, with Smudge, as usual, in her arms, and a most tumultuous welcome followed. And then came Carrie, with her soft kiss and few quiet words. I thought she looked paler and thinner than when I left home, but prettier than ever; and she, too, seemed pleased to see me. I took off my things as quickly as I could - not stopping to look round the somewhat disorderly room, where Jack had worked her sweet will for the last month - and joined the family at the tea-table. And afterward I sat close to mother, and talked to her as I mended one of Dot's shirts.

Now and then my thoughts strayed to a far different scene - to a room lighted up with wax candles in silver sconces, and the white china lamp that always stood on Miss Ruth's little table.

I could see in my mind's eye the trim little figure in black silk and lace ruffles, the diamonds gleaming on the small white hands. Flurry would be on the rug in her white frock, playing with the Persian kittens; most likely her father would be watching her from his armchair.

I am afraid I answered mother absently, for, looking up, I caught her wistful glance at me. Carrie was at her night school, and Uncle Geoffrey had been called out. Jack was learning her lessons in the front parlor, and only Dot kept us company.

"You must find it very different from the Cedars," she said, regretfully; "all that luxury must have spoiled you for home, Esther. Don't think I am complaining, my love, if I say you seem a little dull to-night."

"Oh, mother!" flushing up to my temples with shame and irritation at her words; and then another look at the worn face under the widow's cap restrained my momentary impatience. Dot, who was watching us, struck in in his childish way.

"Do you like the Cedars best, Essie? Would you rather be with Flurry than me?"

My own darling! The bare idea was heresy, and acted on me like a moral *douche*.

"Oh! mother and Dot," I said, "how can you both talk so? I am not spoiled - I refuse to be spoiled. I love the Cedars, but I love my own dear little home best." And at this moment I believed my own words. "Dot, how can you be so faithless - how could I love Flurry best? And what would Allan say? You are our own little boy, you know; he said so, and you belong to us both." And Dot's childish jealousy vanished. As for dear mother, she smiled at me in a sweet, satisfied way.

"That is like our own old Esther. You were so quiet all tea-time, my dear, that I fancied something was amiss. It is so nice having you working beside me again," she went on, with a little gentle artifice. "I have missed your bright talk so much in the evenings."

"Has Carrie been out much?" I asked; but I knew what

the answer would be.

"Generally three evenings in the week," returned mother, with a sigh, "and her home evenings have been so engrossed of late. Mrs. Smedley gives her all sorts of things to do - mending and covering books; I hardly knew what."

"Carrie never sings to us now," put in Dot.

"She is too tired, that is what she always says; but I cannot help thinking a little music would be a healthy relaxation for her; but she will have it that with her it is waste of time," said mother.

Waste of time to sing to mother! I broke my thread in two with indignation at the thought. Yes, I was wanted at home, I could see that; Deborah told me so in her taciturn way, when I went to the kitchen to speak to her and Martha.

I had sad work with my room before I slept that night, when Jack was fast asleep; and I was tired out when I crept shivering into my cold bed. I hardly seemed to have slept an hour before I saw Martha's unlovely face bending over me with the flaming candle, so different from Miss Ruth's trim maid.

"Time to get up, Miss Esther, if you are going to dress Master Dot before breakfast. It is mortal cold, to be sure, and raw as raw; but I have brought you a cup of hot tea, as you seemed a bit down last night."

The good creature! I could have hugged her in my girlish gratitude. The tea was a delicious treat, and put new heart into me. I was quite fresh and rested when I went into Dot's little room. He opened his eyes widely when he saw me.

"Oh, Esther! is it really you, and not that ugly old Martha?" he cried out, joyfully. "I do hate her, to be sure. I will be a good boy, and you shall not have any trouble." And thereupon he fell to embracing me as though he would never leave off.

CHAPTER XIV.

PLAYING IN TOM TIDLER'S GROUND.

We had had an old-fashioned winter - weeks of frost to delight the hearts of the young skaters of Milnthorpe; clear, cold bracing days, that made the young blood in our veins tingle with the sense of new life and buoyancy; long, dark winter evenings, when we sat round the clear, red fire, and the footsteps of the few passengers under our window rang with a sort of metallic sound on the frozen pavements.

What a rush of cold air when the door opened, what snow-powdered garments we used to bring into Deborah's spotless kitchen! Dot used to shiver away from my kisses, and put up a little mittened hand to ward me off. "You are like a snow-woman, Essie," he would say. "Your face is as hard and cold and red as one of the haws Flurry brought me."

"She looks as blooming as a rose in June," Uncle Geoffrey answered once, when he heard Dot's unflattering comparison. "Be off, lassie, and take off those wet boots;" but as I closed the door he added to mother, "Esther is improving, I think; she is less angular, and with that clear fresh color she looks quite bonnie."

"Quite bonnie." Oh, Uncle Geoffrey, you little knew how that speech pleased me.

Winter lasted long that year, and then came March, rough and boisterous and dull as usual, with its cruel east wind and the dust, "a peck of which was worth a king's ransom," as father used to say.

Then came April, variable and bright, with coy smiles forever dissolving in tears; and then May in full blossom and beauty giving promise of summer days.

We used to go out in the lanes, Flurry and I, to gather the spring flowers that Miss Ruth so dearly loved. We made a primrose basket once for her room, and many a cowslip ball for Dot, and then there were dainty little bunches of violets for mother and Carrie, only Carrie took hers to a dying girl in Nightingale lane.

The roads round Milnthorpe were so full of lovely things hidden away among the mosses, that I proposed to Flurry that we should collect basketsful for Carrie's sick people. Miss Ruth was delighted with the idea, and asked Jack and Dot to join us, and we all drove down to a large wood some miles from the town, and spent the whole of the spring afternoon playing in a new Tom Tidler's ground, picking up gold and silver. The gold lay scattered broadcast on the land, in yellow patches round the trunks of trees, or beyond in the gleaming meadows; and we worked until the primroses lay heaped up in the baskets in wild confusion, and until our eyes ached with the yellow gleam. I could hear Dot singing softly to himself as he picked industriously. When he and Flurry got tired they seated themselves like a pair of happy little birds on the low bough of a tree. I could hear them twittering softly to

Rosa Nouchette Carey

each other, as they swung, with their arms interlaced, backward and forward in the sunlight; now and then I caught fragments of their talk.

"We shall have plenty of flowers to pick in heaven," Dot was saying as I worked near them.

"Oh, lots," returned Flurry, in an eager voice, "red and white roses, and lilies of the valley, miles of them - millions and millions, for all the little children, you know. What a lot of children there will be, Dot, and how nice to do nothing but play with them, always and forever."

"We must sing hymns, you know," returned Dot, with a slight hesitation in his voice. Being a well brought up little boy, he was somewhat scandalized by Flurry's views; they sounded somewhat earthly and imperfect.

"Oh, we can sing as we play," observed Flurry, irreverently; she was not at all in a heavenly mood this afternoon. "We can hang up our harps, as they do in the Psalms, you know, and just gather flowers as long as we like."

"It is nice to think one's back won't ache so much over it, there," replied poor Dot, who was quite weak and limp from his exertions. "One of the best things about heaven is, though it all seems nice enough, that we shan't be tired. Think of that, Flurry - never to be tired!"

"I am never tired, though I am sleepy sometimes," responded Flurry, with refreshing candor, "You forget the nicest part, you silly boy, that it will never be dark. How I do hate the dark, to be sure."

Dot opened his eyes widely at this. "Do you?" he returned, in an astonished voice; "that is because you are a girl, I suppose. I never thought much about it. I think it is nice and cozy when one is tucked up in bed. I always imagine the day is as tired as I am, and that she has been put to bed too, in a nice, warm, dark blanket."

"Oh, you funny Dot," crowed Flurry. But she would not talk any more about heaven; she was in wild spirits, and when she had swung enough she commenced pelting Dot with primroses. Dot bore it stoutly for awhile, until he could resist no longer, and there was a flowery battle going on under the trees.

It was quite late in the day when the tired children arrived home.

Carrie fairly hugged Dot when the overflowing baskets were placed at her feet.

"These are for all the sick women and little children," answered Dot, solemnly; "we worked so hard, Flurry and I."

"You are a darling," returned Carrie, dimpling with pleasure.

I believe this was the sweetest gift we could have made her. Nothing for herself would have pleased her half so much. She made Jack and me promise to help her carry them the next day, and we agreed, nothing loth. We had quite a festive afternoon in Nightingale lane.

I had never been with Carrie before in her rounds, and I was wonderfully struck with her manner to the poor folk; there was so much tact, such delicate sympathy in all she said and did. I could see surly faces soften and rough voices grow silent as she addressed them in her simple way. Knots of boys and men dispersed to let her pass.

"Bless her sweet face!" I heard one old road-sweeper say; and all the children seemed to crowd round her involuntarily, and yet, with the exception of Dot, she had never seemed to care for children.

I watched her as she moved about the squalid rooms, arranging the primroses in broken bowls, and even teacups, with a sort of ministering grace I had never noticed in her before. Mother had always praised her nursing. She said her touch was so soft and firm, and her movement so noiseless; and she had once advised me to imitate her in this; and as I saw the weary eyes brighten and the languid head raise itself on the pillow at her approach, I could not but own that Carrie was in her natural sphere.

As we returned home with our empty baskets, she told us a great deal about her district, and seemed grateful to us for sharing her pleasure. Indeed, I never enjoyed a talk with Carrie more; I never so thoroughly entered into the interest of her work.

One June afternoon, when I returned home a little earlier than usual, for Flurry had been called down to go out with her father, I found Miss Ruth sitting with mother.

I had evidently disturbed a most engrossing conversation, for mother looked flushed and a little excited, as she always did when anything happened out of the common, and Miss Ruth had the amused expression I knew so well.

"You are earlier than usual, my dear," said mother, with an odd little twitch of the lip, as though something pleased her. But here Dot, who never could keep a secret for five minutes, burst out in his shrill voice:

"Oh, Essie, what do you think? You will never believe it - you and I and Flurry are going to Roseberry for six whole weeks."

"You have forgotten me, you ungrateful child," returned Miss Ruth in a funny tone; "I am nobody, I suppose, so long as you get your dear Esther and Flurry."

Dot was instinctively a little gentleman. He felt he had made a mistake; so he hobbled up to Miss Ruth, and laid his hand on hers: "We couldn't do without you - could we, Essie?" he said in a coaxing voice. "Esther does not like ordering dinners; she often says so, and she looks ready to cry when Deb brings her the bills. It will be ever so much nicer to have Miss Ruth, won't it, Esther?" But I was too bewildered to answer him.

"Oh, mother, is it really true? Can you really spare us, and for six whole weeks? Oh, it is too delightful! But Carrie, does she not want the change more than I?"

I don't know why mother and Miss Ruth exchanged glances at this; but mother said rather sadly:

"Miss Lucas has been good enough to ask your sister, Esther; she thought you might perhaps take turns; but I am sorry to say Carrie will not hear of it. She says it will spoil your visit, and that she cannot be spared."

"Our parochial slave-driver is going out of town," put in Miss Ruth dryly. She could be a little sarcastic sometimes when Mrs. Smedley's name was implied. In her inmost heart she had no more love than I for the bustling lady.

"She is going to stay with her niece at Newport, and so her poor little subaltern, Carrie, cannot be absent from her post. One day I mean to give a piece of my mind to that good lady," finished Miss Ruth, with a malicious sparkle in her eyes.

"Oh, it's no use talking," sighed mother, and there was quite a hopeless inflection in her voice. "Carrie is a little weak, in spite of her goodness. She is like her mother in that - the strongest mind governs her. I have no chance against Mrs. Smedley."

"It is a shame," I burst out; but Miss Ruth rose from her chair, still smiling.

"You must restrain your indignation till I have gone, Esther," she said, in mock reproof. "Your mother and I have done all we could, and have coaxed and scolded for the last half-hour. The Smedley influence is too strong for us. Never mind, I have captured you and Dot; remember, you must be ready for us on Monday week;" and with that she took her departure.

Mother followed me up to my room, on pretense of looking over Jack's things, but in reality she wanted a chat with me.

The dear soul was quite overjoyed at the prospect of

my holiday; she mingled lamentations over Carrie's obstinacy with expressions of pleasure at the treat in store for Dot and me.

"And you will not be lonely without us, mother?"

"My dear, how could I be so selfish! Think of the benefit the sea air will be to Dot! And then, I can trust him so entirely to you." And thereupon she began an anxious inquiry as to the state of my wardrobe, which lasted until the bell rang.

But, in spite of the delicious anticipations that filled me, I was not wholly satisfied, and when mother had said good-night to us I detained Carrie.

She came back a little reluctantly, and asked me what I wanted with her. She looked tired, almost worn out, and the blue veins were far too perceptible on the smooth, white forehead. I noticed for the first time a hollowness about the temples; the marked restlessness of an over-conscientious mind was wearing out the body; the delicacy of her look filled me with apprehension.

"Oh, Carrie!" I said, vehemently, "you are not well; this hot weather is trying you. Do listen to me, darling. I don't want to vex you, but you must promise me to come to Roseberry."

To my surprise she drew back with almost a frightened look on her face; well, not that exactly, but a sort of scared, bewildered expression.

"Don't, Esther. Why will none of you give me any peace? Is it not enough that mother and Miss Lucas have been talking to me, and now you must begin! Do you know how much it costs me to stand firm against you all? You distress me, you wear me out with your talk."

"Why cannot we convince you?" I returned, with a sort of despair. "You are mother's daughter, not Mrs. Smedley's: you owe no right of obedience to that woman."

"How you all hate her!" she sighed. "I must look for no sympathy from any of you - your one thought is to thwart me in every way."

"Carrie!" I almost gasped, for she looked and spoke so unlike herself.

"I don't mean to be unkind," she replied in a softening tone; "I suppose you all mean it for the best. Once for all, Esther, I cannot come to Roseberry. I have promised Mrs. Smedley to look after things in her absence, and nothing would induce me to forfeit my trust."

"You could write to her and say you were not well," I began; but she checked me almost angrily.

"I am well, I am quite well; if I long for rest, if the prospect of a little change would be delightful, I suppose I could resist even these temptations. I am not worse than many other girls; I have work to do, and must do it. No fears of possible breakdowns shall frighten me from my duty. Go and enjoy your holiday, and do not worry about me, Esther." And then she kissed me, and took up her candle.

I was sadly crestfallen, but no arguments could avail, I thought; and so I let her go from me. And yet if I had known the cause of her sudden irritability, I should not so soon have given up all hope. I little knew how sorely she was tempted; how necessary some brief rest and change of scene was to her overwrought nerves. If I had only been patient and pleaded with her, I think I must have persuaded her; but, alas! I never knew how nearly she had yielded.

There was no sleep for Dot that night. I found him in a fever of excitement, thumping his hot pillows and flinging himself about in vain efforts to get cool. It was no good scolding him; he had these sleepless fits sometimes; so I bathed his face and hands, and sat down beside him, and laid my head against the pillow, hoping that he would quiet down by-and-by. But nothing would prevent his talking.

"I wish I were out with the flowers in the garden," he said; "I think it is stupid being tucked up in bed in the summer. Allan is not in bed, is he? He says he is often called up, and has to cross the quadrangle to go to a great bare room where they bind up broken heads. Should you like to be a doctor, Essic?"

"If I were a man," I returned, confidently, "I should be either a clergyman or a doctor; they are the grandest and noblest of professions. One is a cure of bodies, and the other is a cure of souls."

"Oh, but they hurt people," observed Dot, shrinking a little; "they have horrid instruments they carry about with them."

"They only hurt people for their own good, you silly

little boy. Think of all the dark sick rooms they visit, and the poor, helpless people they comfort. They spend their lives doing good, healing dreadful diseases, and relieving pain."

"I think Allan's life will be more useful than Fred's," observed Dot. Poor little boy! Constant intercourse with grown-up people was making him precocious. He used to say such sharp, shrewd things sometimes.

I sighed a little when he spoke of Fred. I could imagine him loitering through life in his velveteen coat, doing little spurts of work, but never settling down into thorough hard work.

Allan's descriptions of his life were not very encouraging. His last letter to me spoke a little dubiously about Fred's prospects.

"He is just a drawing-master, and nothing else," wrote Allan. "Uncle Geoffrey's recommendations have obtained admittance for him into one or two good houses, and I hear he has hopes of Miss Hemming's school in Bayswater. Not a very enlivening prospect for our elegant Fred! Fancy that very superior young man sinking into a drawing-master! So much for the hanging committee and the picture that is to represent the Cameron genius.

"I went down to Acacia road on Thursday evening, and dimly perceived Fred across an opaque cloud of tobacco smoke. He and some kindred spirits were talking art jargon in this thick atmosphere.

"Fred looked a Bohemian of Bohemians in his gaudy dressing-gown and velvet smoking-cap. His hair is longer than ever, and he has become aesthetic in his tastes. There was broken china enough to stock a small shop. I am afraid I am rather too much a Philistine for their notions. I got some good downright stares and shrugs over my tough John Bull tendencies.

"Tell mother Fred is all right, and keeping out of debt, and so one must not mind a few harmless vagaries."

"Broken china, indeed!" muttered Uncle Geoff when I had finished reading this clause. "Broken fiddlesticks! Why, the lad must be weak in his head to spend his money on such rubbish." Uncle Geoffrey was never very civil to Fred.

Dot did not say any more, and I began a long story, to keep his tongue quiet. As it was purposely uninteresting, and told in a monotonous voice, it soon had the effect of making him drowsy. When I reached this point, I stole softly from the room. It was bright moonlight when I lay down in bed, and all night long I dreamed of a rippling sea and broad sands, over which Dot and I were walking, hand in hand.

CHAPTER XV.

LIFE AT THE BRAMBLES.

It was a lovely evening when we arrived at Roseberry.

"We lead regular hermit lives at the Brambles, away from the haunts of men," observed Miss Ruth; but I was too much occupied to answer her. Dot and I were peeping through the windows of the little omnibus that was conveying us and our luggage to the cottage. Miss Ruth had a pretty little pony carriage for country use; but she would not have it sent to the station to meet us - the omnibus would hold us all, she said. Nurse could go outside; the other two servants who made up the modest establishment at the Brambles had arrived the previous day.

Roseberry was a straggling little place, without much pretension to gentility. A row of white lodging-houses, with green verandas, looked over the little parade; there was a railed-in green enclosure before the houses, where a few children played.

Half a dozen bathing-machines were drawn up on the beach; beyond was the Preventive station, and the little white cottages where the Preventive men lived, with neat little gardens in front.

The town was rather like Milnthorpe, for it boasted only one long street. A few modest shops, the Blue Boar Inn, and a bow-windowed house, with "Library" painted on it in large characters, were mixed up with pleasant-looking dwelling houses. The little gray church was down a country road, and did not look as though it belonged to the town, but the schools were in High street. Beyond Roseberry were the great rolling downs.

We had left the tiny parade and the lodging houses behind us, and our little omnibus seemed jolting over the beach - I believe they called it a road but it was rough and stony, and seemed to lead to the shore. It was quite a surprise when we drove sharply round a low rocky point, and came upon a low gray cottage, with a little garden running down to the beach.

Truly a hermit's abode, the Brambles; not another house in sight; low, white chalky cliffs, with the green downs above them, and, far as we could see, a steep beach, with long fringes of yellow sands, with the grey sea breaking softly in the distance, for it was low tide, and the sun had set.

"Is this too lonely for you, Esther?" asked Miss Ruth, as we walked up the pebbly path to the porch. It was a deep stone porch, with seats on either side, and its depth gave darkness to the little square hall, with its stone fireplace and oak settles.

"What a delicious place!" was my answer, as I followed her from one room into another. The cottage was a perfect nest of cozy little rooms, all very tiny, and leading into each other.

There was a snug dining-room that led into Mr. Lucas' study, and beyond that two little drawing-rooms, very small, and simply though prettily furnished. They were perfect summer rooms, with their Indian matting and muslin curtains, with wicker chairs and lounges, and brackets with Miss Ruth's favorite china.

Upstairs the arrangements were just as simple; not a carpet was to be seen, only dark polishes floors and strips of Indian matting, cool chintz coverings, and furniture of the simplest maple and pine wood - a charming summer retreat, fitted up with unostentatious taste. There was a tiny garden at the back, shut in by a low chalk cliff, a rough zigzag path that goats might have climbed led to the downs, and there was a breach where we could enjoy the sweet air and wide prospect.

It was quite a cottage garden. All the old-fashioned flowers bloomed there; little pink cabbage roses, Turks-caps, lilies, lupins, and monkshood and columbines. Everlasting peas and scarlet-runners ran along the wall, and wide-lipped convolvuli, scarlet weeds of poppies flaunted beside the delicate white harebells, sweet-william and gillyflowers, and humble southernwood, and homely pinks and fragrant clove carnations, and pansies of every shade in purple and golden patches.

"Oh, Essie, it reminds me of our cottage; why, there are the lilies and the beehives, and there is the porch where you said you should sit on summer evenings and mend Allan's socks." And Dot leaned on his crutches and looked round with bright wide-open eyes.

Our little dream cottage; well, it was not unlike it, only the sea and the downs and the low chalk cliffs were added. How Dot and I grew to love that garden! There was an old medlar tree, very gnarled and crooked, under which Miss Ruth used to place her little tea-table; the wicker chairs were brought out and there we often used to spend our afternoons, with little blue butterflies hovering round us, and the bees humming among the sweet thyme and marjoram, and sometimes an adventurous sheep looking down on us from the cliff.

We led a perfect gypsy life at the Brambles; no one called on us, the vicar of Roseberry was away, and a stranger had taken his duty; no interloper from the outer world broke the peaceful monotony of our days, and the sea kept up its plaintive music night and day, and the larks sang to us, and the busy humming of insect life made an undertone of melody, and in early mornings the little garden seemed steeped in dew and fragrance. We used to rise early, and after breakfast Flurry and I bathed. There was a little bathing-room beyond the cottage with a sort of wooden bridge running over the beach, and there Flurry and I would disport ourselves like mermaids.

After a brisk run on the sands or over the downs, we joined Miss Ruth on the beach, where we worked and talked, or helped the children build sand-castles, and deck them with stone and sea-weeds. What treasures we collected for Carrie's Sunday scholars; what stores of bright-colored seaweed - or sea flowers, as Dot persisted in calling them - and heaps of faintly-tinged shells!

Flurry's doll family had accompanied us to the Brambles. "The poor dear things wanted change of air!" Flurry had decided; and in spite of my dissuasion, all the fair waxen creatures and their heterogeneous wardrobe had been consigned to a vast trunk.

Flurry's large family had given her infinite trouble when we settled for our mornings on the beach. She traveled up and down the long stony hillocks to the cottage until her little legs ached, to fetch the twelve dolls. When they were all deposited in their white sun-bonnets under a big umbrella, to save their complexions, which, notwithstanding, suffered severely, then, and then only, would Flurry join Dot on the narrow sands.

Sometimes the tide rose, or a sudden shower came on, and then great was the confusion. Once a receding wave carried out Corporal Trim, the most unlucky of dolls, to sea. Flurry wrung her hands and wept so bitterly over this disaster that Miss Ruth was quite frightened, and Flossy jumped up and licked his little mistress' face and the faces of the dolls by turns.

"Oh, the dear thing is drownded," sobbed Flurry, as Corporal Trim floundered hopelessly in the surge. Dot's soft heart was so moved by her distress that he hobbled into the water, crutches and all, to my infinite terror.

"Don't cry. Flurry; I've got him by the hair of his head," shouted Dot, valiantly shouldering the dripping doll. Flurry ran down the beach with the tears still on her cheeks, and took the wretched corporal and hugged him to her bosom.

"Oh, my poor drownded Trim," cried Flurry tenderly, and a strange procession formed to the cottage. Flurry with the poor victim in her arms and Flossy jumping and barking delightedly round her, and snatching at the wet rags; Dot, also, wet and miserable, toiling up the beach on his crutches; Miss Ruth and I following with the eleven dolls.

The poor corporal spent the rest of the day watching his own clothes drying by the kitchen fire, where Dot kept him company; Flurry trotted in and out, and petted them both. I am afraid Dot, being a boy, often found the dolls a nuisance, and could have dispensed with their company. There was a grand quarrel once when he flatly refused to carry one. "I can't make believe to be a girl," said Dot, curling his lip with infinite contempt.

"We used to spend our afternoons in the garden. It was cooler than the beach, and the shade of the old medlar was refreshing. We sometimes read aloud to the children, but oftener they were working in their little gardens, or playing with some tame rabbits that belonged to Flurry. Dot always hobbled after Flurry wherever she went; he was her devoted slave. Flurry sometimes treated him like one of her dolls, or put on little motherly airs, in imitation of Miss Ruth.

"You are tired, my dear boy; pray lean on me," we heard her once say, propping him with her childish arm. "Sit down in the shade, you must not heat yourself;" but Dot rather resented her care of him, after the fashion of boys, but on the whole they suited each other perfectly.

In the evenings we always walked over the downs or drove with Miss Ruth in her pony carriage through the leafy lanes, or beside the yellow cornfields. The children used to gather large nosegays of poppies and

Rosa Nouchette Carey

cornflowers, and little pinky convolvuli. Sometimes we visited a farmhouse where some people lived whom Miss Ruth knew.

Once we stopped and had supper there, a homely meal of milk, and brown bread, and cream cheese, with a golden honeycomb to follow, which we ate in the farmyard kitchen. What an exquisite time we had there, sitting in the low window seat, looking over a bright clover field. A brood of little yellow chickens ran over the red-brick floor, a black retriever and her puppies lay before the fire - fat black puppies with blunt noses and foolish faces, turning over on their backs, and blundering under every one's feet.

Dot and Flurry went out to see the cows milked, and came back with long stories of the dear little white, curly-tailed pigs. Flurry wrote to her father the next day, and begged that he would buy her one for a pet. Both she and Dot were indignant when he told them the little pig they admired so much would become a great ugly sow like its mother.

Mrs. Blake, the farmer's wife, took a great fancy to Dot, and begged him to come again, which both the children promised her most earnestly to do. They both carried off spoils of bright red apples to eat on the way.

It was almost dark when we drove home through the narrow lanes; the hedgerows glimmered strangely in the dusk; a fresh sea-ladened wind blew in our faces across the downs, the lights shone from the Preventive station, and across the vague mist glimmered a star or two. How fragrant and still it was, only the soft washing of the waves on the beach to break the silence!

Miss Ruth shivered a little as we rattled down the road leading to the Brambles. Dorcas, mindful of her mistress' delicacy, had lighted a little fire in the inner drawing-room, and had hot coffee waiting for us.

It looked so snug and inviting that the children left it reluctantly to go to bed; but Miss Ruth was inexorable. This was our cozy hour; all through the day we had to devote ourselves to the children - we used to enjoy this quiet time to ourselves. Sometimes I wrote to mother or Carrie, or we mutually took up our books; but oftener we sat and talked as we did on this evening, until Nurse came to remind us of the lateness of the hour.

Mr. Lucas paid us brief visits; he generally came down on Saturday evening and remained until Monday. Miss Ruth could never coax him to stay longer; I think his business distracted him, and kept his trouble at bay. In this quiet place he would have grown restless. He had bought the Brambles to please his wife, and she, and not Miss Ruth, had furnished it. They had spent happy summers there when Flurry was a baby. The little garden had been a wilderness until then; every flower had been planted by his wife, every room bore witness to her charming taste. No wonder he regarded it with such mingled feelings of pain and pleasure.

Mr. Lucas made no difference to our simple routine. Miss Ruth and Flurry used to drive to the little station to meet him, and bring him back in triumph to the seven o'clock nondescript meal, that was neither dinner nor tea, nor supper, but a compound of all. I used to go up with the children after that meal, that he and Miss Ruth might enjoy their chat undisturbed. When I returned to the drawing-room Miss Ruth was invariably alone.

"Giles has gone out for a solitary prowl," she would say; and he rarely returned before we went upstairs. Miss Ruth knew his habits, and seldom waited up to say good-night to him.

"He likes better to be alone when he is in this mood," she would say sometimes. Her tact and cleverness in managing him were wonderful; she never seemed to watch him, she never let him feel that his morbid fits were noticed and humored, but all the same she knew when to leave him alone, and when to talk to him; she could be his bright companion, or sit silently beside him for hours. On Sunday mornings Mr. Lucas always accompanied us to church, and in the afternoon he sat with the children on the beach. Dot soon got very fond of him, and would talk to him in his fearless way, about anything that came into his head; Miss Ruth sometimes joined them, but I always went apart with my book.

Mr. Lucas was so good to me that I could not bear to hamper him in the least by my presence; with grown-up people he was a little stiff and reserved, but with children he was his true self.

Flurry doted on her father, and Dot told me in confidence that "he was the nicest man he had ever known except Uncle Geoffrey."

I could not hear their talk from my nest in the cliff, but I am afraid Dot's chief occupation was to hunt the little scurrying crabs into a certain pool he had already fringed with seaweed. I could see him and Flurry carrying the big jelly-fishes, and floating them carefully. They had left their spades and buckets at home, out of respect for the sacredness of the day; but neither Flurry's clean white frock nor Dot's new suit hindered them from scooping out the sand with their hands, and making rough and ready ramparts to keep in their prey.

Mr. Lucas used to lie on the beach with his straw hat over his eyes, and watch their play, and pet Flossy. When he was tired of inaction he used to call to the children, and walk slowly and thought fully on. Flurry used to run after him.

"Oh, do wait for Dot, father," she would plead; nothing would induce her to leave her infirm and halting little playfellow. One day, when Mr. Lucas was impatient of his slow progress, I saw him shoulder him, crutches and all, and march off with him, Dot clapping his hands and shouting with delight. That was the only time I followed them; but I was so afraid Dot was a hindrance, and wanted to capture him, I walked quite a mile before I met them coming back.

Mr. Lucas was still carrying Dot; Flurry was trotting beside him, and pretending to use Dot's crutches.

"We have been ever so far, Essie," screamed Dot when he caught sight of me. "We have seen lots of seagulls, and a great cave where the smugglers used to hide."

"Oh, Dot, you must not let Mr. Lucas carry you," I said, holding out my arms to relieve him of his burden. "You must stay with me, and I will tell you a story."

"He is happier up here, aren't you, Frankie boy?" returned Mr. Lucas, cheerfully.

"Oh, but he will tire you," I faltered.

"Tire me, this little bundle of bones!" peeping at Dot over his shoulder; "why, I could walk miles with him. Don't trouble yourself about him, Miss Esther. We understand each other perfectly."

And then he left me, walking with long, easy strides over the uneven ground, with Flurry running to keep up with him.

They used to go on the downs after tea, and sit on the little green beach, while Miss Ruth and I went to church.

Miss Ruth never would use her pony carriage on Sunday. A boy used to draw her in a wheel-chair. She never stayed at home unless she was compelled to do so. I never knew any one enjoy the service more, or enter more fully into it.

No matter how out of tune the singing might be, she always joined in it with a fervor that quite surprised me. "Depend upon it, Esther," she used to say, "it is not the quality of our singing that matters but how much our heart joins with the choir. Perfect praise and perfect music cannot be expected here; but I like to think old Betty's cracked voice, when she joins in the hymns, is as sweet to angels' ears as our younger notes."

The children always waited up for us on Sunday evening, and afterward Miss Ruth would sing with them; sometimes Mr. Lucas would walk up and down the gravel paths listening to them, but oftener I could catch the red light of his cigar from the cliff seat.

I wonder what sad thoughts came to him as the voices floated out to him, mixed up with the low ripple of waves on the sand.

"Where loyal hearts and true" - they were singing that, I remember; Flurry in her childish treble. And Flurry's mother, lying in her quiet grave - did the mother in paradise, I wonder, look down from her starry place on her little daughter singing her baby hymn, and on that lonely man, listening from the cliff seat in the darkness?

Rosa Nouchette Carey

CHAPTER XVI.

THE SMUGGLERS' CAVE.

The six weeks passed only too rapidly, but Dot and I were equally delighted when Miss Ruth petitioned for a longer extension of absence, to which dear mother returned a willing consent.

A little note was enclosed for me in Miss Ruth's letter.

"Make your mind quite easy, my dear child," she wrote, "we are getting on very well, and really Jack is improving, and does all sorts of little things to help me; she keeps her room tidier, and I have not had to find fault with her for a week.

"We do not see much of Carrie; she comes home looking very pale and fagged; your uncle grumbles sometimes, but I tell him words are wasted, the Smedley influence is stronger than ever.

"But you need not think I am dull, though I do miss my bright, cheery Esther, and my darling Frankie. Jack and I have nice walks, and Uncle Geoffrey takes me sometimes on his rounds, and two or three times Mr. Lucas has sent the carriage to take us into the country; he says the horses need exercise, now his sister is away, but I know it is all his kindness and thought for us. I will willingly spare you a little longer, and am only thankful that the darling boy is deriving so much benefit from the sea air."

Dear, unselfish mother, always thinking first of her children's interest, and never of her own wishes; and yet I could read between the lines, and knew how she missed us, especially Dot, who was her constant companion.

But it was really the truth that the sea air was doing Dot good. He complained less of his back, and went faster and faster on his little crutches; the cruel abscesses had not tried him for months, and now it seemed to me that the thin cheeks were rounding out a little. He looked so sunburned and rosy, that I wished mother could have seen him. It was only the color of a faintly-tinged rose, but all the same it was wonderful for Dot. We had had lovely weather for our holiday; but at the beginning of September came a change. About a week after mother's letter had arrived, heavy storms of wind and rain raged round the coast.

Miss Ruth and Dot were weather-bound, neither of them had strength to brave the boisterous wind; but Flurry and I would tie down our hats with our veils and run down the parade for a blow. It used to be quite empty and deserted; only in the distance we could see the shiny hat of the Preventive man, as he walked up and down with his telescope.

I used to hold Flurry tightly by the hand, for I feared she would be blown off her feet. Sometimes we were nearly drenched and blinded with the salt spray.

The sea looked so gray and sullen, with white curling

waves leaping up against the sea wall; heaps of froth lay on the parade, and even on the green enclosure in the front of the houses. People said it was the highest tide they had known for years.

Once I was afraid to take Flurry out, and ran down to the beach alone. I had to plant my feet firmly in the shingles, for I could hardly stand against the wind. What a wild, magnificent scene it was, a study in browns and grays, a strange colorless blending of faint tints and uncertain shading.

As the waves receded there was a dark margin of heaped-up seaweed along the beach, the tide swept in masses of tangled things, the surge broke along the shore with a voice like thunder, great foamy waves leaped up in curling splendor and then broke to pieces in the gray abyss. The sky was as gray as the sea; not a living thing was in sight except a lonely seagull. I could see the gleam of the firelight through one of the windows of the cottage. It looked so warm and snug. The beach was high and dry round me, but a little beyond the Brambles the tide flowed up to the low cliffs. Most people would have shivered in such a scene of desolation, for the seagull and I had it all to ourselves, but the tumult of the wind and waves only excited me. I felt wild with spirits, and could have shouted in the exuberance of my enjoyment.

I could have danced in my glee, as the foamy snowflakes fell round me, and my face grew stiff and wet with the briny air. The white manes of the sea-horses arched themselves as they swept to their destruction. How the wind whistled and raved, like a hunted thing! "They that go down to the sea in ships, and do their business in the deep waters," those words seemed to flash to me across the wild tumult, and I thought of all the wonders seen by the mariners of old.

"Oh, Esther, how can you be so adventurous?" exclaimed Miss Ruth, as I thrust a laughing face and wet waterproof into the room; she and the children were sitting round the fire.

"Oh, it was delicious," I returned. "It intoxicated me like new wine; you cannot imagine the mighty duet of the sea and wind, the rolling sullen bass, and the shrill crescendo."

"It must have been horrible," she replied, with a little shiver. The wild tempestuous weather depressed her; the loud discordance of the jarring elements seemed to fret the quiet of her spirit.

"You are quite right," she said to me as we sat alone that evening, "this sort of weather disturbs my tranquillity; it makes me restless and agitates my nerves. Last night I could not sleep; images of terror blended with my waking thoughts. I seemed to see great ships driving before the wind, and to hear the roaring of breakers and crashing of timbers against cruel rocks; and when I closed my eyes, it was only to see the whitened bones of mariners lying fathoms deep among green tangled seaweed."

"Dear Miss Ruth, no wonder you look pale and depressed after such a night. Would you like me to sleep with you? the wind seems to act on me like a lullaby. I felt cradled in comfort last night."

"You are so strong," she said, with a little sadness in her voice. "You have no nerves, no diseased sensibilities; you do not dread the evils you cannot see, the universe does not picture itself to you in dim terrors."

"Why, no," I returned, wonderingly, for such suggestions were new to me.

"Sleep your happy sleep, my dear," she said, tenderly, "and thank God for your perfect health, Esther. I dozed a little myself toward morning, before the day woke in its rage, and then I had a horrible sort of dream, a half-waking scare, bred of my night-terrors.

"I thought I was tossing like a dead leaf in the gale; the wind had broken bounds, and carried me away bodily. Now I was lying along the margin of waves, and now swept in wide circles in the air.

"The noise was maddening. The air seemed full of shrieks and cries, as though the universe were lost and bewailing itself, 'Lamentation and mourning and woe,' seemed written upon the lurid sky and sea. I thought of those poor lovers in Dante's 'Inferno,' blown like spectral leaves before the infernal winds of hell; but I was alone in this tumultuous torrent.

"I felt myself sinking at last into the dim, choking surge - it was horribly real, Esther - and then some one caught me by the hair and drew me out, and the words came to me, 'for so He bringeth them to the haven where they would be.'"

"How strange!" I exclaimed in an awed tone, for Miss Ruth's face was pale, and there was a touch of sadness in her voice.

"It was almost a vision of one's life," she returned, slowly; "we drift hither and thither, blown by many a gust of passion over many an unseen danger. If we be not engulfed, it is because the Angel of His Providence watches over us; 'drawn out of many waters,' how many a life history can testify of that!"

"We have our smooth days as well," I returned, cheerfully, "when the sun shines, and there are only ripples on the waters."

"That is in youth," she replied; "later on the storms must come, and the wise mariner will prepare himself to meet them. We must not always be expecting fair weather. Do you not remember the lines of my favorite hymn:

"'And oh, the joy upon that shore
To tell our shipwrecked voyage o'er.'

"Really, I think one of the great pleasures in heaven will be telling the perils we have been through, and how He has brought us home at last."

Miss Ruth would not let me sleep with her that night; but to my great relief, for her pale, weary looks made me anxious, the wind abated, and toward morning only the breaking surge was heard dashing along the shore.

"I have rested better," were the first words when we met, "but that one night's hurly-burly has wrecked me a little," which meant that she was only fit for bed.

But she would not hear of giving up entirely, so I drew her couch to the fire, and wrapped her up in shawls and left Dot to keep her company, while Flurry and I went out. In spite of the lull the sea was still very unquiet, and the receding tide gave us plenty of amusement, and we spent a very happy morning. In the afternoon, Miss Ruth had some errands for me to do in the town - wools to match, and books to change at the library, after which I had to replenish our exhausted store of note-paper.

It was Saturday, and we had decided the pony carriage must go alone to the station to meet Mr. Lucas. He generally arrived a little before six, but once he had surprised us walking in with his portmanteau, just as we were starting for our afternoon's walk. Flurry begged hard to accompany me; but Miss Ruth thought she had done enough, and wished her to play with Dot in the dining-room at some nice game. I was rather sorry at Miss Ruth's decision, for I saw Flurry was in one of her perverse moods. They occurred very seldom, but gave me a great deal of trouble to overcome them. She could be very naughty on such occasions, and do a vast amount of mischief. Flurry's break-outs, as I called them, were extremely tiresome, as Nurse Gill and I knew well. I was very disinclined to trust Dot in her company, for her naughtiness would infect him, and even the best of children can be troublesome sometimes. Flurry looked very sulky when I asked her what game they meant to play, and I augured badly from her toss of the head and brief replies. She was hugging Flossie on the window-seat, and would not give me her attention, so I turned to Dot and begged him to be a good boy and not to disturb Miss Ruth, but take care of Flurry.

Dot answered amiably, and I ran off, determining to be back as soon as I could. I wished Nurse Gill could sit with the children and keep them in good temper, but she was at work in Miss Ruth's room and could not come down.

My errands took longer than I thought; wool matching is always a troublesome business, and the books Miss Ruth wanted were out, and I had to select others; it was more than an hour before I set off for home, and then I met Nurse Gill, who wanted some brass rings for the curtains she was making, and had forgotten to ask me to get them.

The wind was rising again, and I was surprised to find Miss Ruth in the porch with her handkerchief tied over her head, and Dorcas running down the garden path.

"Have you seen them, Miss Esther?" asked the girl, anxiously.

"Who - what do you mean?" I inquired.

"Miss Florence and Master Dot; we have been looking for them everywhere. I was taking a cup of tea just now to mistress, and she asked me to go into the dining-room, as the children seemed so quiet; but they were not there, and Betty and I have searched the house and garden over, and we cannot find them."

"Oh, Esther, come here," exclaimed Miss Ruth in agony, for I was standing still straining my eyes over the beach to catch a glimpse of them. "I am afraid I was very wrong to send you out, and Giles will be here presently, and Dorcas says Dot's hat is missing from the peg, and Flurry's sealskin hat and jacket."

Dot out in this wind! I stood aghast at the idea, but the next moment I took Miss Ruth's cold little hands

Rosa Nouchette Carey

in mine.

"You must not stand here," I said firmly; "come into the drawing-room, I will talk to you there, and you too, Dorcas. No, I have not seen them," as Miss Ruth yielded to my strong grasp, and stood shivering and miserable on the rug. "I came past the Preventive station and down the parade, and they were not there."

"Could they have followed Nurse Gill?" struck in Dorcas.

"No, for I met her just now, and she was alone. I hardly think they would go to the town. Dot never cared for the shops, or Flurry either. Perhaps they might be hidden in one of the bathing machines. Oh, Miss Ruth," with an access of anxiety in my voice, "Dot is so weakly, and this strong wind will blow him down; it must be all Flurry's naughtiness, for nothing would have induced him to go out unless she made him."

"What are we to do?" she replied, helplessly. This sudden terror had taken away her strength, she looked so ill. I thought a moment before I replied.

"Let Dorcas go down to the bathing machines," I said, at last, "and she can speak to the Preventive man; and if you do not mind being alone, Miss Ruth, and you must promise to lie down and keep quiet, Betty might go into the town and find Nurse Gill. I will just run along the beach and take a look all around."

"Yes, do," she returned. "Oh, my naughty, naughty Flurry!" almost wringing her hands.

"Don't frighten yourself beforehand," I said, kissing her and speaking cheerfully, though I did feel in a state about Dot; and what would mother and Mr. Lucas say? "I daresay Dorcas or I will bring them back in a few minutes, and then won't they get a scolding!"

"Oh, no; I shall be too happy to scold them," she returned, with a faint smile, for my words put fresh heart in her, and she would follow us into the porch and stand looking after us.

I scrambled over the shingles as fast as I could, for the wind was rising, and I was afraid it would soon grow dusk. Nothing was in sight; the whole shore was empty and desolate - fearfully desolate, even to my eyes.

It was no use going on, I thought; they must be hiding in the bathing machines after all. And I was actually turning round when something gray on the beach attracted my attention, and I picked it up. To my horror, it was one of Dot's woolen mittens that mother had knitted for him, and which he had worn that very afternoon.

I was on their track, after all. I was sure of it now; but when I lifted my eyes and saw the dreary expanse of shore before me, a blank feeling of terror took possession of me. They were not in sight! Nothing but cloudy skies and low chalky cliffs, and the surge breaking on the shingles.

All at once a thought that was almost an inspiration flashed across me - the smugglers' cave! Flurry was always talking about it; it had taken a strong hold of her imagination, and both she and Dot had been wild to explore it, only Miss Ruth had never encouraged the idea. She thought caves were damp, dreary places, and not fit for delicate children. Flurry must have tempted Dot to accompany her on this exploring expedition. I was as convinced of the fact as though I had overheard the children's conversation. She would coax and cajole him until his conscience was undermined. How could he have dragged himself so far on his crutches? for the cave was nearly half a mile away from where I stood, and the wind was rising fearfully. And now an icy chill of terror came over me from head to foot - the tide was advancing! It had already covered the narrow strip of sand; in less than an hour it would reach the cliffs, for the shore curved a little beyond the cottage, and with the exception of the beach before the Brambles, the sea covered the whole of the shingles.

I shall never, to my dying day, forget that moment's agony when my mind first grasped the truth of the deadly peril those thoughtless babes had incurred. Without instant help, those little children must be drowned, for the water flowed into the cave. Even now it might be too late. All these thoughts whirled through my brain in an instant.

Only for a moment I paused and cast one despairing glance round me. The cottage was out of sight. Nurse Gill, and Dorcas, and Betty were scouring the town; no time to run back for help, no hope of making one's voice heard with the wind whistling round me.

"Oh, my God! help me to save these children!" I cried, with a sob that almost choked me. And then I dashed like a mad thing toward the shore.

My despair gave me courage, but my progress was

difficult and slow. It was impossible to keep up that pace over the heavy shingles with the wind tearing round me and taking away my breath.

Several times I had to stand and collect my energies, and each time I paused I called the children's names loudly. But, alas! the wind and the sea swallowed up the sound.

How fast the tide seemed coming up! The booming of the breakers sounded close behind me. I dared not look - I dared not think. I fought and buffeted the wind, and folded my cloak round me.

"Out of the depth I have cried unto Thee." Those were the words I said over and over to myself.

I had reached the cave at last, and leaned gasping and nearly faint with terror before I began searching in its dim recesses.

Great masses of slimy seaweed lay heaped up at the entrance; a faint damp odor pervaded it. The sudden roar of wind and sea echoed in dull hollowness, but here at least my voice could be heard.

"Flurry-Dot!" I screamed. I could hear my own wild shriek dying away through the cave. To my delight, two little voices answered:

"Here we are Esther! Come along, we are having such a game! Flurry is the smuggler, and I am the Preventive man, and Flossy is my dog, and - oh, dear! what is the matter?" And Dot, who had hobbled out of a snug, dry little corner near the entrance, looked up with frightened eyes as I caught him and Flurry in my arms. I suppose my face betrayed my fears, for I could not at that moment gasp out another word.

CHAPTER XVII.

A LONG NIGHT.

"What is the matter, Essie?" cried Dot, piteously, as I held him in that tight embrace without speaking. "We were naughty to come, yes, I know, but you said I was to take care of Flurry, and she would come. I did not like it, for the wind was so cold and rough, and I fell twice on the shingles; but it is nice here, and we were having such a famous game."

"Esther is going to be cross and horrid because we ran away, but father will only laugh," exclaimed Flurry, with the remains of a frown on her face. She knew she was in the wrong and meant to brave it out.

Oh, the poor babes, playing their innocent games with Death waiting for them outside!

"Come, there is not an instant to lose," I exclaimed, catching up Dot in my arms; he was very little and light, and I thought we could get on faster so, and perhaps if the sea overtook us they would see us and put out a boat from the Preventive station. "Come, come," I repeated, snatching Flurry's hand, for she resisted a little: but when I reached the mouth of the cave she uttered a loud cry, and tugged fiercely at my hand to get free.

Rosa Nouchette Carey

"Oh, the sea, the dreadful sea!" she exclaimed, hiding her face; "it is coming up! Look at the waves - we shall be drownded!"

I could feel Dot shiver in my arms, but he did not speak, only his little hands clung round my neck convulsively. Poor children! their punishment had already begun.

"We shall be drowned if you don't make haste," I returned, trying to speak carefully, but my teeth chattered in spite of myself. "Come, Flurry, let us run a race with the waves; take hold of my cloak, for I want my hands free for Dot." I had dropped his crutches in the cave; they were no use to him - he could not have moved a step in the teeth of this wind.

Poor Flurry began to cry bitterly, but she had confidence in my judgment, and an instinct of obedience made her grasp my cloak, and so we commenced our dangerous pilgrimage. I could only move slowly with Dot; the wind was behind us, but it was terribly fierce. Flurry fell twice, and picked herself up sobbing; the horrors of the scene utterly broke down her courage, and she threw her arms round me frantically and prayed me to go back.

"The waves are nearly touching us!" she shrieked; and then Dot, infected by her terrors, began to cry loudly too. "We shall be drownded, all of us, and it is getting dark, and I won't go, I won't go!" screamed the poor child trying to push me back with her feeble force.

Then despair took possession of me; we might have done it if Flurry had not lost all courage; the water would not have been high enough to drown us; we could have waded through it, and they would have seen us from the cottage and come to our help. I would have saved them; I knew I could; but in Flurry's frantic state it was impossible. Her eyes dilated with terror, a convulsive trembling seized her. Must we go back to the cave, and be drowned like rats in a hole? The idea was horrible, and yet it went far back. Perhaps there was some corner or ledge of rock where we might be safe; but to spend the night in such a place! the idea made me almost as frantic as Flurry. Still, it was our only chance, and we retraced our steps but still so slowly and painfully that the spray of the advancing waves wetted our faces, and beyond - ah! - I shut my eyes and struggled on, while Flurry hid her head in the folds of my cloak.

We gained the smugglers' cave, and then I put down Dot, and bade him pick up his crutchers and follow me close, while I explored the cave. It was very dark, and Flurry began to cry afresh, and would not let go of my hand; but Dot shouldered his crutches, and walked behind us as well as he could.

At each instant my terror grew. It was a large winding cave, but the heaps of seaweed everywhere, up to the very walls, proved that the water filled the cavern. I became hysterical too. I would not stay to be drowned there, I muttered between my chattering teeth; drowned in the dark, and choked with all that rotten garbage! Better take the children in either hand, and go out and meet our fate boldly. I felt my brain turning with the horror, when all at once I caught sight of a rough broken ledge of rock, rising gradually from the back of the cave. Seaweed hung in parts high up, but it seemed to me in the dim twilight there was a portion of the rock bare; if so, the sea did not cover it - we might find a dry foothold.

"Let go my hand a moment, Flurry," I implored; "I think I see a little place where we may be safe. I will be back in a moment, dear." But nothing could induce her to relax her agonized grasp of my cloak. I had to argue the point. "The water comes all up here wherever the seaweed, is," I explained. "You think we are safe, Flurry, but we can be drowned where we stand; the sea fills the cave." But at this statement Flurry only screamed the louder and clung closer. Poor child! she was beside herself with fright.

So I said to Dot:

"My darling is a boy, and boys are not so frightened as girls; so you will stay here quietly while Flurry and I climb up there, and Flossy shall keep you company."

"Don't be long," he implored, but he did not say another word. Dear, brave little heart, Dot behaved like a hero that day. He then stooped down and held Flossy, who whined to follow us. I I think the poor animal knew our danger, for he shivered and cowered down in evident alarm, and I could hear Dot coaxing him.

It was very slippery and steep, and I crawled up with difficulty, with Flurry clambering after me, and holding tightly to my dress. Dot watched us wistfully as we went higher and higher, leaving him and Flossy behind. The seaweed impeded us, but after a little while we came to a bare piece of rock jutting out over the cave, with a scooped-out corner where all of us could huddle, and it seemed to me as though the shelf went on for a yard or two beyond it. We were above water-mark there; we should be quite safe, and a delicious glimmer of hope came over me.

I had great difficulty in inducing Flurry to stay behind while I crawled down for Dot. She was afraid to be alone in that dark place, with the hollow booming of wind and waves echoing round her; but I told her sternly that Dot and Flossy would be drowned and then she let me go.

Dot was overjoyed to welcome me back, and then I lifted him up and bade him crawl slowly on his hands and knees, while I followed with his crutches, and Flossy crept after us, shivering and whining for us to take him up. As we toiled up the broken ledge it seemed to grow darker, and we could hardly see each other's faces if we tried, only the splash of the first entering wave warned me that the sea would soon have been upon us.

I was giddy and breathless by the time we reached the nook where Flurry was, and then we crept into the corner, the children clasping each other across me, and Flossy on my lap licking our faces alternately. Saved from a horrible death! For a little while I could do nothing but weep helplessly over the children and thank God for a merciful deliverance.

As soon as the first hysterical outburst of emotion was over, I did my best to make the children as comfortable as I could under such forlorn circumstances. I knew Flurry's terror of darkness, and I could well imagine how horribly the water would foam and splash beneath us, and I must try and prevent them from seeing it.

I made Dot climb into my lap, for I thought the hard rock would make his poor back ache, and I could keep

Rosa Nouchette Carey

him from being chilled; and then I induced Flurry to creep under my heavy waterproof cloak - how thankful I was I put it on! - and told her to hold Flossy in her arms, for the little creature's soft fur would be warm and comfortable; and then I fastened the cloak together, buttoning it until it formed a little tent above them. Flurry curled her feet into my dress and put her head on my shoulder, and she and Dot held each other fast across me, and Flossy rolled himself up into a warm ball and went to sleep. Poor little creatures! They began to forget their sorrows a little, until Flurry suddenly recollected that it was tea-time, and her father had arrived; and then she began crying again softly.

"I'm so hungry," she sobbed; "aren't you Dot?"

"Yes, but I don't mean to mind it," returned Dot, manfully. "Essie is hungry too." And he put up his hand and stroked my neck softly. The darling, he knew how I suffered, and would not add to my pain by complaining.

I heard him say to Flurry in a whisper, "It is all our fault; we ought to be punished for running away; but Essie has done nothing wrong. I thought God meant to drown us, as He did the disobedient people." But this awful reminder of her small sins was too much for Flurry.

"I did not mean to be wicked," she wailed. "I thought it would be such fun to play at smugglers in the cave, and Aunt Ruth and Esther never would let me."

"Yes, and I begged you not to run away, and you would," retorted Dot in an admonishing tone. "I did not want come, too, because it was so cold, and the wind blew so; but I promised Essie to take care of you, so I went. I think you were quite as bad as the people whom God drowned, because they would not be good and mind Noah."

"But I don't want to be drowned," responded Flurry, tearfully. "Oh, dear, Dot, don't say such dreadful things! I am good now, and I will never, never disobey auntie again. Shall we say our prayers, Dot, and ask God not to be so very angry, and then perhaps He will send some one to take us out of this dark, dreadful place?"

Dot approved of this idea, and they began repeating their childish petitions together, but my mind strayed away when I tried to join them.

Oh, how dark and desolate it was! I shivered and clasped the children closer to me as the hollow moaning of the waves reverberated through the cavern. Every minute the water was rising; by-and-by the spray must wet us even in our sheltered corner. Would the children believe me when I told them we were safe? Would not Flurry's terrors return at the first touch of the cold spray? The darkness and the noise and the horror were almost enough to turn her childish brain; they were too much for my endurance.

"Oh, heavens!" I cried to myself, "must we really spend a long, hideous night in this place? We are safe! safe!" I repeated; but still it was too horrible to think of wearing out the long, slow hours in such misery.

It was six now; the tide would not turn until three in the morning; it had been rising for three hours now; it would not be possible to leave the cave and make our way by the cliff for an hour after that. Ten hours - ten long, crawling hours to pass in this cramped position! I thought of dear mother's horror if she knew of our peril, and then I thought of Allan, and a lump came in my throat.

Mr. Lucas would be scouring the coast in search of us. What a night for the agonized father to pass! And poor, fragile Miss Ruth, how would she endure such hours of anxiety? I could have wrung my hands and moaned aloud at the thought of their anguish, but for the children - the poor children who were whispering their baby prayers together; that kept me still. Perhaps they might be even now at the mouth of the cave, seeking and calling to us. A dozen times I imagined I could hear the splash of oars and the hoarse cries of the sailors; but how could our feeble voices reach them in the face of the shrieking wind? No one would think of the smugler's cave, for it was but one of many hollowed out of the cliff. They would search for us, but very soon they would abandon it in despair; they knew I had gone to seek the children; most likely I had been too late, and the rising tide had engulfed us, and swept us far out to sea. Miss Ruth would think of her dreams and tremble, and the wretched father would sit by her, stunned and helpless, waiting for the morning to break and bring him proof of his despair.

The tears ran down my cheeks as these sad thoughts passed through my mind, and a strong inward cry for deliverance, for endurance, for some present comfort in this awful misery, shook my frame with convulsive shudders. Dot felt them, and clasped me tighter, and Flurry trembled in sympathy; my paroxysm disturbed them, but my prayer was heard, and the brief agony passed.

I thought of Jeremiah in his dungeon, of Daniel in the lions' den, of the three children in the fiery furnace, and the Form that was like the Son of God walking with them in the midst of the flames; and I knew and felt that we were as safe on that rocky shelf, with the dark, raging waters below us, as though we were by our own bright hearth fire at home; then my trembling ceased, and I recovered voice to talk to the children.

I wanted them to go to sleep; but Flurry said, in a lamentable voice, that she was too hungry, and the sea made such a noise; so I told them about Shadrach, Meshech, and Abednego; and after I had finished that, all the Bible stories I could remember of wonderful deliverance; and by-and-by we came to the storm on the Galilean lake.

Flurry leaned heavily against me. "Oh, it is getting colder," she gasped; "Flossy keeps my hands warm, and the cloak is thick, and yet I can't help shivering." And I could feel Dot shiver, too. "The water seems very near us, I wish I did not feel afraid of it Esther," she whispered, after another minute; but I pretended not to hear her.

"Yes, it is cold, but not so cold as those disciples must have felt," I returned; "they were in a little open boat, Flurry, and the water dashed right over them, and the vessel rocked dreadfully" - here I paused - "and it was dark, for Jesus was not yet come to them."

"I wish He would come now," whispered Dot.

"That is what the disciples wished, and all the time they little knew that He was on His way to them, and watching them toiling against the wind, and that very soon the wind would cease, and they would be safe on the shore. We do not like being in this dark cave, do we, Flurry darling? And the sea keeps us awake; but He knows that, and He is watching us; and by-and-by, when the morning comes, we shall have light and go home."

Flurry said "Yes," sleepily, for in spite of the cold and hunger she was getting drowsy; it must have been long past her bedtime. We had sat on our dreary perch three hours, and there were six more to wait. I noticed that the sound of my voice tranquillized the children; so I repeated hymns slowly and monotonously until they nodded against me and fell into weary slumbers. "Thank God!" I murmured when I perceived this, and I leaned back against the rock, and tried to close my eyes; but they would keep opening and staring into the darkness. It was not black darkness - I do not think I could have borne that; a sort of murky half-light seemed reflected from the water, or from somewhere, and glimmered strangely from a background of inky blackness.

It was bitterly cold now; my feet felt numbed, and the spray wetted and chilled my face. I dared not move my arm from Dot, he leaned so heavily against it, and Flurry's head was against him. She had curled herself up like Flossy, and I had one hand free, only I could not disentangle it from the cloak. I dared not change my cramped position, for fear of waking them. I was too thankful for their brief oblivion. If I could only doze for a few moments; if I could only shut out the black waters for a minute! The tumults of my thoughts were indescribable. My whole life seemed to pass before me; every childish folly, every girlish error and sin, seemed to rise up before me; conversations I had forgotten, little incidents of family life, dull or otherwise; speeches I had made and repented, till my head seemed whirling. It must be midnight now, I thought. If I could only dare; but a new terror kept me wide awake. In spite of my protecting arms, would not Dot suffer from the damp chilliness? He shivered in his sleep, and Flurry moaned and half woke, and then slept again. I was growing so numbed and cramped that I doubted my endurance for much longer. Dot seemed growing heavier, and there was the weight of Flurry and Flossy. If I could only stretch myself! And then I nearly cried out, for a sudden flash seemed to light the cavern. One instant, and it was gone; but that second showed a grewsome scene - damp, black walls, with a frothing turbulous water beneath them, and hanging arches exuding moisture. Darkness again. From whence had that light flashed? As I asked myself the question it came again, startling me with its sudden brilliancy; and this time it was certainly from some aperture overhead, and a little beyond where we sat.

Gone again, and this time utterly; but not before I caught a glimpse of the broad rocky shelf beyond us. The light had flashed down not a dozen yards from where we stood; it must have been a lantern; if so, they were still seeking us, this time on the cliffs. It was only midnight, and there were still four weary hours to wait, and every moment I was growing more chilled and numbed. I began to dread the consequences to myself as well as to the children. If I could only crawl along the shelf and explore, perhaps there might be some opening to the cliff. I had not thought of this before, until the light brought the idea to my mind.

I perceived, too, that the glimmering half-light came from above, and not from the mouth of the cave. For a

Rosa Nouchette Carey

moment the fear of losing my balance and falling back into the water daunted me, and kept me from moving; but the next minute I felt I must attempt it. I unfastened my cloak and woke Dot softly, and then whispered to him that I was cramped and in pain, and must move up and down the platform; and he understood me, and crawled sleepily off my lap; then I lifted Flurry with difficulty, for she moaned and whimpered at my touch.

My numbness was so great I could hardly move my limbs; but I crawled across Flurry somehow, and saw Dot creep into my place, and covered them with my cloak; and then I commenced to move slowly and carefully on my hands and knees up the rocky path.

CHAPTER XVIII.

"YOU BRAVE GIRL!"

They told me afterward that this was a daring feat, and fraught with awful peril, for in that painful groping in the darkness I might have lost my balance and fallen back into the water.

I was conscious of this at the time; but we cannot die until our hour is come, and in youth one's faith is more simple and trusting; to pray is to be heard, to grasp more tightly by the mantle of His Providence, so I committed myself to Heaven, and crept slowly along the face of the rock. In two or three minutes I felt cold air blowing down upon my face, and, raising myself cautiously, I found I was standing under an aperture, large enough for me to crawl through, which led to the downs. For one moment I breathed the fresh night air and caught the glimmer of starlight, and then I crept back to the children.

Flurry was awake and weeping piteously, and Dot was trying to comfort her in a sleepy voice; but she was quiet the moment I told them about the hole.

"I must leave you behind, Dot," I said, sorrowfully, "and take Flurry first;" and the brave little fellow said:

"All right, Essie," and held back the dog, who was whining to follow.

I put my arm round Flurry, and made her promise not to lose hold of the rock. The poor child was dreadfully frightened, and stopped every now and then, crying out in horror that she was falling into the water, but I held her fast and coaxed her to go on again; and all the time the clammy dews of terror stood on my forehead. Never to my dying day shall I forget those terrible moments.

But we were mercifully preserved, and to my joy I felt the winds of heaven blowing round us, and in another moment Flurry had crawled through the hole in the rock, and was sitting shivering on the grass.

"Now I must go back for Dot and Flossy," I exclaimed; but as I spoke and tried to disengage myself from Flurry's nervous grasp, I heard a little voice below.

"I am here, Essie, and I have got Flossy all safe. Just stoop down and take him, and then I shall clamber up all right."

"Oh, my darling, how could you?" The courageous child had actually dragged himself with the dog under one arm all along the dangerous path, to spare me another journey.

I could scarcely speak, but I covered his cold little face with kisses as he tottered painfully into my arms - my precious boy, my brave, unselfish Dot!

"I could not bring the crutches or the cloak, Essie," he whispered.

"Never mind them," I replied, with a catch in my voice. "You are safe; we are all safe - that is all I can take in. I must carry you, Dot, and Flurry shall hold my dress, and we shall soon be home."

"Where is your hat, Essie?" he asked, putting up his hand to my hair. It was true I was bareheaded, and yet I had never missed it. My cloak lay below in the cavern. What a strange sight I must have presented if any one could have seen us! My hair was blowing loosely about my face; my dress seemed to cling round my feet.

How awfully dark and desolate the downs looked under that dim, starry light. Only the uncertain glimmer enabled me to keep from the cliffs or discern the right path. The heavy booming of the sea and the wind together drowned our voices. When it lulled I could hear Flurry sobbing to herself in the darkness, and Flossy, whining for company, as he followed us closely. Poor Dot was spent and weary, and lay heavily against my shoulder. Every now and then I had to stop and gather strength, for I felt strangely weak, and there was an odd beating at my heart. Dot must have heard my panting breath, for he begged me more than once to put him down and leave him, but I would not.

My strength was nearly gone when we reached the shelving path leading down to the cottage, but I still dragged on. A stream of light came full upon us as we turned the corner; it came from the cottage.

The door was wide open and the parlor blinds were raised, and the ruddy gleam of lamplight and firelight streamed full on our faces.

No one saw us as we toiled up the pebbled path; no one waited for us in the porch. I have a faint recollection that I stood in the hall, looking round me for a moment in a dazed fashion; that Flossy barked, and a door burst open; there was a wave of light, and a man's voice saying something. I felt myself swaying with Dot in my arms; but some one must have caught us, for when I came to myself I was lying on the couch by the drawing-room fire, and Miss Ruth was kneeling beside me raining tears over my face.

"And Dot!" I tried to move and could not, and fell back on my pillow. "The children!" I gasped, and there was a sudden movement in the room, and Mr. Lucas stood over me with his child in his arms. Was it my fancy, or were there tears in his eyes, too?

"They are here, Esther," he said, in a soothing voice. "Nurse is taking care of your boy." And then he burst out, "Oh, you brave girl! you noble girl!" in a voice of strong emotion, and turned away.

"Hush, Giles, we must keep her quiet," admonished his sister. "We do not know what the poor thing has been through, but she is as cold as ice. And feel how soaking her hair is!"

Had it rained? I suppose it had, but then the children must be wet too!

Miss Ruth must have noticed my anxious look, for she kissed me and whispered:

"Don't worry, Esther; we have fires and hot baths ready. Nurse and the others will attend to the children; they will soon be warmed and in bed. Let me dry your hair and rub your cold hands; and drink this, and you will soon be able to move."

The cordial and food they gave me revived my numb faculties, and in a little while I was able, with assistance, to go to my room. Miss Ruth followed me, and tenderly helped me to remove my damp things; but I would not lie down in my warm bed until I had seen with my own eyes that Flurry was already soundly asleep and Dot ready to follow her example.

"Isn't it delicious?" he whispered, drowsily, as I kissed him; and then Miss Ruth led me back to my room, and tucked me up and sat down beside me.

"Now tell me all about it," she said, "and then you will be able to sleep." For a strong excitement had succeeded the faintness, and in spite of my aching limbs and weariness I had a sensation as though I could fly.

But when I told her she only shuddered and wept, and before I had half narrated the history of those dismal hours she was down on her knees beside the bed, kissing my hands.

"Do let me," she sobbed, as I remonstrated. "Oh, Esther, how I love you! How I must always love you for this!"

"No, I am not Miss Ruth any longer; I am Ruth. I am your own friend and sister, who would do anything to show her gratitude. You dear girl! - you brave girl! - as Giles called you."

This brought to my lips the question, "How had Mr.

Lucas borne this dreadful suspense?"

"As badly as possible," she answered, drying her eyes. "Oh, Esther! what we have all been through. Giles came in half an hour after you left to search the shore. He was in a dreadful state, as you may imagine. He sent down to the Preventive station at once, and there was a boat got ready, and he went with the men. They pulled up and down for an hour or two, but could find no trace of you."

"We were in the cavern all the time," I murmured.

"That was the strangest part of all," she returned. "Giles remembered the cavern, and they went right into the mouth, and called as loudly as they could."

"We did not hear them; the wind was making such a noise, and it was so dark."

"The men gave up all hope at last, and Giles was obliged to come back. He walked into the house looking as white as death. 'It is all over,' he said; 'the tide has overtaken them, and that girl is drowned with them.' And then he gave a sort of sob, and buried his face in his hands. I turned so faint that for a little time he was obliged to attend to me, but when I was better he got up and left the house. It did not seem as though he could rest from the search, and yet he had not the faintest glimmer of hope. He would have the cottage illuminated and the door left open, and then he lighted his lantern and walked up and down the cliffs, and every time he came back his poor face looked whiter and more drawn. I had got hold of his hand, and was trying to keep him from wandering out again, when all at once we heard Flossy bark. Giles burst open the door, and then he gave a great cry, for there you were, my poor Esther, standing under the hall lamp, with your hair streaming over your shoulders and Dot in your arms, and Flurry holding your dress, and you looked at us and did not seem to see us, and Giles was just in time to catch you as you were reeling. He had you all in his arms at once," finished Miss Ruth, with another sob, "till I took our darling Flurry from him, and then he laid you down and carried Dot to the fire."

"If I could not have saved them I would have died with them; you knew that, Miss Ruth."

"Ruth," she corrected. "Yes, I knew that, and so did Giles. He said once or twice, 'She is strong enough or sensible enough to save them if it were possible, but no one can fight against fate.' Now I must go down to him, for he is waiting to hear all about it, and you must go to sleep, Esther, for your eyes are far too bright."

But, greatly to her surprise and distress, I resisted this advice and broke out into frightened sobs. The sea was in my ears, I said, when I tried to close my eyes, and my arms felt empty without Dot and I could not believe he was safe, though she told me so over and over again.

I was greatly amazed at my own want of control; but nothing could lessen this nervous excitement until Mr. Lucas came up to the door, and Miss Ruth went out to him in sore perplexity.

"What am I to do, Giles? I cannot soothe her in the least."

"Let her have the child," he returned, in his deep voice;

"she will sleep then." And he actually fetched little Dot and put him in Miss Ruth's arms.

"Isn't it nice, Essie?" he muttered sleepily, as he nestled against me.

It was strange, but the moment my arm was round him, and I felt his soft breathing against my shoulder, my eyelids closed of their own accord, and a sense of weariness and security came over me.

Before many minutes were over I had fallen into a deep sleep, and Miss Ruth was free to seek her brother and give him the information for which he was longing.

It was nearly five in the morning when I closed my eyes, and it was exactly the same time on the following afternoon when I opened them.

My first look was for Dot, but he was gone, the sun was streaming in at the window, a bright fire burned in the grate, and Nurse Gill was sitting knitting in the sunshine.

She looked up with a pleasant smile on her homely face as I called to her rather feebly.

"How you have slept, to be sure, Miss Esther - a good twelve hours. But I always say Nature is a safe nurse, and to be trusted. There's Master Dot has been up and dressed these three hours and more, and Miss Flurry too."

"Oh, Nurse Gill, are you sure they are all right?" I asked, for it was almost too good news to be true.

"Master Dot is as right as possible, though he is a little palish, and complains of his back and legs, which is only to be expected if they do ache a bit. Miss Flurry has a cold, but we could not induce her to lie in bed; she is sitting by the fire now on her father's knee, and Master Dot is with them: but there, Miss Ruth said she was to be called as soon as you woke, Miss Esther, though I did beg her not to put herself about, and her head so terribly bad as it has been all day."

"Oh, nurse, don't disturb her," I pleaded, eagerly, "I am quite well, there is nothing the matter with me. I want to get up this moment and dress myself;" for a great longing came over me to join the the little group downstairs.

"Not so fast, Miss Esther," she returned, good-humoredly. "You've had a fine sleep, to be sure, and young things will stand a mortal amount of fatigue; but there isn't a speck of color in your face, my poor lamb. Well, well," as I showed signs of impatience - "I won't disturb Miss Ruth, but I will fetch you some coffee and bread-and-butter, and we will see how you will feel then."

Mrs. Gill was a dragon in her way, so I resigned myself to her peremptory kindness. When she trotted off on her charitable errand, I leaned on my elbow and looked out of the window. It was Sunday evening, I remembered, and the quiet peacefulness of the scene was in strangest contrast to the horrors of yesterday; the wind had lulled, and the big curling waves ceased to look terrible in the sunlight; the white spray tossed lightly hither and thither, and the long line of dark seaweed showed prettily along the yellow sands. The bitter war of winds and waves was over, and the defeated enemy had retired with spent fury, and sunk into silence. Could it be a dream? had we really lived through that dreadful nightmare? But at this moment Nurse Gill interrupted the painful retrospect by placing the fragrant coffee and brown bread-and-butter before me.

I ate and drank eagerly, to please myself as well as her, and then I reiterated my intention to get up. It cost me something, however, to persevere in my resolution. My limbs trembled under me, and seemed to refuse their support in the strangest way, and the sight of my pale face almost frightened me, and I was grateful to Nurse Gill when she took the brush out of my shaking hand and proceeded to manipulate the long tangled locks.

"You are no more fit than a baby to dress yourself, Miss Esther," said the good old creature, in a vexed voice. "And to think of drowning all this beautiful hair. Why, there is seaweed in it I do declare, like a mermaid."

"The rocks were covered with it," I returned, in a weary indifferent voice; for Mrs. Gill's officiousness tired me, and I longed to free myself from her kindly hands.

When I was dressed, I crept very slowly downstairs. My courage was oozing away fast, and I rather dreaded all the kind inquiries that awaited me. But I need not have been afraid.

Dot clapped his hands when he saw me, and Mr. Lucas put down Flurry and came to meet me.

"You ought not to have exerted yourself," he said,

reproachfully, as soon as he looked at me; and then he took hold of me and placed me in the armchair, and Flurry brought me a footstool and sat down on it, Dot climbed up on the arm of the chair and propped himself against me, and Miss Ruth rose softly from her couch and came across the room and kissed me.

"Oh, Esther, how pale you look!" she said, anxiously.

"She will soon have her color back again," returned Mr. Lucas, looking at me kindly. I think he wanted to say something, but the sight of my weakness deterred him. I could not have borne a word. The tears were very near the surface now, so near that I could only close my eyes and lean my head against Dot; and, seeing this, they very wisely left me alone. I recovered myself by-and-by, and was able to listen to the talk that went on around me. The children's tongues were busy as usual; Flurry had gone back to her father, and she and Dot were keeping up a brisk fire of conversation across the hearth-rug. I could not see Mr. Lucas' face, as he had moved to a dark corner, but Miss Ruth's couch was drawn full into the firelight, and I could see the tears glistening on her cheek.

"Don't talk any more about it, my darlings," she said at last. "I feel as though I should never sleep again, and I am sure it is bad for Esther."

"It does not hurt me," I returned, softly. "I suppose shipwrecked sailors like to talk over the dangers they escape; somehow everything seems so far away and strange to-night, as though it had happened months ago." But though I said this I could not help the nervous thrill that seemed to pass over me now and then.

Rosa Nouchette Carey

"Shall I read to you a little?" interrupted Mr. Lucas, quietly. "The children's talk tires your head;" and without waiting for an answer, he commenced reading some of my favorite hymns and a lovely poem, in a low mellow voice that was very pleasant and soothing.

Nurse came to fetch Flurry, and then Dot went too, but Mr. Lucas did not put down the book for a long time. I had ceased to follow the words; the flicker of the firelight played fitfully before my eyes. The quiet room, the shaded lamplight, the measured cadence of the reader's voice, now rising, now falling, lulled me most pleasantly. I must have fallen asleep at last, for Flossy woke me by pushing his black nose into my hand; for when I sat up and rubbed my eyes Mr. Lucas was gone, and only Miss Ruth was laughing softly as she watched me.

"Giles went away half an hour ago," she said amused at my perplexed face. "He was so pleased when he looked up and found you were asleep. I believe your pale face frightened him, but I shall tell him you look much better now."

"My head feels less bewildered," was my answer.

"You are beginning to recover yourself," she returned, decidedly; "now you must be a good child and go to bed;" and I rose at once.

As I opened the drawing-room door, Mr. Lucas came out from his study.

"Were you going to give me the slip?" he said, pleasantly. "I wanted to bid you good-by, as I shall be off in the morning before you are awake."

"Good by," I returned, rather shyly, holding out my hand; but he kept it a moment longer than usual.

"Esther, you must let me thank you," he said, abruptly. "I know but for you I must have lost my child. A man's gratitude for such a mercy is a strong thing, and you may count me your friend as long as I live."

"You are very good," I stammered, "but I have done nothing; and there was Dot, you know." I am afraid I was very awkward, but I dreaded his speaking to me so, and the repressed emotion of his face and voice almost frightened me.

"There, I have made you quite pale again," he said, regretfully. "Your nerves have not recovered from the shock. Well, we will speak of this again; good-night, my child, and sleep well," and with another kind smile he left me.

CHAPTER XIX.

A LETTER FROM HOME.

I was so young and healthy that I soon recovered from the shock, and in a few days I had regained strength and color. Mr. Lucas had gone to see mother, and the day after his visit she wrote a fond incoherent letter, full of praises of my supposed heroism. Allan, to whom I had narrated everything fully, wrote more quietly, but the underlying tenderness breathed in every word for Dot and me touched me greatly. Dot had not suffered much; he was a little more lame, and his back ached more constantly. But it was Flurry who came off worst; her cold was on her chest, and when she threw it off she had a bad cough, and began to grow pale and thin; she was nervous, too, and woke every night calling out to me or Dot, and before many days were over Miss Ruth wrote to her brother and told him that Flurry would be better at home.

We were waiting for his answer, when Miss Ruth brought a letter to my bedside from mother, and sat down, as usual, to hear the contents, for I used to read her little bits from my home correspondence, and she wanted to know what Uncle Geoffrey thought about Flurry. My sudden exclamation frightened her.

"What is wrong, Esther? It is nothing about Giles?"

"Oh, no!" I returned, the tears starting to my eyes, "but I must go home at once; Carrie is very ill, they are afraid it is an attack of rheumatic fever. Mother writes in such distress, and there is a message from Uncle Geoffrey, asking me to pack up and come to them without delay. There is something about Flurry, too; perhaps you had better read it."

"I will take the letter away with me. Don't hurry too much, Esther; we will talk it over at breakfast, and there is no train now before eleven, and nurse will help you to pack."

That was just like Miss Ruth - no fuss, no unnecessary words, no adding to my trouble by selfish regrets at my absence. She was like a man in that, she never troubled herself about petty details, as most women do, but just looked straight at the point in question.

Her calmness reassured me, and by breakfast-time I was able to discuss matters quietly.

"I have sent nurse to your room, Esther," she said, as she poured out the coffee; "the children have had their bread and milk, and have gone out to play; it is so warm and sunny, it will not hurt Flurry. The pony carriage will be round here at half-past ten, so you will have plenty of time, and I mean to drive you to the station myself."

"You think of everything," I returned, gratefully. "Have you read the letter? Does it strike you that Carrie is so very ill?"

"I am afraid so," she admitted, reluctantly; "your mother says she has been ailing some time, only she would not take care of herself, and then she got wet, and took her class in her damp things. I am afraid you have a long spell of nursing before you; rheumatic fever sometimes lasts a long time. Your uncle says something about a touch of pleurisy as well."

I pushed away my plate, for I could not eat. I am ashamed to say a strong feeling of indignation took possession of me.

"She would not give up," I burst out, angrily: "she would not come here to recruit herself, although she owned she felt ill; she has just gone on until her strength was exhausted and she was not in a state for anything, and now all this trouble and anxiety must come on mother, and she is not fit for it."

"Hush, Esther; you must not feel like this," she returned, gently. "Poor Carrie will purchase wisdom dearly; depend upon it, the knowledge that she has brought on this illness through her own self-will will be the sharpest pang of all. You must go home and be a comfort to them all, as you have been our comfort," she added, sweetly; "and, Esther, I have been thinking over things, and you must trust Dot to me. We shall all return to the Cedars, most likely to-morrow, and I will promise not to let him out of my sight."

And as I regarded her dubiously, she went on still more eagerly:

"You must let me keep him, Esther. Flurry is so poorly, and she will fret over the loss of her little companion; and with such a serious illness in the house, he would only be an additional care to you."

And as she seemed so much in earnest, I consented reluctantly to wait for mother's decision; for, after all, the child would be dull and neglected, with Jack at school, and mother and me shut up in Carrie's sick room. So in that, as in all else, Miss Ruth was right.

Dot cried a little when I said good-by to him; he did not like seeing me go away, and the notion of Carrie's illness distressed him, and Flurry cried, too, because he did, and then Miss Ruth laughed at them both.

"You silly children," she said, "when we are all going home to-morrow, and you can walk over and see Esther every day, and take her flowers and nice things for Carrie." Which view of the case cheered them immensely, and we left them with their heads very close together, evidently planning all sorts of surprises for Carrie and me.

Miss Ruth talked very cheerfully up to the last moment, and then she grew a little silent and tearful.

"I shall miss you so, Esther, both here and at the Cedars," she said tenderly. "I feel it may be a long time before you come to us again; but there, I mean to see plenty of you," she went on, recovering herself. "I shall bring Dot every day, if it be only for a few minutes!" And so she sent me away half comforted.

It was a dreary journey, and I was thankful when it was over; there was no one to meet me at the station, so I took one of the huge lumbering flies, and a sleepy old horse dragged me reluctantly up the steep Milnthorpe streets.

It was an odd coincidence, but as we passed the bank

and I looked out of the window half absently, Mr. Lucas came down the steps and saw me, and motioned to the driver to stop.

"I am very sorry to see you here," he said, gravely. "I met Dr. Cameron just now, and he told me your mother had written to recall you."

"Did he say how Carrie was?" I interrupted anxiously.

"She is no better, and in a state of great suffering; it seems she has been imprudent, and taken a severe chill; but don't let me keep you, if you are anxious to go on." But I detained him a moment.

"Flurry seems better this morning," I observed; "her cough is less hard."

He looked relieved at that.

"I have written for them to come home to-morrow, and to bring Dot, too; we will take care of him for you, and make him happy among us, and you will have enough on your hands."

And then he drew back, and went slowly down High street, but the encounter had cheered me; I was beginning to look on Mr. Lucas as an old friend.

Uncle Geoffrey was on the door-step as I drove up, and we entered the house together.

"This is a bad business, I am afraid," he said, in a subdued voice, as he closed the parlor door; "it goes to one's heart to see that pretty creature suffer. I am glad, for all our sakes, that Allan will be here next week."

And then I remembered all at once that the year was out, and that Allan was coming home to live; but he had said so little about it in his last letters that I was afraid of some postponement.

"He is really coming, then?" I exclaimed, in joyful surprise; this was good news.

"Yes, next Thursday; and I shall be glad of the boy's help," he replied, gruffly; and then he sat down and told me about Carrie.

Foolish girl, her zeal had indeed bordered upon madness. It seems Uncle Geoffrey had taxed her with illness a fortnight ago, and she had not denied it; she had even consented to take the remedies prescribed her in the way of medicine, but nothing would induce her to rest. The illness had culminated last Sunday; she had been caught in a heavy rain, and her thin summer walking dress had been drenched, and yet she had spent the afternoon as usual at the schools. A shivering fit that evening had been the result.

"She has gradually got worse and worse," continued Uncle Geoffrey; "it is not ordinary rheumatic fever; there is certainly sciatica, and a touch of pleurisy; the chill on her enfeebled, worn-out frame has been deadly, and there is no knowing the mischief that may follow. I would not have you told before this, for after a nasty accident like yours, a person is not fit for much. Let me look at you, child. I must own you don't stem much amiss. Now listen to me, Esther. I have elected Deborah head-nurse, and you must work under her orders. Bless me," catching a glimpse of a crimson disappointed face, for I certainly felt crestfallen at this, "a chit like you cannot be expected to know everything. Deb is a splendid nurse; she has a head on her shoulders, that woman," with a little chuckle; "she has just put your mother out of the room, because she says that she is no more use than a baby, so you will have to wheedle yourself into her good graces if you expect to nurse Carrie."

"Why did you send for me, if you expect me to be of no use?" I returned, with decided temper, for this remark chafed me; but he only chuckled again.

"Deborah sent for you, not I," he said, in an amused voice. "'Couldn't we have Miss Esther home?' she asked; 'she has her wits about her,' which I am afraid was a hit at somebody."

This soothed me down a little, for my dignity was sadly affronted that Deborah should be mistress of the sick room. I am afraid after all that I was not different from other girls, and had not yet outgrown what mother called the "porcupine stage" of girlhood, when one bristles all over at every supposed slight, armed at every point with minor prejudices, like "quills upon the fretful porcupine."

Uncle Geoffrey bade me run along, for he was busy, so I went upstairs swallowing discontent with every step, until I looked up and saw mother's pale sad face watching me from a doorway, and then every unworthy feeling vanished.

"Oh, my darling, thank Heaven I have you again!" she murmured, folding me in her loving arms; "my dear child, who has never given me a moment's anxiety." And then I knew how heavily Carrie's willfulness had weighed on that patient heart.

She drew me half weeping into Carrie's little room, and we sat down together hand in hand. The invalid had been moved into mother's room, as it was large and sunny, and I could hear Deborah moving quietly as I passed the door.

Mother would not speak about Carrie at first; she asked after Dot, and was full of gratitude to Miss Ruth for taking care of him; and then the dear soul cried over me, and said she had nearly lost us both, and that but for me her darling boy would have been drowned. Mr. Lucas had told her so.

"He was full of your praises, Esther," she went on, drying her eyes; "he says he and Miss Ruth will be your fast friends through life; that there is nothing he would not do to show his gratitude; it made me so proud to hear it."

"It makes me proud, too, mother; but I cannot have you talking about me, when I am longing to hear about Carrie."

Mother sighed and shook her head, and then it was I noticed a tremulous movement about her head, and, oh! how gray her hair was, almost white under her widow's cap.

"There is not much to say," she said, despondently; "your uncle will not tell me if she be in actual danger, but he looks graver every day. Her sufferings are terrible; just now Deborah would not let me remain, because I fretted so, as though a mother can help grieving over her child's agony. It is all her own fault, Esther, and that makes it all the harder to bear."

I acquiesced silently, and then I told mother that I had come home to spare her, and do all I could for Carrie - as much as Deborah would allow.

"You must be very prudent, then," she replied, "for Deborah is very jealous, and yet so devoted, that one cannot find fault with her. Perhaps she is right, and I am too weak to be of much use, but I should like you to be with your sister as much as possible."

I promised to be cautious, and after a little more talk with mother I laid aside my traveling things and stole gently into the sick room.

Deborah met me on the threshold with uplifted finger and a resolute "Hush!" on her lips. She looked more erect and angular than ever, and there was a stern forbidding expression on her face; but I would not be daunted.

I caught her by both her hands, and drew her, against her will, to the door.

"I want to speak to you," I whispered; and when I had her outside, I looked straight into her eyes. "Oh, Deb," I cried, "is it not dreadful for all of us? and I have been in such peril, too. What should we do without you, when you know all about nursing, and understand a sick room so well? You are everything to us, Deborah, and we are so grateful, and now you must let me help you a little, and spare you fatigue. I daresay there are many little things you could find for me to do."

I do not know about the innocence of the dove, but certainly the wisdom of the serpent was in my speech; my humility made Deborah throw down her arms at once. "Any little thing that I can do," I pleaded, and her face relaxed and her hard gray eyes softened.

"You are always ready to help a body, Miss Esther, I will say that, and I don't deny that I am nearly ready to drop with fatigue through not having my clothes off these three nights. The mistress is no more help than a baby, not being able to lift, or to leave off crying."

"And you will let me help you?" I returned, eagerly, a little too eagerly, for she drew herself up.

"I won't make any promises, Miss Esther," she said, rather stiffly; "the master said I must have help, and I am willing to try what you can do, though you are young and not used to the ways of a sick room," finished the provoking creature; but I restrained my impatience.

"Any little thing that I can do," I repeated, humbly; and my forbearance had its reward, for Deborah drew aside to let me pass into the room, only telling me, rather sharply, to say as little possible and keep my thoughts to myself. Deborah's robust treatment was certainly bracing, and it gave me a sort of desperate courage; but the first shock of seeing Carrie was dreadful.

The poor girl lay swathed in bandages, and as I entered the room her piteous moanings almost broke my heart. Burning with fever, and racked by pain, she could find no ease or rest.

As I kissed her she shuddered, and her eyes looked at me with a terrible sadness in them.

"Oh, my poor dear, how sorry I am!" I whispered. I

dared not say more with Deborah hovering jealously in the back-ground.

"Don't be sorry," she groaned; "I deserved it. I deserve it all." And then she turned away her face, and her fair hair shaded it from me. Did I hear it aright; and was it a whispered prayer for patience that caught my ear as she turned away.

Deborah would not let me stay long. She sent me down to have tea and talk to mother, but she promised that I should come up again by-and-by. I was surprised as I opened the parlor door to find Mr. Lucas talking to Uncle Geoffrey and mother with Jack looking up at him with awe-struck eyes. He came forward with an amused smile, as he noticed my astonished pause.

"You did not expect to see me here," he said, in his most friendly manner; "but I wanted to inquire after your sister. Mrs. Cameron has been so good as to promise me a cup of tea, so you must make it."

That Mr. Lucas should be drinking tea at mother's table! somehow, I could not get over my surprise. I had never seen him in our house before, and yet in the old times both he and his wife had been frequent visitors. Certainly he seemed quite at home.

Mother had lighted her pretty china lamp, and Uncle Geoffrey had thrown a log of wood on the fire, and the parlors looked bright and cozy, and even Jack's hair was brushed and her collar for once not awry. I suppose Mr. Lucas found it pleasant, for he stayed quite late, and I wondered how he could keep his dinner waiting so long; but then Uncle Geoffrey was such a clever man, and could talk so well. I thought I should have to leave them at last, for it was nearly the time that Deborah wanted me; but just then Mr. Lucas looked across at me and noticed something in my face.

"You want to be with your sister," he said, suddenly interpreting my thoughts, "and I am reducing my cook to despair. Good-by, Mrs. Cameron. Many thanks for a pleasant hour." And then he shook hands with us all, and left the room with Uncle Geoffrey.

"What an agreeable, well-bred man," observed mother. "I like him exceedingly, and yet people call him proud and reserved."

"He is not a bit," I returned, indignantly; and then I kissed mother, and ran upstairs.

Rosa Nouchette Carey

CHAPTER XX.

"YOU WERE RIGHT, ESTHER."

For many, many long weeks, I might say months, my daily life was lived in Carrie's sick room.

What a mercy it is that we are not permitted to see the course of events - that we take moment by moment from the Father's hand, not knowing what lies before us!

It was September when I had that little altercation with Deborah on the threshold, and when she drew aside for me to pass into that dimly-lighted sickroom; it was Christmas now, and I was there still. Could I have foreseen those months, with their record of suffering, their hours of changeless monotony, well might my courage have failed. As it was, I watched the slow progression of nights and days almost indifferently; the walls of the sickroom closed round me, shutting me out from the actual world, and concentrating my thoughts on the frail girl who was fighting against disease and death.

So terrible an illness I pray to Heaven I may never see again; sad complications producing unheard-of tortures, and bringing the sufferer again and again to the very brink of death.

"If I could only die: if I were only good enough to be allowed to die!" that was the prayer she breathed; and there were times when I could have echoed it, when I would rather have parted with her, dearly as I loved her, than have seen her so racked with agony; but it was not to be. The lesson was not completed. There are some who must be taught to live, who have to take back "the turned lesson," as one has beautifully said, and learn it more perfectly.

If I had ever doubted her goodness in my secret soul, I could doubt no longer, when I daily witnessed her weakness and her exceeding patience. She bore her suffering almost without complaint, and would often hide from us how much she had to endure.

"'It is good to be still.' Do you remember that, Esther?" she said once; and I knew she was quoting the words of one who had suffered.

After the first day I had no further difficulty with Deborah; she soon recognized my usefulness, and gave me my share of nursing without grudging. I took my turn at the night-watching, and served my first painful apprenticeship in sick nursing. Mother could do little for us; she could only relieve me for a couple of hours in the afternoon, during which Uncle Geoffrey insisted that I should have rest and exercise.

Allan did not come home when we expected him; he had to postpone his intention for a couple of months. This was a sad disappointment, as he would have helped us so much, and mother's constant anxiety that my health should not suffer by my close confinement was a little trying at times. I was quite well, but it was no wonder that my fresh color faded a little, and that I grew a little quiet and subdued. The absence of life and change must be pernicious to young people; they want air, movement, a certain stirring of activity and bustle to keep time with their warm natures.

Every one was very kind to me. Uncle Geoffrey would take me on his rounds, and often Miss Ruth and Flurry would call for me, and drive me into the country, and they brought me books and fruit and lovely flowers for Carrie's room; and though I never saw Mr. Lucas during his few brief visits he never failed to send me a kind message or to ask if there was anything he could do for us.

Miss Ruth, or Ruth, as I always called her now, would sometimes come up into the sickroom and sit for a few minutes. Carrie liked to see her, and always greeted her with a smile; but when Mrs. Smedley heard of it, and rather peremptorily demanded admittance, she turned very pale, and calling me to her, charged me, in an agitated voice, never to let her in. "I could not see her, I could not," she went on, excitedly. "I like Miss Ruth; she is so gentle and quiet. But I want no one but you and mother."

Mother once - very injudiciously, as Uncle Geoffrey and I thought - tried to shake this resolution of Carrie's.

"Poor Mrs. Smedley seems so very grieved and disappointed that you will not see her, my dear. This is the third time she has called this week, and she has been so kind to you."

"Oh, mother, don't make me see her!" pleaded Carrie, even her lips turning white; and of course mother kissed her and promised that she should not be troubled. But when she had left the room Carrie became very much agitated.

"She is the last I ought to see, for she helped to bring me to this; she taught me to disobey my mother - yes, Esther, she did indeed!" as I expostulated in a shocked manner. "She was always telling me that my standard was not high enough - that I ought to look above even the wisest earthly parents. She said my mother had old-fashioned notions of duty; that things were different in her young days; that, in spite of her goodness, she had narrow views; that it was impossible for her even to comprehend me."

"Dear Carrie, surely you could not have agreed with her?" I asked, gently; but her only answer was a sigh as she sank back upon her pillows.

It was the evening Allan was expected, I remember. It was December now, and for nine weeks I had been shut up in that room, with the exception of my daily walk or drive.

Deborah had gone back to her usual work; it was impossible to spare her longer. But she still helped in the heaviest part of the nursing, and came from time to time to look after us both.

Dot had remained for six weeks at the Cedars; but mother missed him so much that Uncle Geoffrey decided to bring him home; and how glad and thankful I was to get my darling back!

I saw very little of him, however, for, strange to say, Carrie did not care for him and Jack to stay long in the room. I was not surprised that Jack fidgeted her, for she was restless and noisy, and her loud voice and awkward manners would jar sadly on an invalid; but Dot was different.

In a sick room he was as quiet as a little mouse, and he had such nice ways. It grieved me to see Carrie shade her eyes in that pained manner when he hobbled in softly on his crutches.

"Carrie always cries when she sees me!" Dot said once, with a little quiver of his lips. Alas! we neither of us understood the strange misery that even the sight of her afflicted little brother caused her.

Mother had gone downstairs when she had made her little protest about Mrs. Smedley, and we were left alone together. I was resting in the low cushioned chair Ruth had sent me in the early days of Carrie's illness, and was watching the fire in a quiet fashion that had become habitual to me. The room looked snug and pleasant in the twilight; the little bed on which I slept was in the farthest corner; a bouquet of hothouse flowers stood on the little round table, with some books Mr. Lucas had sent up for me. It must have looked cheerful to Carrie as she lay among the pillows; but to my dismay there were tears on her cheeks - I could see them glistening in the firelight.

"Do you feel less well to-night, dear?" I asked, anxiously, as I took a seat beside her; but she shook her head.

"I am better, much better," was her reply, "thanks to you and Deborah and Uncle Geoffrey," but her smile was very sad as she spoke. "How good you have been to me, Esther - how kind and patient! Sometimes I have looked at you when you were asleep over there, and I have cried to see how thin and weary you looked in your sleep, and all through me."

"Nonsense," I returned, kissing her; but my voice was not quite clear.

"Allan will say so to-night when he sees you - you are not the same, Esther. Your eyes are graver, and you seem to have forgotten how to laugh, and it is all my fault."

"Dear Carrie, I wish you would not talk so."

"Let me talk a little to-night," she pleaded. "I feel better and stronger, and it will be such a relief to tell you some of my thoughts. I have been silent for nine weeks, and sometimes the pent-up pain has been more than I could bear."

"My poor Carrie," stroking the thin white hand on the coverlid.

"Yes, I am that," she sighed. "Do you remember our old talks together? Oh, how wise you were, Esther, but I would not listen to you; you were all for present duties. I can recollect some of your words now. You told me our work lay before us, close to us, at our very feet, and yet I would stretch out my arms for more, till my own burdens crushed me, and I fell beneath them."

"You attempted too much," I returned; "your intention was good, but you overstrained your powers."

"You are putting it too mildly," she returned, with a great sadness in her voice. "Esther, I have had time to think since I have lain here, and I have been reviewing your life and mine. I wanted to see where the fault lay, and how I had missed my path. God was taking away my work from me; the sacrifice I offered was not acceptable."

"Oh, my dear, hush!" But she lifted her hand feebly and laid on my lips.

"It was weeks before I found it out, but I think I see it clearly now. We were both in earnest about our duty, we both wanted to do the best we could for others; but, Esther, after all it was you who were right; you did not turn against the work that was brought to you - your teaching, and house, and mother, and Dot, and even Jack - all that came first, and you knew it; you have worked in the corner of the vineyard that was appointed to you, and never murmured over its barrenness and narrow space, and so you are ripe and ready for any great work that may be waiting for you in the future. 'Faithful in little, faithful in much' - how often have I applied those words to you!"

I tried to stem the torrent of retrospection, but nothing would silence her; as she said herself, the pent up feelings must have their course. But why did she judge herself so bitterly? It pained me inexpressibly to hear her.

"If I had only listened to you!" she went on; "but my spiritual self-will blinded me. I despised my work. Oh, Esther! you cannot contradict me; you know how bitterly I spoke of the little Thornes; how I refused to take them into my heart; how scornfully I spoke of my ornamental brickmaking."

I could not gainsay her words on that point; I knew her to be wrong.

"I wanted to choose my work; that was the fatal error. I spurned the little duties at my feet, and looked out for some great work that I must do. Teaching the little Thornes was hateful to me; yet I could teach ragged children in the Sunday-school for hours. Mending Jack's things and talking to mother were wearisome details; yet I could toil through fog and rain in Nightingale lane, and feel no fatigue. My work was impure, my motives tainted by self-will. Could it be accepted by Him who was subject to His parents for thirty years, who worked at the carpenter's bench, when He could have preached to thousands?" And here she broke down, and wept bitterly.

What could I answer? How could I apply comfort to one so sorely wounded? And yet through it all who could doubt her goodness?

"Dear Carrie," I whispered, "if this be all true, if there be no exaggeration, no morbid conscientiousness in all you say, still you have repented, and your punishment has been severe."

"My punishment!" she returned, in a voice almost of despair. "Why do you speak of it as past, when you know I shall bear the consequences of my own imprudence all my life long? This is what is secretly fretting me. I try to bow myself to His will; but, oh! it is so hard not to be allowed to make amends, not to be allowed to have a chance of doing better for the future, not to be allowed to make up for all my deficiencies in the past; but just to suffer and be a burden."

I looked at her with frightened eyes. What could she mean, when she was getting better every day, and Uncle Geoffrey hoped she might be downstairs by Christmas Day?

"Is it possible you do not know, Esther?" she said incredulously; but two red spots came into her thin cheeks. "Have not mother and Uncle Geoffrey told you?"

"They have told me nothing," I repeated. "Oh, Carrie, what do you mean? You are not going to die?"

"To die? Oh, no!" in a tone of unutterable regret. "Should I be so sorry for myself if I thought that? I am getting well - well," with a slight catching of her breath - "but when I come downstairs I shall be like Dot."

I do not know what I said in answer to this terrible revelation. Uncle Geoffrey had never told me; Carrie had only extorted the truth from him with difficulty. My darling girl a cripple! It was Carrie who tried to comfort me as I knelt sobbing beside her.

"Oh, Esther, how you cry! Don't, my dear, don't. It makes me still more unhappy. Have I told you too suddenly? But you must know. That is why I could not bear to see Dot come into the room. But I mean to get over my foolishness."

But I attempted no answer. "Cruel, cruel!" were the only words that forced themselves through my teeth.

"You shall not say that," she returned, stroking my hair. "How can it be cruel if it be meant for my good? I have feared this all along, Esther; the mischief has set in in one hip. It is not the suffering, but the thought of my helplessness that frightens me." And here her sweet eyes filled with tears.

Oh, how selfish I was, when I ought to have been comforting her, if only the words would come! And then a sudden thought came to me.

"They also serve who only stand and wait," and I repeated the line softly, and a sort of inspiration came over me.

"Carrie," I said, embracing her, "this must be the work the loving Saviour has now for you to do. This is the Cross He would have you take up, and He who died to save the sinful and unthankful will give you grace sufficient to your need."

"Yes, I begin to think it is!" she returned; and a light came into her eyes, and she lay back in a satisfied manner. "I never thought of it in that way; it seemed my punishment - just taking away my work and leaving me nothing but helplessness and emptiness."

"And now you will look at it as still more difficult work. Oh, Carrie, what will mine be compared to that - to see you patient under suffering, cheerfully enduring, not murmuring or repining? What will that be but preaching to us daily?"

"That will do," she answered faintly; "I must think it out. You have done more for me this afternoon than any one has." And seeing how exhausted she was, I left her, and stole back to my place.

She slept presently, and I sat still in the glimmering

firelight, listening to the sounds downstairs that told of Allan's arrival; but I could not go down and show my tear-stained face. Deborah came up presently to lay the little tea-table, and then Carrie woke up, and I waited on her as usual, and tried to coax her failing appetite; and by-and-by came the expected tap at the door.

Of course it was Allan; no one but himself would come in with that alert step and cheerful voice.

"Well, Carrie, my dear," he said, affectionately, bending over her as she looked up at him - whatever he felt at the sight of her changed face he kept to himself; he kissed me without a word and took his seat by the bedside.

"You know, Allan?" she whispered, as he took her hand.

"Yes, I know; Uncle Geoffrey has told me; but it may not be as bad as you think - you have much for which to be thankful; for weeks he never thought you would get over it. What does it matter about the lameness, Carrie, when you have come back to us from the very jaws of death?" and his voice trembled a little.

"I felt badly about it until Esther talked to me," she returned. "Esther has been such a nurse to me, Allan."

He looked at me as she said this, and his eyes glistened. "Esther is Esther," he replied, laconically; but I knew then how I satisfied him.

"When we were alone together that night - for I waited downstairs to say good-night to him, while Deborah stayed with Carrie - he suddenly drew me toward him and looked in my face.

"Poor child," he said, tenderly, "it is time I came home to relieve you; you have grown a visionary, unsubstantial Esther, with large eyes and a thin face; but somehow I never liked the look of you so well."

That made me smile. "Oh, Allan, how nice it is to have you with me again!"

"Nice! I should think so; what walks we will have, by the bye. I mean to have Carrie downstairs before a week is over; what is the good of you both moping upstairs? I shall alter all that."

"She is too weak too move," I returned, dubiously.

"But she is not too weak to be carried. You are keeping her too quiet, and she wants rousing a little; she feeds too much on her own thoughts, and it is bad for her; she is such a little saint, you know," continued Allan, half jestingly, "she wants to be leavened a little with our wickedness.

"She is good; you would say so if you heard her."

"Not a bit more good than some other people - Miss Ruth, for example;" but I could see from his mischievous eyes that he was not thinking of Ruth. How well and handsome he was looking: he had grown broader, and there was an air of manliness about him - "my bonnie lad," as I called him.

I went to bed that night with greater contentment in my heart, because Allan had come home; and even Carrie seemed cheered by the hopeful view he had taken of her case.

"He thinks, perhaps, that after some years I may not be quite so helpless," she whispered, as I said good-night to her, and her face looked composed and quiet in the fading firelight; "anyhow, I mean to bear it as well as I can, and not give you more trouble."

"I do not think it a trouble," was my answer as her arms released me; and as I lay awake watching the gleaming shadows in the room, I thought how sweet such ministry is to those we love, their very helplessness endearing them to us. After all, this illness had drawn us closer together, we were more now as sisters should be, united in sympathy and growing deeper into each other's hearts. "How pleasant it is to live in unity!" said the Psalmist; and the echo of the words seemed to linger in my mind until I fell asleep.

CHAPTER XXI.

SANTA CLAUS.

After all Allan's sanguine prognostication was not fulfilled. The new year had opened well upon us before Carrie joined the family circle downstairs.

But the sickroom was a different place now, when we had Allan's cheery visits to enliven our long evenings. A brighter element seemed introduced into the house. I wondered if Carrie felt as I did! if her heart leaped up with pleasure at the sound of his merry whistle, or the light springing footsteps that seemed everywhere!

His vigorous will seemed to dominate over the whole household; he would drag me out peremptorily for what he called wholesome exercise, which meant long, scrambling walks, which sent me home with tingling pulses and exuberant spirits, until the atmosphere of the sick room moderated and subdued them again.

He continued to relieve me in many ways; sometimes he would come in upon us in his quick, alert way, and bundle me and my work-basket downstairs, ordering me to talk to mother, while he gave Carrie a dose of his company. Perhaps the change was good for her, for I always fancied she looked less depressed when I saw her again.

Rosa Nouchette Carey

Our choice of reading displeased him not a little; the religious biographies and sentimental sacred poetry that Carrie specially affected were returned to the bookshelves by our young physician with an unsparing hand; he actually scolded me in no measured terms for what he called my want of sense.

"What a goose you are, Esther," he said, in a disgusted voice; "but, there, you women are all alike," continued the youthful autocrat. "You pet one another's morbid fancies, and do no end of harm. Because Carrie wants cheering, you keep her low with all these books, which feed her gloomy ideas. What do you say? she likes it; well, many people like what is not good for them. I tell you she is not in a fit state for this sort of reading, and unless you will abide by my choice of books I will get Uncle Geoffrey to forbid them altogether."

Carrie looked ready to cry at this fierce tirade, but I am afraid I only laughed in Allan's face; still, we had to mind him. He set me to work, I remember, on some interesting book of travels, that carried both of us far from Milnthorpe, and set us down in wonderful tropical regions, where we lost ourselves and our troubles in gorgeous descriptions.

One evening I came up and found Allan reading the "Merchant of Venice," to her, and actually Carrie was enjoying it.

"He reads so well," she said, rather apologetically, as she caught sight of my amused face; she did not like to own even to me that she found it more interesting than listening to Henry Martyn's life.

It charmed us both to hear the sound of her soft laugh;

and Allan went downstairs well satisfied with the result of his prescription.

On Christmas Eve I had a great treat. Ruth wanted me to spend the evening with her; and as she took Carrie into her confidence, she got her way without difficulty. Carrie arranged every thing; mother was to sit with her, and then Allan and Deborah would help her to bed. I was to enjoy myself and have a real holiday, and not come home until Allan fetched me.

I had quite a holiday feeling as I put on my new cashmere dress. Ruth had often fetched me for a drive, but I had not been inside the Cedars for months, and the prospect of a long evening there was delicious.

Flurry ran out into the hall to meet me, and even Giles' grave face relaxed into a smile as he hoped "Miss Cameron was better;" but Flurry would hardly let me answer, she was so eager to show me the wreaths auntie and she had made, and to whisper that she had hung out a stocking for Santa Claus to fill, and that Santa Claus was going to fill one for Dot too.

"Come in, you naughty little chatterbox, and do not keep Esther in the hall," exclaimed Ruth, from the curtained doorway; and the next minute I had my arms round her. Oh, the dear room! how cozy it looked after my months of absence; no other room, not even mother's pretty drawing-room at Combe Manor, was so entirely to my taste.

There was the little square tea-table, as usual, and the dark blue china cups and saucers, and the wax candles in their silver sconces, and white china lamp, and the soft glow of the ruddy firelight playing into the dim corner.

Ruth drew up the low rocking chair, and took off my hat and jacket, and smoothed my hair.

"How nice you look Esther, and what a pretty dress! Is that Allan's present? But you are still very thin, my dear.

"Oh, I am all right," I returned, carelessly, for what did it matter how I looked, now Carrie was better? "Dear Ruth," I whispered, as she still stood beside me, "I can think of nothing but the pleasure of being with you again."

"I hope you mean to include me in that last speech," said a voice behind me; and there was Mr. Lucas standing laughing at us. He had come through the curtained doorway unheard, and I rose in some little confusion to shake hands.

To my surprise, he echoed Miss Ruth's speech; but then he had not seen me for three months. I had been through so much since we last met.

"What have they been doing to you, my poor child?" Those were actually his words, and his eyes rested on my face with quite a grieved, pitying expression.

"Allan told me I was rather unsubstantial-looking," I returned, trying to speak lightly; but somehow the tears came to my eyes. "I was so tired before he came home, but now I am getting rested."

"I wonder at Dr. Cameron letting a child like you work so hard," he retorted, quite abruptly. He had called me child twice, and I was eighteen and a half, and feeling so old - so old. I fancy Ruth saw my lip quiver, for she hastily interposed:

"Let her sit down, Giles, and I will give her some tea. She looks as cold as a little starved robin."

And after that no one spoke again of my altered looks. It troubled me for a few minutes, and then it passed out of my mind.

After all, it could not be helped if I were a little thin and worn. The strain of those three months had been terrible; the daily spectacle of physical suffering before my eyes, the wakeful nights, the long monotonous days, and then the shock of knowing that Carrie must be a cripple, had all been too much for me.

We talked about it presently, while Flurry sat like a mouse at my feet, turning over the pages of a new book of fairy tales. The kind sympathy they both showed me broke down the barrier of my girlish reserve, and I found comfort in speaking of the dreary past. I did not mind Mr. Lucas in the least: he showed such evident interest in all I told them. After dinner he joined us again in the drawing-room, instead of going as usual for a short time to his study.

"When are you coming back to stay with us?" he asked, suddenly, as he stirred the logs until they emitted a shower of sparks.

"Yes," echoed his sister, "Carrie is so much better now that we think it is high time for you to resume your duties; poor Flurry has been neglected enough."

My answer was simply to look at them both; the idea of renewing work had never occurred to me; how could Carrie spare me? And yet ought I not to do my part all the more, now she was laid by? For a moment the sense of conflicting duties oppressed me.

"Please do not look pale over it," observed Mr. Lucas, kindly; "but you do not mean, I suppose, to be always chained to your sister's couch? That will do neither of you any good."

"Oh, no, I must work, of course," I returned, breathlessly. "Carrie will not be able to do anything, so it is the more necessary for me, but not yet - not until we have her downstairs."

"Then we will give you three weeks' grace," observed Mr. Lucas, coolly. "It is as you say, with your usual good sense, absolutely necessary that one of you should work; and as Flurry has been without a governess long enough, we shall expect you to resume your duties in three weeks' time."

I was a little perplexed by this speech, it was so dignified and peremptory; but looking up I could see a little smile breaking out at the corner of his mouth. Ruth too seemed amused.

"Very well," I returned in the same voice; "I must be punctual, or I shall expect my dismissal."

"Of course you must be punctual," he retorted; and the subject dropped, but I perceived he was in earnest under his jesting way. Flurry's governess was wanted back, that was clear.

As for me, the mere notion of resuming my daily work at the Cedars was almost too delightful to contemplate. I had an odd idea, that missing them all had something to do with my sober feelings. I felt it when I went up to kiss Flurry in her little bed; the darling child was lying awake for me.

She made me lie down on the bed beside her, and hugged me close with her warm arms, and her hair fell over my face like a veil, and then prattled to me about Santa Claus and the wonderful gifts she expected.

"Will Santa Claus bring you anything, Esther?"

"Not much, I fear," was my amused answer. We were rather a gift-loving family, and at Combe Manor our delight had been to load the breakfast table on Christmas day with presents for every member of the family, including servants; but of course now our resources were limited, and I expected few presents; but in my spare time I had contrived a few surprises in the shape of work. A set of embroidered baby linen for Flurry's best doll, dainty enough for a fairy baby; a white fleecy shawl for mother, and another for Carrie, and a chair-back for Ruth; she was fond of pretty things, but I certainly did not look for much in return.

Allan had brought me that pretty dress from London, and another for Carrie, and he had not Fortunatus' purse, poor fellow!

"I have got a present for you," whispered Flurry, and I could imagine how round and eager her eyes were; I think with a little encouragement she would have told me what it was; but I assured her that I should enjoy the surprise.

"It won't keep you awake trying to guess, will it?" she asked, anxiously; and when I said no, she seemed a little disappointed.

"Dot has got one too," she observed, presently; but I knew all about that. Dot was laboriously filling an album with his choicest works of art. His fingers were always stained with paint or Indian ink at meal times, and if I unexpectedly entered the room, I could see a square-shaped book being smuggled away under the tablecloth.

I think these sudden rushes were rather against the general finish of the pictures, causing in some places an unsightly smudge or a blotchy appearance. In one page the Tower of Babel was disfigured by this very injudicious haste, and the bricks and the builders were wholly indistinguishable for a sad blotch of ochre; still, the title page made up for all such defects: "To my dear sister, Esther, from her affectionate little brother, Frankie."

"Aunt Ruth has one, too," continued Flurry; but at this point I thought it better to say good-night. As it was, I found Allan had been waiting for me nearly half-an-hour, and pretended to growl at me for my dawdling, though in reality he was thoroughly enjoying his talk with Ruth.

Carrie was awake when I entered the room; she was lying watching the fire. She welcomed me with her sweetest smile, and though I fancied her cheek was wet as I kissed it, her voice was very tranquil.

"Have you had a pleasant evening, Esther?"

"Very pleasant. Have you missed me very much, darling?"

"I always miss you," she replied, gently; "but Allan has done his best to make the time pass quickly. And then dear mother was so good; she has been sitting with me ever so long; we have had such a nice talk. Somehow I begin to feel as if I had never known what mother was before."

I knew Carrie wanted to tell me all about it, but I pretended I was tired, and that it was time to be asleep. So she said no more; she was submissive to us even in trifles now; and very soon I heard the sound of her soft, regular breathing.

As for me, I laid wide awake for hours; my evening had excited me. The thought of resuming my happy duties at the Cedars pleased and exhilarated me. How kind and thoughtful they had been for my comfort, how warmly I had been welcomed!

I fell to sleep at last, and dreamed that Santa Claus had brought me a mysterious present. The wrappers were so many that Deborah woke me before I reached the final. I remember I had quite a childish feeling of disappointment when my pleasant dream was broken.

What a Christmas morning that was! Outside the trees were bending with hoar frost, a scanty whiteness lay on the lawn, and the soft mysterious light of coming snow seemed to envelope everything. Inside the fire burned ruddily, and Carrie lay smiling upon her pillows, with a little parcel in her outstretched hands. I thought of my unfinished dream, and told it to her as I unfolded the silver paper that wrapped the little box.

"Oh, Carrie!" I exclaimed, for there was her little amethyst cross and beautiful filagree chain; that had been father's gift to her, the prettiest ornament she possessed, and that had been my secret admiration for years.

"I want you to have it," she said, smiling, well pleased at my astonished face. "I can never wear it again, Esther; the world and I have parted company. I shall like to see you in it. I wish it were twice as good; I wish it were of priceless value, for nothing is too good for my dear little sister."

I was very near crying over the little box, and Carrie was praising the thickness and beauty of her shawl, when in came Dot, with his scrap-book under his arm, and Jack, with a wonderful pen-wiper she had concocted, with a cat and kitten she had marvelously executed in gray cloth.

Nor was this all. Downstairs a perfect array of parcels was grouped round my plate. There was a book from Allan, and a beautiful little traveling desk from Uncle Geoffrey. Mother had been searching in her jewel case, and had produced a pearl-ring, which she presented to me with many kisses.

But the greatest surprise of all was still in store for me. Flurry's gift proved to be a very pretty little photograph of herself and Flossy, set in a velvet frame. Ruth's was an ivory prayer-book: but beside it lay a little parcel, directed in Mr. Lucas' handwriting, and a note inside begging me to accept a slight tribute of his gratitude. I opened it with a trembling hand, and there was an exquisite little watch, with a short gold chain attached to it - a perfect little beauty, as even Allan declared it to be.

I was only eighteen, and I suppose most girls would understand my rapture at the sight. Until now a silver watch with a plain black guard had been my only possession; this I presented to Jack on the spot, and was in consequence nearly hugged to death.

"How kind, how kind!" was all I could say; and mother seemed nearly as pleased as I was. As for Uncle Geoffrey and Allan, they took it in an offhand and masculine fashion.

"Very proper, very prettily done," remarked Uncle Geoffrey, approvingly. "You see he has reason to be grateful to you, my dear, and Mr. Lucas is just the man to acknowledge it in the most fitting way."

"I always said he was a brick," was Allan's unceremonious retort. "It is no more than he ought to have done, for your pluckiness saved Flurry." But to their surprise I turned on them with hot cheeks.

"I have done nothing, it is all their kindness and goodness to me: it is far too generous. How ever shall I thank him?" And then I snatched up my treasure, and ran upstairs to show it to Carrie; and I do not think there was a happier girl that Christmas morning than Esther Cameron.

The one drawback to my pleasure was - how I was to thank Mr. Lucas? But I was spared this embarrassment, for he and Flurry waited after service in the porch for us, and walked down High street.

He came to my side at once with a glimmer of fun in

his grave eyes.

"Well, Miss Esther, has Santa Claus been good to you? or has he taken too great a liberty?"

"Oh, Mr. Lucas," I began, in a stammering fashion, but he held up his hand peremptorily.

"Not a word, not a syllable, if you please; the debt is all on my side, and you do not fancy it can be paid in such a paltry fashion. I am glad you are not offended with me, that is all." And then he proceeded to ask kindly after Carrie.

His manner set me quite at my ease, and I was able to talk to him as usual. Dot was at the window watching for our approach. He clapped his hands delightedly at the sight of Mr. Lucas and Flurry.

"I suppose I must come in a moment to see my little friend," he said, in a kindly voice, and in another moment he was comfortably seated in our parlor with Dot climbing on his knee.

I never remember a happier Christmas till then, though, thank God, I have known still happier ones since. True, Carrie could not join the family gathering downstairs; but after the early dinner we all went up to her room, and sat in a pleasant circle round the fire.

Only Fred was missing; except the dear father who lay in the quiet churchyard near Combe Manor; but we had bright, satisfactory letters from him, and hoped that on the whole he was doing well.

We talked of him a good deal, and then it was that Dot

announced his grand purpose of being an artist.

"When I am a man," he finished, in a serious voice, "I mean to work harder than Fred, and paint great big pictures, and perhaps some grand nobleman will buy them of me."

"I wonder what your first subject will be, Frankie?" asked Allan, in a slightly amused voice. He was turning over Dot's scrap-book, and was looking at the Tower of Babel in a puzzled way.

"The Retreat of the Ten Thousand under Xenophon," was the perfectly startling answer, at which Allan opened his eyes rather widely, and Uncle Geoffrey laughed. Dot looked injured and a little cross.

"People always laugh when I want to talk sense," he said, rather loftily.

"Never mind, Frankie, we won't laugh any more," returned Allan, eager to soothe his favorite; "it is a big subject, but you have plenty of years to work it out in, and after all the grand thing in me is to aim high." Which speech, being slightly unintelligible, mollified Dot's wrath.

CHAPTER XXII.

ALLAN AND I WALK TO ELTHAM GREEN.

The next great event in our family annals was Carrie's first appearance downstairs.

Uncle Geoffrey had long wished her to make the effort, but she had made some excuse and put it off from day to day; but at last Allan took it into his head to manage things after his usual arbitrary fashion, and one afternoon he marched into the room, and, quietly lifting Carrie in his arms, as though she were a baby, desired me to follow with, her crutches, while he carried her downstairs.

Carrie trembled a good deal, and turned very white, but she offered no remonstrance; and when Allan put her down outside the parlor door, she took her crutches from me in a patient uncomplaining way that touched us both.

I always said we ought to have prepared Dot, but Allan would not hear of my telling him; but when the door opened and Carrie entered, walking slowly and painfully, being still unused to her crutches, we were all startled by a loud cry from Dot.

"She is like me! Oh, poor, poor Carrie!" cried the little

fellow, with a sob; and he broke into such a fit of crying that mother was quite upset. It was in vain we tried to soothe him; that Carrie drew him toward her with trembling arms and kissed him, and whispered that it was God's will, and she did not mind so very much now; he only kept repeating, "She is like me - oh, dear - oh dear! she is like me," in a woe-begone little voice.

Dot was so sensitive that I feared the shock would make him ill, but Allan came at last to the rescue. He had been called out of the room for a moment, and came back to find a scene of dire confusion - it took so little to upset mother, and really it was heartbreaking to all of us to see the child's grief.

"Hallo, sonny, what's up now?" asked Allan, in a comical voice, lifting up Dot's tear-stained face for a nearer inspection.

"Oh, she is like me," gasped Dot; "she has those horrid things, you know; and it's too bad, it's too bad!" he finished, with another choking sob.

"Nonsense," returned Allan, with sturdy cheerfulness; "she won't use them always, you silly boy."

"Not always!" returned Dot, with a woe-begone, puckered-up face.

"Of course not, you little goose - or gander, I mean; she may have to hobble about on them for a year or two, perhaps longer; but Uncle Geoff and I mean to set her all right again - don't we, Carrie?" Carrie's answer was a dubious smile. She did not believe in her own recovery; but to Dot, Allan's words were full of complete comfort.

"Oh, I am so glad, I am so glad!" cried the unselfish little creature. "I don't mind a bit for myself; I shouldn't be Dot without my sticks, but it seemed so dreadful for poor Carrie."

And then, as she kissed him, with tears in her eyes, he whispered "that she was not to mind, for Allan would soon make her all right: he always did."

Carrie tried to be cheerful that evening, but it cost her a great effort. It was hard returning to everyday life, without strength or capacity for its duties, with no bright prospect dawning in the future, only a long, gray horizon of present monotony and suffering. But here the consolation of the Gospel came to her help; the severe test of her faith proved its reality; and her submission and total abnegation of will brought her the truest comfort in her hour of need.

Looking back on this part of our lives, I believe Carrie needed just this discipline; like many other earnest workers she made an idol of her work. It cost her months of suffering before she realized that God does not always need our work; that a chastened will is more acceptable to Him than the labor we think so all-sufficient. Sad lesson to poor human pride, that believes so much in its own efforts, and yet that many a one laid by in the vigor of life and work, has to learn so painfully. Oh, hardest of all work, to do nothing while others toil round us, to wait and look on, knowing God's ways are not our ways, that the patient endurance of helplessness is the duty ordained for us!

Carrie had to undergo another ordeal the following

day, for she was just settled on her couch when Mrs. Smedley entered unannounced.

I had never liked Mrs. Smedley; indeed, at one time I was very near hating her; but I could not help feeling sorry for the woman when I saw how her face twitched and worked at the sight of her favorite.

Carrie's altered looks must have touched her conscience. Carrie was a little nervous, but she soon recovered herself.

"You must not be sorry for me," she said, taking her hand, for actually Mrs. Smedley could hardly speak; tears stood in her hard eyes, and then she motioned to me to leave them together.

I never knew what passed between them, but I am sure Mrs. Smedley had been crying when I returned to the room. She rose at once, making some excuse about the lateness of the hour - and then she did what she never had done before - kissed me quite affectionately, and hoped they would soon see me at the vicarage.

"There, that is over," said Carrie, as if to herself, in a relieved tone; but she did not seem disposed for any questioning, so I let her close her eyes and think over the interview in silence.

The next day was a very eventful one. I had made up my mind to speak to mother and Carrie that morning, and announce my intention of going back to the Cedars. I was afraid it would be rather a blow to Carrie, and I wanted to get it over.

In two or three days the three weeks' leave of absence

would be over - Ruth would be expecting to hear from me. The old saying, "*L'homme propose, Dieu dispose*," was true in this case. I had little idea that morning, when I came down to breakfast, that all my cherished plans were to be set aside, and all through old Aunt Podgill.

Why, I had never thought of her for years; and, as far as I can tell, her name had not been mentioned in our family circle, except on the occasion of dear father's death, when Uncle Geoffrey observed that he or Fred must write to her. She was father's and Uncle Geoffrey's aunt, on their mother's side, but she had quarreled with them when they were mere lads, and had never spoken to them since. Uncle Geoffrey was most in her black books, and she had not deigned to acknowledge his letter.

"A cantankerous old woman," I remember he had called her on that occasion, and had made no further effort to propitiate her.

It was rather a shock, then, to hear Aunt Podgill's name uttered in a loud voice by Allan, as I entered the room, and my surprise deepened into astonishment to find mother was absolutely crying over a black-edged letter.

"Poor Mrs. Podgill is dead," explained Uncle Geoffrey, in rather a subdued voice, as I looked at him.

But the news did not affect me much; I thought mother's handkerchief need hardly be applied to her eyes on that account.

"That is a pity, of course; but, then, none of us knew

her," I remarked, coldly. "She could not have been very nice, from your account, Uncle Geoffrey, so I do not know why we have to be so sorry for her death," for I was as aggrieved as possible at the sight of mother's handkerchief.

"Well, she was a cantankerous old woman," began Uncle Geoffrey; and then he checked himself and added, "Heaven forgive me for speaking against the poor old creature now she is dead."

"Yes, indeed, I have a great respect for Aunt Podgill," put in Allan; and I thought his voice was rather curious, and there was a repressed mirthful gleam in his eyes, and all the time mother went on crying.

"Oh, my dear," she sobbed at last, "I am very foolish to be so overcome; but if it had only come in Frank's - in your father's time, it might - it might have saved him;" and here she broke down.

"Ah, to be sure, poor thing!" ejaculated Uncle Geoffrey in a sympathizing tone; "that is what is troubling her; but you must cheer up, Dora, for, as I have always told you, Frank was never meant to be a long-lived man."

"What are you all talking about?" I burst out, with vexed impatience. "What has Mrs. Podgill's death to do with father? and why is mother crying? and what makes you all so mysterious and tiresome?" for I was exasperated at the incongruity between mother's tears and Allan's amused face.

"Tell her," gasped out mother: and Uncle Geoffrey, clearing his voice, proceeded to be spokesman, only Allan interrupted him at every word.

"Why, you see, child, your mother is just a little upset at receiving some good news - "

"Battling good news," put in Allan.

"It is natural for her, poor thing! to think of your father; but we tell her that if he had been alive things would have shaped themselves differently - "

"Of course they would," from that tiresome Allan.

"Aunt Podgill, being a cantankerous - I mean a prejudiced - person, would never have forgotten her grudge against your father; but as in our last moments 'conscience makes cowards of us all,' as Shakespeare has it" - Uncle Geoffrey always quoted Shakespeare when he was agitated, and Allan said, "Hear, hear!" softly under his breath - "she could not forget the natural claims of blood; and so, my dear," clearing his throat a little more, "she has left all her little fortune to your mother; and a pretty little penny it is, close upon seven hundred a year, and the furniture besides."

"Uncle Geoffrey!" now it was my turn to gasp. Jack and Dot burst out laughing at my astonished face; only Dot squeezed my hand, and whispered, "Isn't it splendid, Essie?" Mother looked at me tearfully.

"It is for your sakes I am glad, that my darling girls may not have to work. Carrie can have every comfort now; and you can stay with us, Esther, and we need not be divided any longer."

"Hurrah," shouted Dot, waving his spoon over his head; but I only kissed mother without speaking; a strange, unaccountable feeling prevented me. If we were rich - or rather if we had this independence - I must not go on teaching Flurry; my duty was at home with mother and Carrie.

I could have beaten myself for my selfishness; but it was true. Humiliating as it is to confess it, my first feeling was regret that my happy days at the Cedars were over.

"You do not seem pleased," observed Allan, shrewdly, as he watched me.

"I am so profoundly astonished that I am not capable of feeling," I returned hastily; but I blushed a little guiltily.

"It is almost too good to believe," he returned. "I never liked the idea of you and Carrie doing anything, and yet it could not be helped; so now you will all be able to stay at home and enjoy yourselves."

Mother brightened up visibly at this.

"That will be nice, will it not, Esther? And Dot can have his lessons with you as usual. I was so afraid that Miss Ruth would want you back soon, and that Carrie would be dull. How good of your Aunt Podgill to make us all so happy! And if it were not for your father - " and here the dear soul had recourse to her handkerchief again.

If I was silent, no one noticed it; every one was so eager in detailing his or her plans for the future. It was quite a relief when the lengthy breakfast was over, and I was free to go and tell Carrie; somehow in the general excitement no one thought of her. I reproached myself still more for my selfishness, and called myself all manner of hard names when I saw the glow of pleasure on her pale face.

"Oh, Esther, how nice! How pleased dear mother must be! Now we shall have you all to ourselves, and you need not be spending all your days away from us."

How strange! Carrie knew of my warm affection for Ruth and Flurry, and yet it never occurred to her that I should miss my daily intercourse with them. It struck me then how often our nearest and dearest misunderstand or fail to enter into our feelings.

The thought recurred to me more than once that morning when I sat at my work listening to the discussion between her and mother. Carrie seemed a different creature that day; the wonderful news had lifted her out of herself, and she rejoiced so fully and heartily in our good fortune that I was still more ashamed of myself, and yet I was glad too.

"It seems so wonderful to me, mother," Carrie was saying, in her sweet serious way, "that just when I was laid by, and unable to keep myself or any one else, that this provision should be made for us."

"Yes, indeed; and then there is Dot, too, who will never be able to work," observed mother.

It was lucky Dot did not hear her, or we might have had a reproachful *resume* of his artistic intentions.

"Dear mother, you need not be anxious any longer over the fortune of your two cripples," returned Carrie, tenderly. "I shall not feel so much a burthen now; and then we shall have Esther to look after us." And they both looked at me in a pleased, affectionate way. What could I do but put down my work and join in that innocent, loving talk?

At our early dinner that day Allan seemed a little preoccupied and silent, but toward the close of the meal he addressed me in his off-hand fashion.

"I want you to come out with me this afternoon; mother can look after Carrie."

"It is a half holiday; may I come too?" added Jack, coaxingly.

"Wait till you are asked, Miss Jacky," retorted Allan good-humoredly. "No, I don't want your ladyship's company this afternoon; I must have Esther to myself." And though Jack grumbled and looked discontented, he would not change his decision.

I had made up my mind to see Ruth, and tell her all about it; but it never entered my head to dispute Allan's will if he wanted me to walk with him. I must give up Ruth, that was all; and I hurried to put on my things, that I might not keep him waiting, as he possessed his full share of masculine impatience.

I thought that he had some plan to propose to me, but to my surprise he only talked about the most trivial subjects - the weather, the state of the roads, the prospects of skating.

"Where are we going?" I asked at last, for we were passing the Cedars, and Allan rarely walked in that direction; but perhaps he had a patient to see.

"Only to Eltham Green," he returned briefly.

The answer was puzzling. Eltham Green was half a mile from the Cedars, and there was only one house there, beside a few scattered cottages; and I knew Uncle Geoffrey's patient, Mr. Anthony Lambert, who lived there, had died about a month ago.

As Allan did not seem disposed to be communicative, I let the matter rest, and held my peace; and a few minutes quick walking brought us to the place.

It was a little common, very wild and tangled with gorse, and in summer very picturesque. Some elms bordered the road, and there was a large clear-looking pond, and flocks of geese would waddle over the common, hissing and thrusting out their yellow bills to every passer-by.

The cottages were pretty and rustic-looking, and had gay little gardens in front. They belonged to Mr. Lucas; and Eltham Cottage, as Mr. Lambert's house was called, was his property also.

Flurry and I had always been very fond of the common, where Flossy had often run barking round the pond, after a family of yellow ducklings.

"Eltham Cottage is still to let," I observed, looking up at the board; "it is such a pretty house"

Allan made no response to that, but bade me enter, as he wanted to look at it.

It was a long, two-storied cottage, with a veranda all round it, and in summer a profusion of flowers - roses and clematis, and a splendid passionflower - twined round the pillars and covered the porch.

The woman who admitted us ushered us into a charming little hall, with a painted window and a glass door opening on to the lawn. There was a small room on one side of it, and on the other the dining room and drawing-room. The last was a very long, pleasant room, with three windows, all opening French fashion on to the veranda, and another glass door leading into a pretty little conservatory.

The garden was small, but very tastefully laid out; but there was a southern wall, where peaches and nectarines were grown, and beehives stood, and some pretty winding walks, which led to snug nooks, where ferns or violets were hidden.

"What a sweet place!" I exclaimed, admiringly, at which Allan looked exultant; but he only bade me follow him into the upper rooms.

These were satisfactory in every respect. Some were of sunny aspect, and looked over the garden and some large park-like meadows; the front ones commanded the common.

"There is not a bad room in the house," said Allan; and then he made me admire the linen-presses and old-fashioned cupboards, and the bright red-tiled kitchen looking out on a laurestinus walk.

"It is a dear house!" I exclaimed, enthusiastically, at which Allan looked well-pleased. Then he took me by the arm, and drew me to a little window-seat on the upper landing - a proceeding that reminded me of the days at Combe Manor, when I sat waiting for him, and looking down on the lilies.

"I am glad you think so," he said, solemnly; "for I wanted to ask your advice about an idea of mine; it came into my head this morning when we were all talking and planning, that this house would be just the thing for mother."

"Allan!" I exclaimed, "you really do not mean to propose that we should leave Uncle Geoffrey?"

"No, of course not," with a touch of impatience, for he was always a little hasty if people did not grasp his meaning at once, "but, you, see, houses in Milnthorpe are scarce, and we are rather too tight a fit at present. Besides, it is not quiet enough for Carrie: the noise of the carts and gigs on Monday morning jars her terribly. What I propose is, that you should all settle down here in this pretty countrified little nook, and take Uncle Geoff and Deb with you, and leave Martha and me to represent the Camerons in the old house in the High street."

"But, Allan - " I commenced, dubiously, for I did not like the idea of leaving him behind; but he interrupted me, and put his views more forcibly before me.

Carrie wanted quiet and country air, and so did Dot, and the conservatory and garden would be such a delight to mother. Uncle Geoffrey would be dull without us, and there was a nice little room that could be fitted up for him and Jumbles; he would drive in to his work every morning and he - Allan - could walk out and see us on two or three evenings in the week.

"I must be there, of course, to look after the practice. I am afraid I am cut out for an old bachelor, Esther, like Uncle Geoff, for I do not feel at all dismal at the thought of having a house to myself," finished Allan with his boyish laugh.

CHAPTER XXIII.

TOLD IN THE SUNSET.

What a clever head Allan had! I always said there was more in that boy than half a dozen Freds! To think of such a scheme coming into his mind, and driving us all nearly wild with excitement!

Allan's strong will bore down all opposition. Mother's feeble remonstrances, which came from a sheer terror of change; even Uncle Geoffrey's sturdy refusal to budge an inch out of the old house where he had lived so long, did not weigh a straw against Allan's solid reasoning.

It took a vast amount of talking, though, before our young autocrat achieved his final victory, and went off flushed and eager to settle preliminaries with Mr. Lucas. It was all sealed, signed, and delivered before he came back.

The pretty cottage at Eltham was to be ours, furnished with Aunt Podgill's good old-fashioned furniture, and in the early days of April we were to accomplish our second flitting.

The only remaining difficulty was about Jack; but this Uncle Geoffrey solved for us. The gig would bring him into Milnthorpe every morning, and he could easily drive Jack to her school, and the walk back would be good for her. In dark, wintry weather she could return with him, or, if occasion required it, she might be a weekly boarder.

Mr. Lucas came back with Allan, and formally congratulated mother on her good fortune.

I do not know if it were my fancy, but he seemed a little grave and constrained in his manners that evening, and scarcely addressed me at all until the close of his visit.

"Under the circumstances I am afraid Flurry will have to lose her governess," he said, not looking at me, however, but at mother; and though I opened my lips to reply, my mother answered for me.

"Well, yes, I am afraid so. Carrie depends so much on her sister."

"Of course, of course," he returned, hastily; and actually he never said another word, but got up and said good-by to mother.

But I could not let him go without a word after all his kindness to me; so, as Allan had gone out, I followed him out into the hall, though he tried to wave me back.

"It is cold; I shall not open the hail door while you stand there, Miss Esther,"

"Oh, I do not mind the cold one bit," I returned, nervously; "but I want to speak to you a moment, Mr. Lucas. Will you give Ruth my love, and tell her I will come and talk to her to-morrow, and - and I am so sorry to part with Flurry."

"You are not more sorry than she will be," he returned, but not in his old natural manner; and then he begged me so decidedly to go back into the warm room that I dared not venture on another word.

It was very unsatisfactory; something must have put him out, I thought, and I went back to mother feeling chilled and uncomfortable. Oh, dear! how dependent we are for comfort on the words and manners of those around us.

I went to the Cedars the following afternoon, and had a long comfortable talk with Ruth. She even laid aside her usual quiet undemonstrativeness, and petted and made much of me, though she laughed a little at what she called my solemn face.

"Confess now, Esther, you are not a bit pleased about all this money!"

"Oh, indeed I am," I returned, quite shocked at this. "I am so delighted for mother and Dot and Carrie."

"But not for yourself," she persisted.

There was no deceiving Ruth, so I made a full confession, and stammered out, in great confusion, that I did not like losing her and Flurry; that it was wrong and selfish, when Carrie wanted me so; but I knew that even at Eltham I should miss the Cedars.

She seemed touched at that. "You are a faithful soul, Esther; you never forget a kindness, and you cannot bear even a slight separation from those you love. We have spoiled you, I am afraid."

"Yes, indeed," I returned, rather sadly, "you have been far too good to me."

"That is a matter of opinion. Well, what am I to say to comfort you, when you find fault with even your good luck? Will it make you any better to know we shall all miss you dreadfully? Even Giles owned as much; and as for Flurry, we had quite a piece of work with her."

"Mr. Lucas never even said he was sorry," I returned, in a piqued voice. It was true I was quite spoiled, for I even felt aggrieved that he did not join us in the drawing-room, and yet I knew he was in the house.

"Oh, you do not know Giles," she answered, brightly; "he is one of the unselfish ones, he would not have damped what he thought your happiness for the world. You see, Esther, no one in their senses would ever believe that you were really sorry at your stroke of good fortune; it is only I who know you, my dear, that can understand how that is."

Did she understand? Did I really understand myself? Anyhow, I felt horribly abashed while she was speaking. I felt I had been conducting myself in an unfledged girlish fashion, and that Ruth, with her staid common sense, was reproving me.

I determined then and there that no more foolish expression of regret should cross my lips; that I would keep all such nonsense to myself; so when Flurry ran in very tearful and desponding, I took Ruth's cue, and talked to her as cheerfully as possible, giving her such vivid descriptions of the cottage and the garden, and the dear little honeysuckle arbor where Dot and she could have tea, that she speedily forgot all her regrets in delicious anticipations.

"Yes, indeed," observed Ruth, as she benevolently contemplated us, "I expect Flurry and I will be such constant visitors that your mother will complain that there is no end of those tiresome Lucases. Run along, Flurry, and see if your father means to come in and have some tea. Tell him Esther is here."

Flurry was a long time gone, and then she brought back a message that her father was too busy, and she might bring him a cup there, and that she was to give his kind regards to Miss Cameron, and that was all.

I went home shortly after that, and found mother and Carrie deep in discussion about carpets and curtains. They both said I looked tired and cold, and that Ruth had kept me too long.

"I think I am getting jealous of Ruth," Carrie said, with a gentle smile.

And somehow the remark did not please me; not that Carrie really meant it, though; but it did strike me sometimes that both mother and she thought that Ruth rather monopolized me.

My visits to the Cedars became very rare after this, for we were soon engrossed with the bustle of moving. For more than six weeks I trudged about daily between our house and Eltham Cottage. There were carpets to be fitted, and the furniture to be adapted to each room, and when that was done, Allan and I worked hard in the conservatory; and here Ruth often joined us, bringing with her a rare fern or plant from the well-stocked greenhouses at the Cedars. She used to sit and watch us at our labors, and say sometimes how much she wished she could help us, and sometimes she spent an hour or two with Carrie to make up for my absence.

I rather reveled in my hard work, and grew happier every day, and the cottage did look so pretty when we had finished.

Ruth was with me all the last afternoon. We lighted fires in all the rooms, and they looked so cozy. The table in the dining-room was spread with Aunt Podgill's best damask linen and her massive old-fashioned silver; and Deborah was actually baking her famous griddle cakes, to the admiration of our new help, Dorcas, before the first fly, with mother and Carrie and Dot, drove up to the door. I shall never forget mother's pleased look as she stood in the little hall, and Carrie's warm kiss as I welcomed them.

"How beautiful it all looks!" she exclaimed; "how home-like and bright and cozy; you have managed so well, Esther!"

"Esther always manages well," observed dear mother, proudly. The extent to which she believed in me and my resources was astonishing. She followed me all over the house, praising everything. I was glad Ruth heard her, and knew that I had done my best for them all. Allan accompanied the others, and we had quite a merry evening.

Ruth stayed to tea. "She was really becoming one of us!" as mother observed; and Allan took her home. We all crowded into the porch to see them off; even Carrie, who was getting quite nimble on her crutches. It was a warm April night; the little common was flooded with moonlight; the spring flowers were sleeping in the white rays, and the limes glistened like silver. Uncle Geoffrey and I walked with them to the gate, while Ruth got into her pony carriage.

I did not like saying good-night to Allan; it seemed so strange for him to be going back to the old house alone; but he burst into one of his ringing laughs when I told him so.

"Why, I like it," he said, cheerily; "it is good fun being monarch of all I survey. Didn't I tell you I was cut out for an old bachelor? You must come and make tea for me sometimes, when I can't get out here." And then, in a more serious voice, he added, "It does put one into such good spirits to see mother and you girls safe in this pretty nest."

I had never been idle; but now the day never seemed long enough for my numerous occupations, and yet they were summer days, too.

The early rising was now an enjoyment to me. I used to work in the garden or conservatory before breakfast, and how delicious those hours were when the birds and I had it all to ourselves; and I hardly know which sang the loudest, for I was very happy, very happy indeed, without knowing why. I think this unreasoning and unreasonable happiness is an attribute of youth.

I had got over my foolish disappointment about the Cedars. Ruth kept her word nobly, and she and Flurry came perpetually to the cottage. Sometimes I spent an afternoon or evening at the Cedars, and then I always saw Mr. Lucas, and he was most friendly and pleasant. He used to talk of coming down one afternoon to see how I was getting on with my fernery, but it was a long time before he kept his promise.

The brief cloud, or whatever it was, had vanished and he was his own genial self. Flurry had not another governess, but Ruth gave her lessons sometimes, and on her bad days her father heard them. It was rather desultory teaching, and I used to shake my head rather solemnly when I heard of it; but Ruth always said that Giles wished it to be so for the present. The child was not strong, and was growing fast, and it would not hurt her to run wild a little.

When breakfast was over, Dot and I worked hard; and in the afternoon I generally read to Carrie; she was far less of an invalid now, and used to busy herself with work for the poor while she lay on her couch and listened. She used to get mother to help her sometimes, and then Carrie would look so happy as she planned how this garment was to be for old Nanny Stables, and the next for her little grandson Jemmy. With returning strength came the old, unselfish desire to benefit others. It put her quite into spirits one day when Mrs. Smedley asked her to cover some books for the Sunday school.

"How good of her to think of it; it is just work that I can do!" she said, gratefully; and for the rest of the day she looked like the old Carrie again.

Allan came to see us nearly every evening. Oh, those delicious summer evenings! how vividly even now they seem to rise before me, though many, many happy years lie between me and them.

Somehow it had grown a sort of habit with us to spend them on the common. Mother loved the sweet fresh air, and would sit for hours among the furze bushes and gorse, knitting placidly, and watching the children at their play, or the cottagers at work in their gardens; and Uncle Geoffrey, in his old felt hat, would sit beside her, reading the papers.

Allan used to tempt Carrie for a stroll over the common; and when she was tired he and Jack and I would saunter down some of the long country lanes, sometimes hunting for glow-worms in the hedges, sometimes extending our walk until the moon shone over the silent fields, and the night became sweet and dewy, and the hedgerows glimmered strangely in the uncertain light.

How cozy our little drawing-room always looked on our return! The lamp would be lighted on the round table, and the warm perfume of flowers seemed to steep the air with fragrance; sometimes the glass door would lie open, and gray moths come circling round the light, and outside lay the lawn, silvered with moonlight. Allan used to leave us regretfully to go back to the old house at Milnthorpe; he said we were such a snug party.

When Carrie began to visit the cottages and to gather the children round her couch on Sunday afternoons, I knew she was her old self again. Day by day her sweet face grew calmer and happier; her eyes lost their sad wistful expression, and a little color touched her wan cheeks.

Truly she often suffered much, and her lameness was a sad hindrance in the way of her usefulness; but her hands were always busy, and on her well days she spent hours in the cottages reading to two or three old people, or instructing the younger ones.

It was touching to see her so thankful for the fragments of work that still fell to her share, content to take the humblest task, if she only might give but "a cup of cold water to one of these little ones;" and sometimes I thought how dearly the Good Shepherd must love the gentle creature who was treading her painful life-path so lovingly and patiently.

I often wondered why Mr. Lucas never kept his promise of coming to see us; but one evening when Jack and Allan and I returned from our stroll we found him sitting talking to mother and Uncle Geoffrey.

I was so surprised at his sudden appearance that I dropped some of the flowers I held in my hand, and he laughed as he helped me to pick them up.

"I hope I haven't startled you," he said, as we shook hands.

"No - that is - I never expected to see you here this evening," I returned, rather awkwardly.

"Take off your hat, Esther," said mother, in an odd tone; and I thought she looked flushed and nervous, just as she does when she wants to cry. "Mr. Lucas has promised to have supper with us, and, my dear, he wants you to show him the conservatory and the fernery."

It was still daylight, though the sun was setting fast; we had returned earlier than usual, for Allan had to go back to Milnthorpe, and he bade us goodnight hastily as I prepared to obey mother.

Jack followed us, but mother called her back, and asked her to go to one of the cottages and fetch Carrie home. Such a glorious sunset met our eyes as we stepped out on the lawn; the clouds were a marvel of rose and violet and golden splendor; the windows of the cottage were glittering with the reflected beams, and a delicious scent of lilies was in the air.

Mr. Lucas seemed in one of his grave moods, for he said very little until we reached the winding walk where the ferns were, and then -

I am not going to repeat what he said; such words are too sacred; but it came upon me with the shock of a thunderbolt what he had been telling mother, and what he was trying to make me understood, for I was so stupid that I could not think what he meant by asking me to the Cedars, and when he saw that, he spoke more plainly.

"You must come back, Esther; we cannot do without you any longer," he continued very gently, "not as Flurry's governess, but as her mother, and as my wife."

He was very patient with me, when he saw how the suddenness and the wonder of it all upset me, that a man like Mr. Lucas could love me, and be so clever and superior and good. How could such a marvelous thing have happened?

And mother knew it, and Uncle Geoffrey, for Mr.

Lucas had taken advantage of my absence to speak to them both, and they had given him leave to say this to me. Well, there could be no uncertainty in my answer. I already reverenced and venerated him above other men, and the rest came easy, and before we returned to the house the first strangeness and timidity had passed; I actually asked him - summoning up all my courage, however - how it was he could think of me, a mere girl without beauty, or cleverness, or any of the ordinary attractions of girlhood.

"I don't know," he answered, and I knew by his voice he was smiling; "it has been coming on a long time; when people know you they don't think you plain, Esther, and to me you can never be so. I first knew what I really felt when I came out of the room that dreadful night, and saw you standing with drenched hair and white face, with Dot in your arms and my precious Flurry clinging to your dress; when I saw you tottering and caught you. I vowed then that you, and none other, should replace Flurry's dead mother;" and when he had said this I asked no more.

CHAPTER XXIV.

RINGING THE CHANGES.

When Mr. Lucas took me to mother, she kissed me and shed abundance of tears.

"Oh, my darling, if only your poor father could know of this," she whispered; and when Uncle Geoffrey's turn came he seemed almost as touched.

"What on earth are we to do without you, child?" he grumbled, wiping his eye-glasses. "There, go along with you. If ever a girl deserved a good husband and got it, you are the one."

"Yes, indeed," sighed mother; "Esther is every one's right hand."

But Mr. Lucas sat down by her side and said something so kind and comforting that she soon grew more cheerful, and I went up to Carrie.

She was resting a little in the twilight, and I knelt down beside her and hid my face on her shoulder, and now the happy tears would find a vent.

"Why, Esther - why, my dear, what does this mean?" she asked, anxiously; and then, with a sudden conviction dawning on her, she continued in an excited voice - "Mr. Lucas is here; he has been saying something, he - he - " And then I managed somehow to stammer out the truth.

"I am so happy; but you will miss me so dreadfully, darling, and so will Dot and mother."

But Carrie took me in her arms and silenced me at once.

"We are all happy in your happiness; you shall not shed a tear for us - not one. Do you know how glad I am, how proud I feel that he should think so highly of my precious sister! Where is he? Let me get up, that I may welcome my new brother. So you and your dear Ruth will be sisters," she said, rallying me in her gentle way, and that made me smile and blush.

How good Carrie was that evening! Mr. Lucas was quite touched by her few sweet words of welcome, and mother looked quite relieved at the sight of her bright face.

"What message am I to take to Ruth?" he said to me, as we stood together in the porch later on that evening.

"Give her my dear love, and ask her to come to me," was my half-whispered answer; and as I went to bed that night Carrie's words rang in my ears like sweetest music - "You and Ruth will be sisters."

But it was Allan who was my first visitor. Directly Uncle Geoffrey told him what had happened, he put on his broad-brimmed straw hat, and leaving Uncle Geoffrey to attend to the patients, came striding down to the cottage.

He had burst open the door and caught hold of me before I could put down Dot's lesson book. The little fellow looked up amazed at his radiant face.

"What a brick you are, Esther, and what a brick he is!" fairly hugging me. "I never was so pleased at anything in my life. Hurrah for Mr. Lucas at the Cedars!" and Allan threw up his hat and caught it. No wonder Dot looked mystified.

"What does he mean?" asked the poor child; "and how hot you look, Essie."

"Listen to me, Frankie," returned Allan, sitting down by Dot. "The jolliest thing in the world has happened. Esther has made her fortune; she is going to have a good husband and a rich husband, and one we shall all like, Dot; and not only that, but she will have a dear little daughter as well."

Dot fairly gasped as he looked at us both, and then he asked me rather piteously if Allan was telling him a funny story to make him laugh.

"Oh, no, dear Dot," I whispered, bringing my face on a level with his, and bravely disregarding Allan's quizzical looks. "It is quite true, darling, although it is so strange I hardly know how to believe it myself. But one day I am going to the Cedars."

"To live there? to leave us? Oh, Essie!" And Dot's eyes grew large and mournful.

"Mr. Lucas wants me, and Flurry. Oh, my darling,

forgive me!" as a big tear rolled down his cheek. "I shall always love you, Dot; you will not lose me. Oh, dear! oh dear! what am I to say to him, Allan?"

"You will not love me the most any longer, Essie."

And as I took him in my arms and kissed him passionately his cheek felt wet against mine.

"Oh, Frankie, fie for shame!" interrupted Allan. "You have made Esther cry, and just now, when she was so happy. I did not think you were so selfish."

But I would not let him go on. I knew where the pain lay. Dot was jealous for the first time in his life, and for a long time he refused to be comforted.

Allan left us together by-and-by, and I took my darling on my lap and listened to his childish exposition of grief and the recital of grievances that were very real to him. How Flurry would always have me, and he (Dot) would be dull and left out in the cold. How Mr. Lucas was a very nice man; but he was so old, and he did not want him for a brother - indeed, he did not want a brother at all.

He had Allan and that big, stupid Fred - for Dot, for once in his sweet life, was decidedly cross. And then he confided to me that he loved Carrie very much, but not half so well as he loved me. He wished Mr. Lucas had taken her instead. She was very nice and very pretty, and all that, and why hadn't he?

But here I thought it high time to interpose.

"But, Dot, I should not have liked that at all. And I am

so happy," I whispered.

"You love him - that old, old man, Essie!" in unmitigated astonishment.

"He is not old at all," I returned, indignantly; for, in spite of his iron-gray hair, Mr. Lucas could hardly be forty, and was still a young-looking man.

Dot gave a wicked little smile at that. In his present mood he rather enjoyed vexing me.

I got him in a better frame of mind by-and-by. I hardly knew what I said, but I kissed him, and cried and told him how unhappy he made me, and how pleased mother and Carrie and Jack were; and after that he left off saying sharp things, and treated me to a series of penitent hugs, and promised that he would not be cross with "my little girl" Flurry; for after that day he always persisted in calling her "my little girl."

Dot had been a little exhausting, so I went down to the bench near the fernery to cool myself and secure a little quiet, and there Ruth found me. I saw her coming over the grass with outstretched hands, and such a smile on her dear face; and though I was so shy that I could scarcely greet her, I could feel by the way she kissed me how glad - how very glad - she was.

"Dear Esther! My dear new sister!" she whispered.

"Oh, Ruth, is it true?" I returned, blushing. "Last night it seemed real, but this morning I feel half in a dream. It will do me good to know that you are really pleased about this."

"Can you doubt it, dearest?" she returned, reproachfully. "Have you not grown so deep into our hearts that we cannot tear you out if you would? You are necessary to all of us, Esther - to Flurry and me as to Giles - "

But I put my hand on her lips to stop her. It was sweet, and yet it troubled me to know what he thought of me; but Ruth would not be stopped.

"He came home so proud and happy last night. 'She has accepted me, Ruth,' he said, in such a pleased voice, and then he told me what you had said about being so young and inexperienced."

"That was my great fear," I replied, in a low voice.

"Your youth is a fault that will mend," she answered, quaintly. "I wish I could remember Giles' rhapsody - 'So true, so unselfish, so womanly and devoted.' By-the-by, I have forgotten to give you his message; he will be here this afternoon with Flurry."

We talked more soberly after a time, and the sweet golden forenoon wore away as we sat there looking at the cool green fronds of the ferns before us, with mother's bees humming about the roses. There was summer over the land and summer in my heart, and above us the blue open sky of God's Providence enfolding us.

I was tying up the rose in the porch, when I saw Mr. Lucas and Flurry crossing the common. Dot, who was helping me, grew a little solemn all at once.

"Here is your little girl, Essie," he said very gravely.

My dear boy, how could he?

"Oh, Esther," she panted, for she had broken away from her father at the sight of us, "auntie has told me you are going to be my own mamma, in place of poor mamma who died. I shall call you mammy. I was lying awake ever so long last night, thinking which name it should be, and I like that best."

"You shall call me what you like, dear Flurry; but I am only Esther now."

"Yes, but you will be mammy soon," she returned, nodding her little head sagely. "Mamma was such a grand lady; so big and handsome, she was older, too - " But here Mr. Lucas interrupted us.

Dot received him in a very dignified manner.

"How do you do?" he said, putting out his mite of a hand, in such an old-fashioned way. I could see Mr. Lucas' lip curl with secret amusement, and then he took the little fellow in his arms.

"What is the matter, Dot? You do not seem half pleased to see me this afternoon. I suppose you are very angry with me for proposing to take Esther away. Don't you want an old fellow like me to be your brother?"

Dot's face grew scarlet. Truth and politeness were sadly at variance, but at last he effected a compromise.

"Esther says you are not so very old, after all," he stammered.

"Oh, Esther says that, does she?" in an amused voice.

"Father is not old at all," interrupted Flurry, in a cross voice.

"Never mind, so that Esther is satisfied," returned Mr. Lucas, soothingly; "but as Flurry is going to be her little girl, you must be my little boy, eh, Dot?"

"I am Esther's and Allan's little boy," replied Dot, rather ungraciously. We had spoiled our crippled darling among us, and had only ourselves to blame for his little tempers.

"Yes, but you must be mine too," he replied, still more gently; and then he whispered something into his ear. I saw Dot's sulky countenance relax, and a little smile chase away his frown, and in another moment his arms closed round Mr. Lucas' neck; the reconciliation was complete.

What a happy autumn that was! But November found us strangely busy, for we were preparing for my wedding. We were married on New Year's Day, when the snow lay on the ground. A quiet, a very quiet wedding, it was. I was married in my traveling dress, at Giles' expressed wish, and we drove straight from the church door to the station, for we were to spend the first few weeks in Devonshire.

Dear Jessie, my old schoolmate, was my only bridesmaid; for Carrie would not hear of fulfilling that office on her crutches.

I have a vague idea that the church was very full and I have a misty recollection of Dot, with very round eyes, standing near Allan; but I can recall no more, for my thoughts were engaged by the solemn vows we were exchanging.

Three weeks afterward, and we were settled in the house that was to be mine for so many happy years; but never shall I forget the sweetness of that home-coming.

Dear Ruth welcomed us on the threshold, and then took my hand and Giles' and led us into the bright firelit room. Two little faces peeped at us from the curtained recess, and these were Dot and Flurry. I had them both in my arms at once. I would not let Giles have Flurry at first till he threatened to take Dot.

Oh, how happy we were. Ruth made tea for us, and I sat in my favorite low chair. The children scrambled up on Giles' knee, and he peeped at me between their eager faces; but I was quite content to let them engross him; it was pleasure enough for me to watch them.

"Why, how grand you look, Essie!" Dot said at last. "Your fingers are twinkling with green and white stones, and your dress rustles like old Mrs. Jameson's."

 "'And she shall walk in silk attire,
  And silver have to spare,'"

sang Giles. "Never mind Dot, Esther. Your brave attire suits you well."

"She looks very nice," put in Ruth, softly; "but she is our dear old Esther all the same."

"Nonsense, auntie," exclaimed Flurry, in her sharp

little voice. "She is not Esther any longer; she is my dear new mammy." At which we all laughed.

I was always mammy to Flurry, though my other darlings called me mother; for before many years were over I had Dots of my own - dear little fat Winnie, her brother Harold, and baby Geoffrey - to whom Ruth was always "auntie," or "little auntie," as my mischievous Harold called her.

As the years passed on there were changes at Eltham Cottage - some of them sad and some of them pleasant, after the bitter-sweet fashions of life.

The first great sorrow of my married life was dear mother's death. She failed a little after Harold's birth, and, to my great grief, she never saw my baby boy, Geoffrey. A few months before he came into the world she sank peacefully and painlessly to rest.

Fred came up to the funeral, and stayed with Allan; he had grown a long beard, and looked very manly and handsome. His pictures were never accepted by the hanging committee; and after a few years he grew tired of his desultory work, and thankfully accepted a post Giles had procured for him in the Colonies. After this he found his place in life, and settled down, and when we last heard from him he was on the eve of marriage with a Canadian girl. He sent us her photograph, and both Giles and I approved of the open, candid face and smiling brown eyes, and thought Fred had done well for himself.

Allan was a long time making his choice; but at last it fell on our new vicar's daughter, Emily Sherbourne; for, three years after our marriage, Mr. Smedley had been attacked by sudden illness, which carried him off.

How pleased I was when Allan told me that he and Emmie had settled it between them. She was such a sweet girl; not pretty, but with a lovable, gentle face, and she had such simple kindly manners, so different from the girls of the present day, who hide their good womanly hearts under such abrupt loud ways. Emily, or, as we always called her, Emmie, was not clever, but she suited Allan to a nicety. She was wonderfully amiable, and bore his little irritabilities with the most placid good humor; nothing put her out, and she believed in him with a credulity that amused Allan largely; but he was very proud of her, and they made the happiest couple in the world, with the exception of Giles and me.

Carrie lost her lameness, after all; but not until she had been up to London and had undergone skillful treatment under the care of a very skillful physician. I shall always remember Dot's joy when she took her first walk without her crutches. She came down to the Cedars with Jack, now a fine well-grown girl, and I shall never forget her sweet April face of smiles and tears.

"How good God has been to me, Essie," she whispered, as we sat together under the cedar tree, while Jack ran off for her usual romp with Winnie and Harold. "I have just had to lie quiet until I learned the lesson He wanted me to learn years ago, and now He is making me so happy, and giving me back my work."

It was just so; Carrie had come out of her painful ordeal strengthened and disciplined, and fit to teach others. No longer the weak, dreamy girl who stretched out over-eager hands for the work God in His wise providence withheld from her, she had emerged from her enforced retirement a bright helpful woman, who carried about her a secret fund of joy, of which no earthly circumstances could deprive her.

"My sweet sister Charity," Allan called her, and the poor of Milnthorpe had reason to bless her; for early and late she labored among them, tending the sick and dying, working often at Allan's side among his poorer patients.

At home she was Uncle Geoffrey's comfort, and a most sweet companion for him and Jack. As for Dot, he lived almost entirely at the Cedars. Giles had grown very fond of him, and we neither of us could spare him. They say he will always be a cripple; but what does that matter, when he spends day after day so happily in the little room Giles has fitted up for him?

We believe, after all, Dot will be an artist. He has taken a lifelike portrait of my Harold that has delighted Giles, and he vows that he shall have all the advantages he can give him; for Giles is very rich - so rich that I almost tremble at the thought of our responsibilities; only I know my husband is a faithful steward, and makes a good use of his talents. Carrie is his almoner, and sometimes I work with her. There are some almshouses which Giles is building in which I take great interest, and where I mean to visit the old people, with Winnie trotting by my side.

Just now Giles came in heated and tired. "What, little wife, still scribbling?"

"Wait a moment, dear Giles," I replied. "I have just finished."

And so I have - the few scanty recollections of Esther Cameron's life.

Printed in the United Kingdom
by Lightning Source UK Ltd.
106570UKS00003B/41